SEPARATE AND PARALLEL

PARALLEL

The Tale of Two Sisters

Beverly Park Williams

ISBN: 1541118987
ISBN 13: 9781541118980
Library of Congress Control Number: 2016920798
CreateSpace Independent Publishing Platform
North Charleston, South Carolina

This book is dedicated to the Disser sisters: my mother, Shirley; and my aunt, Janet. The accounts of their lives and descriptions of family truths were never shared until now.

He who dwells in the shelter of the Most High will abide in the shadow of the Almighty. I will say to the Lord, "My refuge and my fortress, my God, in whom I trust."

(Psalm 91:1–2)

Claire

The morphine pools familiar Bible verses in my mind. One occasionally becomes clear enough to recite, but I am unable to speak it from my dry mouth and chapped lips. I close my eyes, recite the text as I see it, and smile. He is near.

Cramps in my stomach wrench up toward my chest and around my waist and my lower back seizes in pain. I have no other physical sensations. To move my hands, I have to look down at my fingers lying still on the blanket and concentrate. A sip of water from the straw standing tall in a white paper cup...to touch a petal of the single yellow rose resting on the table...the efforts seem endless.

Nurses in crisp white uniforms and peaked caps appear soundlessly beside my bed even when I have no need for them. They know I am dying. Each one rests against my arm, pressing in with differing shapes and weights, praying for a quiet passing. I can hear their gentle and practiced mumblings. It is no comfort to sense their concern.

My life has been so full. And yet I feel there is so much more to do. The girls have been a joy. "Oh, dear lord, keep them in your loving grace. Show them how to be strong when I leave. Let them know I am going to heaven where there will be no migraine headaches, no stomach cramps, and I will not age. Haven't I asked you time and again never to allow me to become old and full of wrinkles? At long last, I will be cradled in beautiful, sweet and peaceful rest," I pray in my continuing conversation with God.

Suddenly, a young boy appears as if through the window beside my bed. His tousled blond hair cannot hide his smiling green eyes. He is holding out his arms to greet me, barely able to contain his excitement. Who is he? He acts as if he knows me. "Clarissa, oh, Clarissa," he exclaims. "I've been waiting for you for so long!"

"Who are you? My name is not Clarissa; it's Claire," I correct him.

"Why, I am your brother, Willie. I died in the orphanage of diphtheria when I was seven." Though his shirt is clean, it is several sizes too big for him, frayed at the collar and torn at the elbows. His pants are held up at his waist with a large metal pin. He has no socks or shoes. His face is scrubbed clean, and his cheeks are red from the effort. I begin to see a family resemblance. Willie looks like me.

"Am I dead?" I ask, shocking myself that I am not more upset by the possibility. "Yes, indeed," Willie confirms. "Isn't it wonderful? We have all of eternity to play!"

His enthusiasm washes over me in warm shudders of relief. The stomach cramps dissipate in waves down my legs and out through my toes. My head is clear of the pressure and ache of the medicines. My turmoil and grief in leaving the girls feels distant from this place, fading, growing dim.

Willie takes my hand and pulls at my elbow to hasten me from the bed. One bare foot after the other, I stretch and stand. Still dressed in my favorite long yellow nightgown with white lace sleeves, I feel none of my own weight on my feet as I take one step and then another.

He leads me to the window, and I am surprised that there is no sight of the city below. Where I had seen homes and buildings and the river just this morning, the scenery is now as blue as a clear sky on a spring day. I do not feel the heat of my fever or chill from the lack of a cotton sheet. With outstretched arms, Willie lifts from me the floor and pulls me, weightless, without regard for the hospital room window.

I turn my face, fearing impact against the window glass, and suddenly feel mist, refreshing and filled with hundreds of scents I try to identify. Familiar hymns and praises that are new to me are being sung and played by hundreds of choirs and orchestras. Above the glorious noise I hear voices. They are calling to me, "Claire! Clarissa, welcome!" Waves of creamy light and sacred peace overtake me.

A nurse is making her regular rounds. When she walks into Claire's room, she immediately recognizes death. The mouth is slightly open and the eyes are wide, with a gaze that is fixed on nothing at all. Though Claire has passed away, Anna walks softly to her bed to gently lift her chin and close both eyelids. The patient is gone, and the family must be called. Claire's body is still in a pose of calm, and the room is quiet.

Laughter and shouts of joy greet Willie and Claire. Family and friends, just as she remembers them, are reaching out to touch her and embrace her. "Hallelujah, precious Clarissa! Hallelujah!" The euphoria is overwhelming.

> When a woman tells the truth she is
> creating the possibility for more truth
> around her.

—Adrienne Rich

Janet and Shirley

Shirley and Janet are the Disser sisters, daughters of Claire Disser (née Clarissa Doppler). As a child, Janet, three years older than her sister Shirley, was small, demure, and mischievous. Shirley, tall and thin, was an independent and fearless girl but rather naive. Born in the 1920s in Cincinnati, Ohio, the girls came into being during a decade of new personal freedoms for women.

Over a span of more than seventy years, women had fought for the right to vote. The historic Nineteenth Amendment, giving women that right, was passed in 1920. While the '20s were the beginning of the end of discrimination for women, they were also the start of a newfound independence for women, often without the support of a husband or family.

History books indicate that in 1920s America, the ideal was that a woman married, had children, and stayed at home. The model family depicted a husband going to work and coming home in the evenings to dinner on the table, well-behaved children, and a dutiful wife.

Sitting across the table from each other, each well in to their seventies, Janet had to laugh at the thought of a "model" mother and father. "We were born to Clarissa, a woman who was both a product and a casualty of this American 'ideal,'" Janet reminded Shirley.

Shirley shot back, "You don't have to tell me about being a casualty. Mother grew up desperate to be part of a family. I think I did too."

Janet sighed and without thinking, "I can echo that desperation."

Shirley: Well, I never knew my father.
Janet: And I never knew my mother.
Shirley: Why don't you let me tell you the story of our mother?

Janet: Go ahead, but it will be your version of the truth.
Shirley: What truth?
Janet: It depends on who is telling our story.

Shirley looked pained at the sides that she and her sister had drawn for each other.

"What was it like for you and Mother?" Janet provoked. "I can tell you all you want to know and most that you don't want to know about growing up as Father's daughter. What was it like growing up as Mother's daughter?" She decided there was no better time than now to hear Shirley's truth.

Hesitating a moment, Shirley drew a deep intake of breath and began to recount the story of their mother. "Mother was a seed of independence, strong and determined," Shirley began. She wanted Janet to respect and love their mother without ever having known her.

"Let me begin by telling you of Mother's quest for truth and happiness," Shirley offered. "It is a fascinating story..."

PART ONE

Mother

My grace is sufficient for you, for my power is made perfect in weakness. Therefore, I will boast all the more gladly about my weaknesses, so that Christ's power may rest on me.

(2 Corinthians 12:9)

Clarissa

Whenever she could escape the watchful eyes of her aunt, Louisa Doppler, Clarissa explored her childhood neighborhood. Early on Sunday mornings was the easiest time to leave the house unnoticed. Aunt Louisa gave Clarissa no chores on Sunday morning. It was enough of a task for Aunt Louisa to prepare herself and coach Uncle John on what to wear and who to greet at the first service at Knox Presbyterian Church. Then there had to be agreement on whom to invite to breakfast at their table at the Hyde Park Country Club.

A special treat Clarissa gave herself was skipping to the first worship service on Sundays at the high Episcopal Church of the Redeemer on Erie Avenue. She had walked past the church on several Sunday mornings and heard glorious music floating out from the windows and doors.

Arriving a few minutes before the service was to begin, Clarissa would sit in the center of the last row. She could rest her head on the back of the pew, close her eyes, and imagine flying among the sky-reaching arches of the dark cathedral.

One of the elderly greeters, Mrs. Laine, always had a piece of wrapped green spearmint candy in her pocket for Clarissa. Mrs. Laine had hands of ice, but they were soft and not much bigger than Clarissa's own. Her hair was fine and white as snow. With a bright smile behind pink lipstick, Mrs. Laine would hug Clarissa and whisper, "Jesus made this day just for you and for me."

"Did he?" Clarissa was curious. "How do you know that, Mrs. Laine?"

She would reply in several different ways, but the meaning was always the same: "Why, we are God's children, you and me. He made us before we were brought into the world as little babies. And he will welcome us back in to his arms when we are at the end of our lives here on earth."

Clarissa wondered how it was that Mrs. Laine had such knowledge about God. Did she live here at the church and he came to visit her? Clarissa was afraid to ask too many questions. Questions at Aunt Louisa's house usually got her in to trouble. Church and the repeated rituals of Sunday morning were briefly therapeutic. The spiritual experience was private. So was the friendship with Mrs. Laine.

One year, Christmas happened to fall on Sunday morning. Mrs. Laine presented Clarissa with a small white Bible. Inside, on the first page, she had inscribed, "To Claressa, my little angel in the first row." How odd it was that Mrs. Laine thought the last row was the first, Clarissa thought. Clarissa had carefully untied the white satin ribbon and lifted the small white Bible from the black linen box. Beautiful color pictures of Jesus and the disciples took her breath away. A white silk ribbon was attached to the binding to mark a reading place, and every page was edged in gold.

"Look at how you have spelled my name," Clarissa said as she tugged at the sleeve of Mrs. Laine's sweater.

She smiled. "Why, I sounded it out, just the way you introduced yourself to me," she said. Clarissa loved the way this woman spoke to her and had chosen to spell her name. She pronounced and spelled it *Claire-essa*, as if it were chosen and whispered by angels.

On the walk from church back to the Doppler house, the serenity of the service fell away from Clarissa with every step. It was not that she hated living with the Dopplers—they were family. But—and this was a very big "but"—her position in the household was clearly that of charity. To be housed and clothed and fed, she was required to work for the Doppler family, her aunt Louisa, her uncle John, and their son, John Jr., who was seven years her senior.

The Doppler home was one of many stately brick homes in the wealthy residential area of Cincinnati known as Hyde Park. The house was located on Grandin Avenue, just blocks away from the Hyde Park Square. Shops and markets created a commercial boundary for the square. In the center was a severe black marble three-tiered fountain surrounded by twelve identical pear trees that blanketed snow-like petals on the walkways in the spring.

Clarissa was constantly made aware of the pristine condition in which the distinguished Doppler home was to be kept. Aunt Louisa reminded her, "This house is a landmark in Hyde Park and must be maintained to the standards of the original owners. That is your job, Clarissa—to keep this property in an elegant and refined state. Why, I never know when we may have guests."

Even though Clarissa was overwhelmed by the cleaning and caring required of a home the size of the Dopplers', she would have preferred to have been, even in the same situation, in one of the other homes on their long street.

Her favorite was a beautiful pale yellow Victorian that stood proud on the corner of Grandin and Erie Avenues.

The Dopplers' home was an unobtrusive tan brick with a limestone foundation. Her uncle John said, "Solid looking, Clarissa—that's what this place is, solid looking. A banker built this house, and it looks like it. You know, conservative, not overdone like some of the other places in the neighborhood."

And yet those were the homes Clarissa liked the most—the ones Uncle John claimed were "overdone." She imagined herself playing under soaring white columns that graced expansive front porches, high-reaching white towers with black pointed railings, and ground-sweeping willows that hung silver arches in the back lawns. Those were the properties Clarissa wanted to live in someday. Not work in…live in.

At six years of age, Clarissa could not remember a time when she was not cleaning the two stories of the Doppler home. There were five bedrooms, four bathrooms, a parlor, a dining room, a study, a simple kitchen, a cook's kitchen, and a library. The only rooms she was not responsible for were the basement and the attic. For the longest time, Clarissa did not venture into the basement or the attic for fear there were other families—unusual people, perhaps—who lived there to whom she had not been introduced.

In all the first-floor rooms except for the simple kitchen and cook's kitchen, there were fireplaces centered on the outside walls with carved wooden mantels and white ceramic tile spill fronts. Her Aunt Louisa had hung austere paintings of deceased family members on every wall.

The four bathrooms had ceramic tile floors and walls in a variety of pastel colors: pink, blue, green, and yellow. The pink one was the prettiest. Pink and white wall tiles were etched with black outlines of ladies in dresses and bloomers holding parasols. A pink tile floor featured green etchings of ferns.

Oak floors polished to a high sheen grounded every living space in a serious pattern; an even number of planks, laid north to south, regardless of the size of the room. A solitary, soaring oak tree in the front yard stood testament to all the trees that had been cut and split for the purpose of defining the house.

Matching crown molding and solid-oak paneled entry doors or pocket doors separated each living area. High ceilings throughout the house made it difficult to wave away cobwebs without carrying a stepstool and broom in and out of every room. A massive oak door with leaded glass panels and transom welcomed guests into a marble and oak foyer featuring a painted atrium ceiling. An artist's rendering of heaven, with clouds and cherubs, flew above the gleaming white Italian marble floor.

The Doppler children, four in all—three girls and one boy—were grown and gone from the house except for the youngest and only son, John Jr. He was tall, with wide shoulders, dark curly hair, and a handsome smile. It was rare that Clarissa spoke to John. When he came home from school, he locked himself in his room to study. If Clarissa saw him in the house, John Jr. was kind and shy. "Hello, little one, how are you?" he would inquire.

"I am fine, sir," Clarissa would reply with the slight curtsy Aunt Louisa required.

Clarissa never spent time in much of the Doppler home except to clean. Her own room was the smallest of the five bedrooms, at the back of the house on the second floor. A small white wrought-iron bed held a straw mattress on top of metal springs supported by four oak boards. Depending on her size at each age, cotton skirts and blouses that had once belonged to the Dopplers' daughters were hung by Aunt Louisa on wooden pegs on the walls. Underpants and socks were stacked on a stool at the end of the bed. A pair of shoes the Doppler girls had worn and outgrown, close enough in size to be used by Clarissa, was placed just under the bed. A bucket stood in the corner for use as a toilet.

She was content to follow the work schedule that was provided each morning by Aunt Louisa. Aunt Louisa regularly reminded Clarissa, "If left on your own, you would be of no use to anyone. And then where would you be? Out on the street with no home and no clothes and no food, that's where."

Aunt Louisa and Uncle John Doppler had taken Clarissa into their home when she was just six months old, on Valentine's Day, 1908. Aunt Louisa's sister Margaret Ann Fein had died giving birth to Clarissa. "Aunt Louisa, do I have family, more than you and Uncle John?" Clarissa wanted to know when she was finally able to gather the courage to ask.

"Child, your mother died giving birth to you. A brother and a sister were taken in by other generous families like your Uncle John and me. Your mother is gone. Uncle John and I are all you have in this world. We adopted you and gave you our family name. You need not ask any further questions about this matter. Do you understand me?" Aunt Louisa looked down at Clarissa and wagged a bony finger in her face.

"Yes, ma'am, I do understand." Clarissa hung her head and contemplated the floor.

"Do not consider such a topic again," Aunt Louisa scolded. She turned to leave the kitchen, snapping her long black taffeta skirt against Clarissa's bare legs.

When Clarissa saw the bulk that was Aunt Louisa climb the center stairs every afternoon and close her bedroom door for a nap, Clarissa retreated to the simple kitchen. Curled up with the family dog in his sheepskin bed under the butcher block table, she could lay her face on the cool tile floor and take a nap. The rhythmic breathing and warm underbelly of the German shepherd that the Dopplers called Caesar lulled her to sleep.

At the sound of Aunt Louisa's bedroom door opening, Caesar would wake up with a start, warning Clarissa that naptime was over. Aunt Louisa was a commanding woman, in appearance and in tone. She was tall and stout, a round face above rolls of neck, topped by black hair held back in a tight knot at the nape of her neck. Her footsteps thundered down the stairs as she called out, "Child, where are you?"

When it was possible for Clarissa to master a cleaning rag, she began as much house cleaning as she could. At the age of six, she could maneuver a wet mop over the floors and was directed to dust and polish the furniture. Cooking and baking, mending, and washing were handled by Aunt Louisa. She fussed, "There is so much meal planning, shopping, and preparation to do. Not to mention the washing and ironing that is required. Honestly, I don't know how I managed with the girls growing up, much less now that I am getting up in years."

That was a cue for Clarissa to offer, "I will help in any way you need for me to, ma'am."

Aunt Louisa would coo in return, without so much as a glance at Clarissa, "Well there are minor chores that you are helping with, but there is and always will be more for you to do."

Mandatory attendance laws required Clarissa to attend the public school, starting with the first grade. On her seventh birthday Aunt Louisa enrolled her in Hyde Park Elementary School. Her first day of school was the Tuesday after the annual Labor Day celebration.

School was a stark contrast to the Doppler home. Even though she was glad to have the time away from the Doppler house, Clarissa was woefully inept and dreadfully inferior to the other students in basic education and social skills.

Mrs. Gertrude Bellman was her first-grade teacher. It did not take long for the new students to realize who did and did not know how to count and how to identify colors. The class segregated themselves by who was "smart" and who was "stupid." Clarissa was one of the stupid kids. Other stupid kids were those who were brought in by large yellow buses from the areas along the Ohio River. They looked like Clarissa. They were dressed in clothes that were not purchased for them but had been handed down from other children. And they were unable to answer any of the teacher's questions.

At the end of the first day of school, Mrs. Bellman waited until most the other children had left the classroom. "Clarissa!" she called out and waved at her before she had a chance to leave the school building. "Will you come here for a moment?" Mrs. Bellman gave Clarissa two well-used books on numbers and colors that the school had decided to replace.

"What do you want me to do with these?" Clarissa was curious. "Why, read and study them at home. I am giving these books to you as a gift. A Doppler must be able to keep up in school," insisted Mrs. Bellman.

Clarissa did not know how to read. As she walked toward home she wondered if she might ask John Jr. to help her. She went in the back door of the Doppler house and ran up the back steps to her room. Before changing clothes to start the housework, she slipped the books under the mattress.

Aunt Louisa must have heard her come in and stomped up the front stairs. "Where are you, Clarissa?" she demanded.

"I am changing my clothes so I can start my chores," Clarissa answered, trying not to sound as if she was hiding anything.

"Now you get to work," Aunt Louisa insisted. "The day is almost gone, and there is much to be done. School will not be an excuse for you to get behind in your chores."

John Jr. came home from school almost two hours later. Clarissa had made her way upstairs to clean the guest bedroom that was close to John's room. She wanted to be near enough to ask him a question. She startled him. "I need your help."

John smiled. "What is it, little one?"

Clarissa stammered, "I can't...I can't read."

John bent down and sweetly said, "I can. May I help you to read?"

Clarissa clapped her hands together in delight and reached up to wrap her arms around his neck. "Oh, if you could I would be very grateful."

John put out his hand to shake hers and laughed. "It is a deal—a secret deal. Why don't we begin lessons this very evening?"

Clarissa could barely contain her excitement. She was to have her own teacher, within the house. Lessons began that evening, John teaching Clarissa how to count on her fingers, resting in her lap. The letters of the alphabet were more difficult. One of the books Mrs. Bellman had given Clarissa showed animals and shapes and foods that began with each letter. John described all the pictures first and then repeated each letter in sequence.

Every evening after dinner, as soon as Aunt Louisa and Uncle John had retired to the library, John and Clarissa sequestered themselves in John's bedroom for lessons. John locked his bedroom door and pulled two chairs up to his massive walnut desk. Under the light of one reading lamp, they alternated between counting and reciting the alphabet.

Several weeks into the school year, Clarissa could count to one hundred, place one letter after another, and recognize words in the two books from Mrs. Bellman. Only at home and in John's presence did Clarissa celebrate the progress she was making.

In class, Clarissa fell far behind the "smart" students. She withdrew and became removed, staying in the classroom even during recess and lunch. At night, she tried as best as she could with John and on her own to learn what she did not understand and to ask questions. John was a marvelous teacher. "You can ask me anything, little one, anything at all," he would say.

Mrs. Bellman was concerned about Clarissa's withdrawal and lack of basic skills. She telephoned Aunt Louisa to explain that Clarissa had been silent and had removed herself from the other children. Aunt Louisa immediately clarified, "There is no reason for your distress. Clarissa will manage quite well on her own, thank you. She has been taken in by Mr. Doppler and me because there was no one else to care for her. Her education is mandatory, so she will attend public school. We do not anticipate that she will excel in her studies." Startled by the abrupt and unexpected response, Mrs. Bellman thanked Mrs. Doppler and hung up the phone.

Aunt Louisa was horrified that a teacher had called to complain about Clarissa. The next morning, she confronted Clarissa. "Mrs. Bellman is worried about you. She telephoned to express her concern. There will be no coddling of you for your schoolwork. And there will be no tolerance for illness. Not a single day of school is to be missed, and you are merely expected to pass from one level to the next. Am I making myself clear?" Clarissa nodded in understanding.

Fearful of their secret being discovered by Aunt Louisa, Clarissa asked John that night, "What will Aunt Louisa do if she finds out about these lessons? Will she throw me out on the street?"

John knew his mother terrified Clarissa. Taking her shoulders in his strong hands, John looked her straight in the eyes and pledged, "You will always have a place with me. I will never let you be thrown out on the street."

Rather than ask how he could do that, Clarissa chose to let his answer settle in the recesses of her heart as the first promise she had ever received. She would hold onto it, count on it, be comforted by it. While the Doppler children had been doted upon, received tutors and loving parental attention, Clarissa was left to discover her own talents and learning abilities. John was her mentor and her friend. He gave her every opportunity, every night, to learn and grow.

Clarissa was never welcomed or befriended by the other children in her neighborhood. Without exception, they teased her, chased her home, called her names, and laughed at her clothes, her shoes, and her having to use the back door of the Doppler house. Even though Clarissa held back after school to walk home alone, the neighborhood children collected just one block away to jump out and chant, "Clarissa is stupid, Clarissa is dumb, Clarissa is too poor to even have fun."

One evening, she couldn't help but tell John what her classmates were doing to her after school. John was silent for a moment and then swore, "If I were here when you came home from school, I would chase them all to their houses and tell their mothers what horrible little monsters they have for children." He could see that she was frightened by his anger. John picked Clarissa up, turned her upside down, and tickled her sides. He made Clarissa laugh out loud, and then they both realized they needed to be quiet so as to not be caught studying.

At the start of her sixth grade in elementary school, Clarissa came home one day just before noon. Aunt Louisa heard the back door open and close and walked down the main hallway just in time to see Clarissa standing in the simple kitchen, crying. Perplexed, Aunt Louisa asked insistently, "Why are you home in the middle of the day?"

Clarissa was embarrassed. "The school nurse sent me home because of a stain on my skirt."

Aunt Louisa was exasperated. "I cannot believe how young you are for this to happen."

"The nurse told me I am not prepared. That I do not know what is happening to me. She sent me home," Clarissa wailed. "Prepared for what?"

Aunt Louisa was annoyed. "Why, you are too little for this."

Clarissa panicked. "This what?"

Aunt Louisa was red in the face and stammered, "For your monthly stains of course. This will happen every month, and you must be ready."

Clarissa was shocked. "This will happen every month?"

Aunt Louisa telephoned the drugstore in O'Bryonville and asked Mr. Grayden to deliver a small size elastic garter belt and a large package of sanitary napkins. When the package arrived, Aunt Louisa presented them to Clarissa, telling her to wear the garter around her waist, to pull the fabric ends of the napkin through the metal rings hanging from the front and back of the garter, and to keep the napkin between her legs. She was to change napkins every time one became soiled. And she must carry napkins with her to school at the expected time each month.

Clarissa was horrified. She could barely walk with the bulk of the sanitary napkin between her legs. Clarissa changed clothes and went to the hose spigot in the backyard to wash the stains out of her underpants and skirt. She scrubbed and scrubbed with a piece of soap. When the stains would not come out, she used a rag with bleach and scrubbed until her hands were red and raw, and yet a shadow of the stains remained. In frustration, she ripped the skirt and underpants into strips to use for cleaning rags and threw the stained strips in the trash bin beside the back door.

Given her change in physical maturity, Aunt Louisa directed Clarissa to move from her second-floor bedroom, the same floor as young John Jr., and "make do" in the attic. Aunt Louisa announced to Clarissa, "I have decided it is not proper for a bleeding female who is not of my own body to be living in the main quarters of the house. Clean that back bedroom in the event of a guest. Then take your things and that bucket up to the attic with you."

That evening, Aunt Louisa declared to the men of the house her decision to move Clarissa to the attic. Neither John Sr. nor John Jr. wanted to know about this physical change in Clarissa, and they had no argument at the ready to disagree. Aunt Louisa had become increasingly bitter with the passing of time. Both John Sr. and John Jr. chose to stay away from her as much as possible. Over the years, there had been diminishing visits from invited guests and family, which had increased the intensity of her contrary disposition.

Clarissa retreated in silence at Aunt Louisa's command and dared not complain about the move to the attic. In the attic, she found a single lightbulb with a long pull chain at the top of the stairs. When the bulb came to life, it revealed all the Doppler discards in the midst of which she was to sleep.

It was obvious no one had been up to the attic for many years. The cobwebs and dust choked her. The first night, she slept without cover in a large wicker rocking chair that she moved under the lightbulb. A string tied the pull chain to the arm of the rocker in case she needed to see in the night.

The next evening, Clarissa retreated to John's room, and he apologized for the change in living conditions. They would continue the nighttime lessons, no matter that Clarissa had changed rooms. After their hour of study, John joined Clarissa in rummaging through the attic. The remains of a two-sided wooden crib and an over-stuffed chair were pushed together for an adequate place to stretch out and sleep. Beneath several boxes of old toys, they discovered a quilt and an embroidered pillow.

The next night, John presented Clarissa with fresh sheets, a feather pillow, and a down blanket that were the spare linens for his bed. Clarissa folded and hid them each morning in a storage box in the attic for fear that Aunt Louisa would come looking for them. Whenever she had the chance, Clarissa washed her linens and hid them again. Eventually, Clarissa stopped hiding the linens and Aunt Louisa stopped mentioning their absence.

To make the attic livable, Clarissa claimed as much available space as possible. At either end of the attic were two floor-to-ceiling windows. When she was able to move about unnoticed, Clarissa took rags and ammonia up the stairs and washed the windows until they were spotless. As weather permitted, she would open the windows and allow fresh air to breathe life into the massive room.

Over a period of years, she moved boxes and old furnishings away from the center of the attic, consolidated keepsakes, and broke down old furniture to fit unseen in the bottom of the trash bins. Standing on stacked boxes, Clarissa continued to swat away the cobwebs that collected in the eaves. Slowly but surely, she created living quarters to her liking. The dark and gloomy space left unattended for years became a spotless, fresh, and spacious hideaway.

John's tutoring had been sufficient for Clarissa to pass each grade in elementary school, as Aunt Louisa had mandated. He even gave her tips on grooming and how to wear her wavy hair. John knew she was growing up to be a lovely young woman—no longer the tow-headed kid who looked like a rag-a-muffin orphan. Now she was a natural beauty. Her strawberry-blond hair and brilliant-green eyes were pretty enough before she was convinced to smile. When she did smile, she was stunning.

The same year Clarissa started at Withrow Junior High School, John enrolled at the University of Cincinnati and took a part-time job at a printing company in downtown Cincinnati to earn his own spending money. Their evening study sessions were sporadic, but John made time for her as much as possible. The thought of his being away from the Doppler house frightened Clarissa. John reminded her, "I made you a promise when you were just a runt. I never break a promise. I will always be here for you."

At the Hyde Park and then the Withrow schools, the administration and teaching staff gave Clarissa little to no attention. Aunt Louisa had declared to school officials at enrollment each year, "Mind you, Clarissa is living with Mr. Doppler and I because she has no other place to be boarded. Mr. Doppler and I must advise that it is acceptable to place Clarissa in a lower level class, as she is not receiving any instruction at the Doppler home. Also, she will not be permitted to stay after school for additional studies or activities. There are chores to be attended to when Clarissa arrives home."

The students bused in from less attractive neighborhoods were her friends during the school day. The wealthy kids who lived in Hyde Park went from teasing to ignoring Clarissa. She continued to wear the Doppler girls' hand-me-downs. Shoes and boots and stockings were Doppler daughter remnants as well. If she asked for repairs to the holes in her stockings or the soles of her ill-fitting shoes, Aunt Louisa would repeat, "Child, you are more than fortunate to be clothed, fed, and sheltered. Do not ask for anything more."

Clarissa walked alone to and from school. She became very self-conscious about her appearance. Clarissa had fallen down the main stairway when she was nine, carrying laundry, and broken her nose. Instead of taking her to the doctor, Aunt Louisa had sopped up the blood until the bleeding stopped and then used sewing tape to pull the skin together until the wound healed. Clarissa thought it had grown back together in a rather crooked way.

The routine after school each day was cleaning the house and washing and ironing clothes. Aunt Louisa cooked supper, and Clarissa was expected to serve the meal to Aunt Louisa and Uncle John in the dining room and then sit down to serve herself. She was then expected to wash the dishes, pots, and pans and scrub the kitchen floor. Studies were to be considered only when all household chores were completed. The summer months brought a change in the daily routine to include gardening, weeding, window washing, scrubbing and airing out the cellar, and sweeping the walks and driveway.

As she entered Withrow High School, the tutoring sessions with John became less frequent and less necessary. Clarissa now had a study break every day at school, and there were plenty of students who offered their help. Male students vied for the seat next to her in the library for study break, finding pleasure in merely sitting at her side to tutor her in any subject.

During her high school years, the best place to do homework and read at the Doppler home was in the simple kitchen. A burled maple table with two matching spindle back chairs sat ready for use. A small milk glass lamp sat at the wall edge of the table that glowed soft white light. There was many a night when Clarissa would fall asleep on an open textbook or her lined notebook at the kitchen table. On his nightly walk from the library to the master bedroom, Uncle John would stop at the kitchen table to wake her with his teasing, "Go on up to your attic, little one."

> **Children of the same family, the same
> blood, with the same first associations and
> habits, have some means of enjoyment
> in their power, which no subsequent
> connections can supply...**
>
> —Jane Austen

John

As hopeful as he was that he had given Clarissa methods and habits for studying, John was also hopeful that he had given Clarissa some sense of family. As she grew into a lovely young woman, John heard lewd comments about Clarissa from friends whose younger siblings were still attending Withrow High School. Fearful that she was too naive in the ways of the world, especially when it came to the world of young men, John inquired as to Clarissa's weekends.

"Weekends? What weekends?" she joked. "I do not know weekends except that those are the two days I do not go to school. I still do the house chores and study."

John was intrigued. "Don't you have friends who come over to the house to see you or ask you to come over to their houses and listen to records?"

Clarissa threw back her head and laughed out loud. "No, I have no such friends. My friends are river rats, and they do not have the money to own any records."

John drove on to his part-time job, still thinking about how he could rescue Clarissa from the confines of the Doppler house and keep his mother from losing what was left of her already fragile sensibility. Then John thought of the perfect escape.

On Sunday morning, John was seated on the single step at the back door waiting for Clarissa to return from church. "Hello, little one. I guess you truly are not so little anymore." John couldn't help but smile at the innocent young woman clutching her Bible. "Let's have a chat, shall we? We should talk, just you and I, before Mother and Father get home from church and breakfast."

"All right," Clarissa said, suspicious. "What do you want to talk about? Have I done something wrong?" John couldn't help but shake his head at her constant concern for fault, even when there was no need for worry.

"Well," he began, "I believe it is time for you to go out into the social world and have some fun. What do you say to that?"

Clarissa was amused. "That sounds like a fairy story, one that I read many years ago and put back in a box in the attic."

John's face became serious. "I want you to enjoy life the way a young woman is supposed to, with my protection and my care."

Clarissa stood and curtsied. "Why thank you, kind sir, but I have no need of a knight in shining armor. As you can see, there is no dragon to slay and I have no treasure to share."

"I am serious," John insisted. "You must be serious too. You will soon graduate and then where will you be?"

Clarissa raised an eyebrow and was sullen. "You sound like your mother."

John slumped against the back door and closed his eyes. Sadly, he answered, "She is right. Where will you be when you graduate? You must think to the future—your future."

"Oh John, I have thought about my future. What will I do? Where shall I go when I graduate? But it frightens me, so I try to stop imagining life without your mother and your father." Clarissa shook her head and sat down hard on the back stoop beside John.

"Life without my mother?" John was incredulous. "Why, she makes your life miserable. She always has and she always will. What started out for Mother as a grandiose example to others of her Christian charity by taking you in has resulted in her realizing that you are a responsibility. Her idea, as Father has reminded her, and her responsibility." John knew it was time to tell Clarissa the truth about his mother. "You make it difficult for my mother to face her responsibility. You give her no reason to throw you out on the street. You are sweet and kind and beautiful. You are sweeter and kinder and more beautiful than any of my sisters, Mother's real daughters. She resents her decision to take you in. And she resents you."

Clarissa was more troubled than ever before. "John, what do you suggest I do?"

"Aha, little one. I knew you would come around to my idea of a social life." John smiled and stood before her. "I am your cousin, best friend, and confidant. And I take this role very seriously. It is on my shoulders to introduce you to your prince. This very Saturday night, I will whisk you away, in secret, to the meeting place of princes and princesses."

Most truths are so naked that people feel sorry for them and cover them up, at least a little bit.

—Edward R. Murrow

Clarissa

For several years, John had frequented the dance hall on Hyde Park Square every Saturday night for an evening out with friends. On alternating Saturday nights, he began escorting Clarissa as his dance partner. John reserved the other Saturday evenings to spend time with college buddies and friends from high school, dancing and drinking. Smart and ambitious with shining brown eyes and brown curly hair, he was a magnet for the single ladies.

John was pleased to be taking on the task of showing Clarissa an occasional night away from the suffocation of his parents' house. "Sneak out with me!" he'd tempt Clarissa on a Saturday afternoon. "Meet me on the back stoop at eight o'clock sharp, and I'll whisk you away to paradise." John was right. For Clarissa, a night away from Aunt Louisa was heaven, regardless of the noise, the crowds, the smoking, and the drinking at the dance hall.

In the bright-pink ladies' room at the otherwise dull-brown dance hall, the girls who swooned over John confided in Clarissa, "Ooh, John is the whole 'package,' you know?" No, Clarissa really didn't know. She had never thought about Cousin John, or any boy for that matter, in that way.

One girl, Maggie, wanted to be his girlfriend. Maggie's infatuation with John was obvious to John and to all his friends. The girls in the ladies' room teased her, "Maggie, tell Clarissa what John has in his package!"

My, how Maggie blushed and stammered, "I...I don't know what you mean. Stop it now, just stop it. He's handsome and polite and a great dancer."

Laura chimed in, "And he's rich and he's smart and he has an incredible bulge in the front of his pants!" The giggling turned to outright shouts of laughter.

Clarissa was already out the door and headed back to the dance floor when she saw how flushed Maggie had become. John had admitted to Clarissa that he could not be serious with any girl. "You must know that I promised all three of my sisters that I would keep a respectable position and care for our parents through their old age." And just in case Clarissa knew it was Maggie who had been chasing him, John assured Clarissa, "I've told Maggie there will be plenty of time in my life to settle down to a wife and a family."

John Jr. was the model son his father had always wanted. A "surprise" child born one week after Aunt Louisa turned forty-two, he had been constantly teased and tormented by his three older sisters. Just as sisters do, John's siblings grew tired of caring for their baby brother and, one by one, they found friends, married, and started their own families.

As time swept away the years, John's sisters visited less frequently. The repeated praise and compliments Aunt Louisa heaped on John grated on everyone's nerves, and the opposite commentary and treatment of Clarissa was disturbing to everyone's sense of civility. John's sisters and their husbands and their children typically visited their childhood home only on holidays and for birthday celebrations, even though they all lived on the same side of town.

With age, Mrs. Doppler had added considerable weight to her large frame. Seemingly with every new pound came frustration over the lack of her daughters' attentions and what she described as the burden of having

Clarissa in the house. Aunt Louisa became increasingly bitter and sarcastic. The vicious circle of her increasing weight and decreasing tolerance made it more difficult for her daughters and their husbands and children to be in her presence for very long.

Although he missed the attention and company of his sisters, John was pleased to become the oldest sibling in the house and to have Clarissa to look after. "I've been the youngest and the one who has received all the torment in the Doppler house, you know." He lowered his voice, frowned, and shook his index finger at Clarissa. She laughed and pinched his waist just above his belt so he would smile and twirl her around on tiptoe. Clarissa was a ray of sunshine in an otherwise dark and damp house. What a pleasant change to be the oldest and the caretaker of one so unlike him in every way—pure and carefree, despite her situation.

John kept Clarissa close to him at the dance hall. Even though the dance floor in the center of the hall was large, the social area around the dance floor was typically packed tight with young people. John's friends could be found on the fringe of the dance floor, not wanting to miss an opportunity to cut in on a dance with a pretty stranger. They kept close to their own circle but always had an eye open for the chance to interrupt a dance and make a new friend.

Clarissa captivated John's friends with her natural beauty and innocence. He had to regularly warn them away from her, with a polite but firm "don't touch" reminder. That didn't stop the young men inside or outside of his circle of friends from trying to steal even part of a dance with her.

Clarissa was a shy and glamorous young girl. Her high breasts and gentle curves attracted longing glances. She wore her long hair loose until John convinced her to wear it in braids pinned in a loose knot on top of her head. He told her it made her look older. "I'll do whatever you want me to, John," Clarissa said. She was serious. "I never want to do anything to embarrass you or to make you not want to take me dancing."

"Don't be silly, little one. There isn't anything you could do that would embarrass me. Are you razzin' with your cousin? Everyone adores you, including me—especially me." John spoke the truth.

She was only sixteen when John entered the two of them in a dance contest, a waltz. Even though the requirement for entry to the hall was eighteen, the manager was so accustomed to John's presence and so enamored with Clarissa that he never questioned her age.

They had been practicing at home two nights a week when Aunt Louisa was out of the house playing card games. John and Clarissa rehearsed until every step was perfect. John purchased a long-waist, high-neck Victorian style cream silk dress for Clarissa to wear. Maggie had helped him pick it out, color and size, with shoes to match.

Clarissa hand-stitched tucks down both side seams to accent her waist and rearranged the lace to accentuate the neckline.

John was taken by surprise at the vision that was Clarissa on that Saturday night. She glowed in the cream silk dress and shoes. Maggie had presented Clarissa with a box of "goodies." She had taken the liberty of purchasing a tube of pale pink lipstick, black mascara, a garter, and a pair of skin-tone silk stockings. The last item in the box, and the most treasured for Clarissa, was a gold hair clip. Clarissa had practiced with the makeup and the clip. She blotted her lipstick until it was a faint coloring on her lips, she applied only one coat of black mascara, and she was able to brush her hair in a French twist so a few curls spilled out over the top of the clip.

She was a gorgeous young lady who was transformed into a beautiful young woman before John's eyes. He was speechless. Clarissa punched him in the arm. "Please say something. Staring doesn't tell me how I look."

John stammered, "Oh…you look utterly amazing. I must keep a close eye on you this evening. Why, every man in the place will want to steal you away and never bring you back." Clarissa blushed and was pleased her efforts met with his approval.

Clarissa was thrilled that the much-anticipated Saturday night had finally arrived. At the dance hall, men whistled and smiled at her. John's friends had more compliments for her than she could imagine. Promptly at nine o'clock, their circle of conversation was interrupted as the tuxedoed emcee with slick black hair announced the start of the waltz contest.

At a registration table, Clarissa and John signed in and received a numbered placard to wear for judging identification. Their number was eleven. John helped Clarissa, and she in turn helped him to hang the cord around each other's necks so the white placards with the two bold ones were visible on their backs.

Clarissa had never seen John so nervous. Little beads of perspiration were visible on his forehead. She wasn't nervous until she saw that John was nervous. John caught the concerned look on her face and chuckled, "Don't you think these spotlights are a bit much? I'm on fire!"

Clarissa sighed in relief. "I hadn't noticed. I'm so nervous. All these people are watching."

John squeezed her hand in his. "They are just looking to see what new dance steps we can teach them after the contest."

With his last word, the contest began as the band leader struck up the orchestra in the first waltz. Twenty minutes later, eighteen of the twenty-five couples had been eliminated. The three dance judges held up the spare set of numbered placards each time they agreed which couples were to be eliminated and escorted from the dance floor.

Finally, the judges were focused on three remaining couples, including John and Clarissa. The band began a final, more traditional waltz selection. Clarissa got goose bumps up and down her arms. This was the very waltz John had selected for their practices. He could feel the tension release in her hands. Her chin raised and her smile broadened.

The judges were conferring behind raised hands. The final moments of the contest had arrived. As the waltz ended, the judges came out to the dance floor to congratulate John and Clarissa as the contest winners. The crowd applauded and whistled in approval. John twirled Clarissa around in the center of the dance floor. She curtsied and he took a bow.

John's group of friends whooped in celebration and streamed out onto the dance floor to escort John and Clarissa back to high-top tables filled with fresh glasses of beer and shots of whiskey. John had never allowed Clarissa to drink, not even a sip. He made an exception on this one night, and Clarissa took her first gulp of beer.

She wrinkled her nose and said, "Oh my, this is a surprise. It tastes like flat old ginger ale."

The whole group laughed and teased John, and one of his friends said, "See, old man, you didn't have to be such a 'big brother' after all. She doesn't even like the stuff."

Clarissa wondered to herself, *Why on earth was everyone so happy to drink it?*

The contest prize was twenty-five dollars. The deciding judge had given the cash to John. On the walk back to the house that night, John gave it all to Clarissa. "This is your seed money, little one. You earned it. Now you have money of your own." Clarissa was thrilled at the feel of it, the weight of it. She had, in fact, earned it and could do with it as she wished. And it was so much!

...let us dance; this amusement will never
do any harm to the world.

—Voltaire

Clarissa

Dance night was her favorite evening, every other week, out of the house and socializing with John and his friends. While Aunt Louisa listened to the radio and busied herself with embroidery in the drawing room, Clarissa crept down the attic steps to meet John at the back door. They walked quickly, in a rush of secrecy and delight, to the Hyde Park dance hall just three blocks away from the Doppler home.

John took pleasure in introducing her. "This is Clarissa Doppler, my precious cousin. I require you treat her as you would your own little sister." The men were disappointed and the ladies were relieved. She was family.

Clarissa stayed close to John until one magical summer evening when Sam Disser came to the dance hall. He was in the midst of a bunch of his high school buddies. They had remained close friends, especially those like Sam, who had never experienced fighting overseas during the Great War.

Sam Disser had grown from a school boy into a man since his service in the war. When he saw Clarissa, he instantly fell in love. She was a five-foot-three beauty with cat-green eyes, ivory skin, and strawberry-blond hair that fell to her shoulders in waves. At just five foot nine, with dark brown hair and brown eyes, Sam was an ordinary-looking fellow. Clarissa, however, was instantly impressed with his air of maturity and confidence, his quiet demeanor, and his manners.

John whispered in her ear, "Now that's a catch for you. He enlisted in the service for his country, and now he is working in his father's construction business."

"Oh John," Clarissa rose on tiptoe to whisper, "I'm not looking for a man. Why, I'm only a girl!" John shook his head and laughed at his little cousin. He couldn't decide if she was more naive or coy and decided she was too naive to be coy.

Despite the teasing John was giving Clarissa about all the attention she was receiving from the older men—war renegades as he called them—Sam managed to persuade John to escort Clarissa for one dance. "I will protect her as my own and regard her as your family treasure," he said.

John was taken aback. "Well, what can I say but you may dance with her. I will be watching you, closely." With winks and knowing nods, Sam's army buddies knew what to do. They engulfed John and convinced him to buy them a round of drinks.

That first dance with Sam was so different from when she and John danced together. They had practiced dancing to music in measured steps. With Sam she did not feel the steps or hear the music. Her heart was pounding so loudly in her chest that it echoed in her ears. She felt a bit dizzy. Sam's eyes remained fixed on her face as if he was memorizing it. He had little to say.

His strong hand at the small of her back made her shiver. While John held Clarissa at a distance from him, Sam pulled her close. The band played one song after another without ceasing, not wanting to interrupt the merriment of a young and happy crowd.

Sam was spellbound by her beauty. Clarissa gazed in his eyes so intently. He had heard of "falling" for a girl, and if this was what it meant, then Sam was ready to take the tumble.

While they danced, Clarissa could smell the starch of Sam's shirt, feel the buckle of his belt pressing against her waist. His strength carried her across the dance floor, her legs felt attached to his, weightless. Suddenly, a friend in John's group noticed them and said, "Sam has stolen our Clarissa away. John—how could you let that happen?"

With one look at how intimately Sam was dancing with Clarissa, John excused himself from the group and navigated through the dancing crowd toward the pair. Annoyed with himself that his friends had realized her absence before he did, John interrupted Sam and Clarissa mid-dance. "Pardon me, but the last dance of the evening is always reserved for Cousin John."

Sam smiled and answered, "Of course," and then he took his leave to rejoin his buddies and John's friends. John held Clarissa at arm's length and in silence until the music stopped.

John was apologetic. "Clarissa, I should have come to your rescue sooner. Such attention from a young man at a first meeting is not a good idea. Let's walk home." John was angry with himself. He knew Sam by his family's business reputation only. He did not know what kind of a man Sam was, his character.

John and Clarissa waved above the crowd on the dance floor and called out their good-byes. Given their earlier than normal departure, teasing from friends echoed in waves behind them.

"You don't have to leave us so soon!"

"Sam didn't mean to steal her away from us!"

When the fresh air of the evening stopped them on the sidewalk outside the hall, Clarissa inquired, "Are you angry with me?"

"No, I am angry with myself for not paying attention to you as I should," John insisted.

"Ah, but you are the best friend I have ever had," exclaimed Clarissa.

"Ha!" John laughed. "I am the only friend you have ever had." Seeing the impact of his honesty on her face, he added, "The best friend you have ever or will ever have, because we share the secrets of study and dancing." She nodded in agreement and smiled.

Clarissa really loved the dancing. She did not really like John's crowd of friends, the jostling of the crowd, or the noise of a multitude of conversations at the dance hall. The men who kept trying to get her alone made her shudder in dread. They would sneak up beside her when they didn't think John was paying attention to whisper requests for a quick walk in the night air or to step outside with them to try a cigarette.

The night Clarissa met Sam was different. She could feel it in her heart, and she could not stop thinking about him. That evening was like a dream, too vague and pleasant to have happened. He had treated her with respect and care. John confessed as they were walking home, "Clarissa, I must say I am concerned about the way I saw Sam holding you while you were dancing."

Clarissa replied dreamily, "I was not concerned." No, not at all, it felt wonderful.

John and Clarissa had taken a leisurely walk home that night. Clarissa had convinced John to take a detour because they had left the dance hall an hour earlier than their usual departure at eleven o'clock. They strolled up and down a few neighboring streets. Clarissa wanted to savor this night, to remember Sam's strength surrounding her, his breath on her cheek. While John shared stories of work and anecdotes about his buddies, Clarissa was memorizing dancing with Sam.

John's return home that night was, as always, greeted with a boisterous "Is that my precious boy?" Predictably, Mrs. Doppler embraced her son in her ample bosom. She had waited up in the drawing room with her reading or sewing, anxious to hear all about the evening's entertainment. Clarissa was left to enter quietly through the back door.

While John kept his mother amused with stories of dancing and conversation with friends, Clarissa made as little noise as possible tiptoeing through the simple kitchen, then up to her attic retreat. Uncle John was never a concern for their surreptitious return. He was always fast asleep by nine o'clock, settled in his massive leather chair in the corner of his study.

Every Saturday night after meeting Clarissa, Sam returned to the Hyde Park dance hall looking for her. The third week she was absent, Sam confided, "John, buddy, I never meant to upset you by dancing with Clarissa. She made such an impact on me. Do you think I could call on her?"

John slapped Sam on the back and wished him well. "You are on your own, buddy boy. I think you must have scared her away from this place. I haven't been able to get her to come dancing with me since the night you two met." He wrote the address on a drink napkin. John explained, "You must know Clarissa resides with us, my parents and me, and has since her birth." He did not know how else to explain her situation and chose not to explain it fully.

Aunt Louisa answered the door at the sound of Sam's persistent knock. Sam was greeted by the soft rounded cheeks and twinkling eyes of Aunt Louisa at her friendliest. When Sam asked, "Please, ma'am, may I have your permission to call on Clarissa?" Aunt Louisa's five-foot-ten frame stepped out on to the porch. Her arms crossed in front of her broad chest and she stared down at Sam. Her pleasant demeanor changed to pursed lips and a haughty stare.

Mrs. Doppler demanded, "How is it that you, a young man who must be years older than any of her schoolmates, have come to know Clarissa?"

He stammered, "We met at the Hyde Park social club a few Saturday evenings ago."

Aunt Louisa exclaimed in horror, "Why, Clarissa would do no such thing, frequenting such a liberal place. My three daughters were required to have a young man make a call to this house for proper introduction. Any well-mannered young man would not become acquainted with a young woman unless it was in the presence of her elders!"

Sam dared not disagree with Mrs. Doppler. He regained a thread of confidence and swallowed hard. "Would there be a time when I may see Clarissa at the approval of Mr. Doppler and yourself?"

Aunt Louisa would not let go of her indignation. "Young man," she hissed, "I will call Clarissa this very minute to hear her side of this unbelievable story."

With that, Mrs. Doppler turned her back and waved Sam into the foyer, muttering, "All damage has obviously already been done to this family's good name." When Clarissa came running to the hallway in answer to Aunt Louisa's high-pitched calls, she stopped short in shock at the sight of Sam.

Rather than get John in trouble, Clarissa confessed, "Aunt Louisa, I am so, so sorry. I did sneak out of the house one night several weeks ago to follow John. I was wrong. It was a horrible mistake. I know it was wrong and I have never returned. Please forgive me."

Mrs. Doppler sent Clarissa away with a wave of her hand. "Go back to the kitchen." Then she turned to face Sam. Dismissing him with a clipped, "Good-bye," Aunt Louisa shooed him out of the foyer and slammed the door so hard the brass knocker clapped not once, but three times. Sam found himself on the Doppler's front porch, confused and disappointed.

Inside the house, Clarissa waited, soundless, at the kitchen sink. She was fearful and hopeful at the same time that Aunt Louisa would come to talk to her. Clarissa did not understand the feelings she was having about Sam. This was the first and only gentleman caller she had ever had. Only a few moments had passed when Clarissa heard the reaction and felt for herself the oppressive weight of dismay and heartache. Aunt Louisa laughed, and laughed, and laughed even harder at her harsh treatment of Sam Disser.

It was a cruel laugh of dismissal and intimidation. Aunt Louisa took great pleasure in administering fear and in dashing hope. It was a laugh that Clarissa knew all too well. Disheartened and rejected, Clarissa climbed the stairs to the attic and crawled into bed, convinced she would never see Sam again.

The only way to tell the truth is to speak with kindness. Only the words of a loving man can be heard.

—Henry David Thoreau

Sam

He could not get her out of his mind. Clarissa was not at all like the girls Sam had known or dated in school and certainly not similar in any way to the girls he had frequently called on when he was in service or since his return home. No, Clarissa was not typical of his society at home or in the army. She had not been influenced by the constant friendship of other girls. Dancing with her, Sam could feel her simple nature. Clarissa clung to him, needed him.

Sam thought of teenagers the same age as Clarissa as silly, empty. He and his friends called the girls they knew Ts because they copied each other in wearing T-bar shoes along with stylish cloche hats and long-waist dresses. These girls were happy to giggle the night away listening to George Gershwin tunes and dancing with one another. A few of them were known as Ts because they did *tease* the boys with hiked skirts and open-mouthed kisses offered in dark parked cars.

Popularity and immediate recognition were a reality for Sam. His father was a successful business man. Their home on Harrison Pike on the west side of the city was one of the largest in the area. The family business was recognized as the premier concrete and construction firm in Cincinnati. Sam and his sister Grace enjoyed the latest books and magazines and listened to all the popular radio programs. Sam's social life included the use of his father's Buick touring car, a telephone, an allowance, and tailored clothes. Personal freedom was all-important for Sam. He put off thoughts of having to work for the rest of his life in his father's company for as long as possible.

Sam had known in his teenage years that his claim to independence and autonomy would cease as soon as he graduated from high school. The long-term goals of his father's generation were simple: Sam was destined to take over the family business and to be a husband and father. His father's repeated direction was that Sam would marry a girl from an established family who would be a suitable homemaker and mother. That was expected in return for his father's hard work and social standing—no exceptions.

Sam's father complained that the youth of today were too "excitable" and would never amount to anything. His daily reminders to Sam that after he had graduated from high school he would be working in the family business fell on deaf ears. In his spare time, Sam joined friends at the movies and all the city's dance halls.

As soon as graduation day drew to a close, Sam signed on to be a plumber's apprentice, in public and private defiance of his father. Then when war was declared, Sam and his buddies enlisted. They were each anxious to escape their own parental restrictions and predetermined plans for their futures. However, upon their return home after the war, not only Sam but each of his friends as well were expected to fall in step with their parents' plans for a traditional life of work in the family business and a proper wife.

Like all dreamers I confuse enchantment with truth.

—Jean-Paul Sartre

Clarissa

Determined to see Clarissa again, Sam convinced himself to try to call on her one more time. He decided it might be best to choose a weekday evening when John Jr. and perhaps even Mr. Doppler would be home to see his determination and offer their support. As he approached the Doppler's house, he was fairly certain Mr. and Mrs. Doppler were at home, because Mr. Doppler's shiny black Buick was in the driveway. This time, Mr. Doppler answered the door. Mrs. Doppler was playing bridge at the home of a friend from church.

Sam had steeled his nerves and said, "I would like to call on Miss Clarissa if that is convenient." Even though John Sr. was momentarily surprised at this unexpected call for their young ward, he admired Sam for his request to see Clarissa in his presence.

Mr. Doppler replied, "Why certainly, young man. May I know your name, please?"

Sam instantly liked Mr. Doppler. He was a jovial man, an older version of John Jr. with a protruding chin and well-fed stomach. As he put out his hand to introduce himself, Mr. Doppler led Sam into the foyer and then into the drawing room and gestured for him to take a seat.

After answering a few questions about his background—parents, religious persuasion, and what his father did for a living—Sam offered to take his leave and come back at a time when Mrs. Doppler could be present as well. Mr. Doppler chuckled. "That won't be necessary. What I say in this house is law. If I like you, then damned well everyone has to like you."

Besides, Mr. Doppler had already heard his wife's ranting and raving about this bold young upstart who showed up one night to see Clarissa as if he had no manners whatsoever. Why, his wife was even crazier than he thought. This young man was fine. Mr. Doppler left the drawing room to summon Clarissa from the kitchen where she was washing the supper dishes.

When she heard faint bursts of conversation and laughter coming from the drawing room, Clarissa had assumed the caller was a friend of her Uncle John's or a neighbor come to call knowing full well that Mrs. Doppler was not at home. In the midst of her reverie, looking out the kitchen window at the rose garden, Mr. Doppler startled Clarissa. "I have come to announce to you a gentleman caller by the name of Sam Disser. He is awaiting your presence in the drawing room."

Clarissa was horrified. She was dressed in a work shirt and pants covered by a red gingham apron. She pleaded, "May I ask you to entertain Mr. Disser so that I may have time to arrange myself?"

"Certainly." He smiled. "Why, I have entertained more young men in that drawing room than you can imagine. Having three daughters made me quite the expert. Do not keep the young man waiting. This gentleman caller may not live very long if your Aunt Louisa has her way." He laughed at his own joke as he walked back from the kitchen to the drawing room. He offered Sam a scotch and settled back into one of the overstuffed chairs with a scotch of his own.

Bounding up the attic steps, Clarissa ran a quick comb through her hair, pulled off the apron, and put cream on her hands, which were red and wrinkled from scrubbing pots and pans. Clarissa had been wondering if she would ever see Sam again, and here he was, in this house, despite Aunt Louisa's initial dismissal. Clarissa was pleased she had made such an impression on Sam that he would return.

Mr. Doppler was a wonderful host and a delightful conversationalist, not at all the way he was with friends and family when Mrs. Doppler was present. When Clarissa joined the men in the drawing room, they were in the midst of discussing an ongoing construction project in the downtown area.

Clarissa had never known Mr. Doppler to be so quick with a joke and as engaging about local history as he was that night with Sam. She was happy to witness their banter. She was flattered when Mr. Doppler told Sam, "Clarissa is a wonderful young woman. She has become quite a blessing to her Aunt Louisa and me."

She couldn't help but wonder, *How much scotch has Uncle John had...or is he being sincere? I've never heard him talk like this or talk this much.*

Uncle John was able to convince Aunt Louisa that there was nothing questionable or untoward about Sam's background or his behavior. Without admitting she was wrong, Aunt Louisa amended her first impression of Sam in a comment at dinner the next evening, directed at Uncle John. "Well, I am certainly relieved to learn that Sam Disser is from a good family. And I am thankful to the Lord God above that a young man has taken interest in Clarissa. Perhaps this will end in marriage and release me from the burden and responsibility of continuing to provide for her." Neither Uncle John nor Clarissa made a comment. Uncle John quietly pushed away from the dinner table without waiting for his dessert and retreated to his evening time alone in the study.

Soon, Aunt Louisa and Uncle John came to expect regular visits from Sam. Mrs. Doppler began excusing herself from the drawing room, noting the easy camaraderie that had been growing between Sam and her husband. She was glad to leave the chaperoning of Sam and Clarissa to her husband, allowing her to retire to her bedroom to embroider or play solitaire and listen to her favorite radio programs. After Mrs. Doppler's departure, Mr. Doppler found it convenient to excuse himself as well, enabling an easy detour from the drawing room directly to his study for his evening scotch and cigar.

Initially, Clarissa was content to hear the mundane details of Sam's work day while they faced one another on the settee in the drawing room. As repetitive as work in the cement business could be, Sam went into great detail about the intricacies of the family's construction business. "Father has taught me the special recipes of all the cement products. He has taken great pains to show me the specific skills required to start a cement project and then pave and sculpt the wet concrete to meet the engineering drawings and specifications."

Clarissa did not know or come to know what the construction or cement businesses entailed, nor did she understand the terminology Sam used to explain each project to her, but he made it all sound so important. In these private conversations, Sam also embellished stories about his time as an enlisted man during the war.

He was encouraged by her questions and complimented by her agreement with his opinions. She listened intently to his views on the economy, business, and politics and was intrigued by Sam's world that had extended far beyond the confines of her life in Hyde Park.

On the weekends, Clarissa's heart would race when she heard Sam's new Ford Runabout pull up in front of the Doppler house. Sam loved that car and kept it in excellent condition. It had a shining black exterior and lustrous black leather seats. Clarissa didn't know when Sam had the time, but he was particular about keeping the vehicle finish pristine and the interior spotless.

After a brief explanation of his plans for their day, Clarissa and Sam would not even wait to hear Aunt Louisa give her approval. As soon as they saw a smile creep up her lips and her mouth open, Clarissa would say, "Thank you, Aunt Louisa. We will be back before dark, Aunt Louisa." Then they were out the front door and headed down the steps and paved walk to the street.

When they were far enough away from the neighborhood, Clarissa would strip the scarf off her carefully brushed hair and hoot with delight at the wind blowing around her face. "Freedom!" she would shout, "freedom!"

and a drive somewhere, anywhere, with Sam was always an adventure. He liked to drive along the Ohio River, making stops along the way to recite stories of the history of the city at each spot. He brought baskets of food for picnics and a blanket for long talks.

Sam was a Civil War buff and took on the role of teacher, explaining to Clarissa his broad knowledge of local history. It was during the Civil War that a series of six artillery batteries were built along the Ohio River to protect the city of Cincinnati. Clarissa was impressed that Sam knew the exact location (or so he claimed) of each of the sites, his favorite one being Battery Hooper in Fort Wright, Kentucky.

"Now," explained Sam, "the Battery Hooper was a hilltop earthworks fortification that was built for the defense of the city of Cincinnati during the Civil War. This fortification, not a fort, was built by the Union army of the North to turn back invading Confederate troops. This battery was critical for the protection of the city and of the Ohio River valley." Clarissa showed true interest, though she was more enraptured by the scenery and nature's peace at the site Sam had chosen.

As their relationship continued, Sam began calling on Clarissa several evenings during the week. When he was able to finish work on time Sam would clean up and join the family for dinner before driving to the Doppler house. As soon as they were able to sneak away, they would motor to Ault Park for moonlit walks and talks in the gardens.

Sam was flattered by Clarissa's attention and adoration. She was enchanted by his constant care and interest.

The Ford was their ticket to intimacy. It allowed them to share personal feelings and to explore each other's bodies. Most evenings, Sam and Clarissa kissed, necked, and fondled each other in the privacy of the Ford. Sam nicknamed it their "room."

One evening, he introduced Clarissa to sexual intercourse in the Ford. Sam had been kissing Clarissa lightly on the face and neck. He whispered in her ear, "I love you, Clarissa. I have from the first moment I saw you. I love you more than I ever dreamed I could love anyone." Sam nibbled on her earlobe and told her again, "I love you. I know I have never said that to you before, but I do love you. I want you to be with me, forever."

As he trailed his kisses down her neck Clarissa agreed, "And I love you, so much." He unbuttoned her sweater and slipped his hands inside her bra to caress her breasts. For the first time, he took her breasts out of her bra and fondled her nipples with his fingers. He rolled her nipples between the tips of his fingers until they were hard and red. When Clarissa arched her back in arousal, Sam bent down and sucked on her nipples, separately at first, and then he pulled her massive breasts together and sucked on both nipples.

Her hands were running through his hair, and she was softly moaning. Sam unzipped her skirt down the back.

He lifted Clarissa up off the seat so he could pull it down to the floor. Then he lifted her up again to do the same with her white panties. Sam turned Clarissa sideways so her head was leaning on the passenger side window ledge. She was staring up at the sky and the stars. He knew she was in ecstasy.

Sam lifted her legs up on each of his shoulders. He buried his face in the soft hair and wet lips between her legs. He sucked the sweet orgasm and felt himself as hard and big as he had ever been. Sam could wait no longer. He unzipped his pants and revealed his fullness to Clarissa. He slipped on a condom and pulled her over on top of him. With her breasts and hardened nipples brushing his chest he shoved his manhood inside of her and exploded.

"That was unbelievable," Sam gasped. "You are so tight and so wet." Clarissa was silent. "Oh, Clarissa, you are mine. I love you." Sam was holding her face in his hands. "Do not be afraid or upset. I know this was your first time. I'm sorry I didn't go slower. I couldn't help myself." Clarissa smiled. The pain between her legs had taken her breath away. Sam had to help her back into her seat.

Their lovemaking took place every time they were together. Sam professed his love to Clarissa again and again and committed to marry her. At first the excitement of his passion and lovemaking overcame Clarissa's fears of being caught in the park with all their clothes on the small leather bench behind the front seats.

As the weekends flew by, Sam's kisses and caresses took less time and his mounting her or pulling her on top of him took less time as well. The physical relief for him was remarkable. "Clarissa, I need your love forever. I love you," Sam repeated again and again.

It was obvious to Clarissa that Sam had sexual experience. He had coached and coaxed her how to relax and accept his physical desire. "You know, the Bible tells us that God made man and made woman so they are a physical fit and give one another pleasure," Sam instructed. "This is how it is done for the pleasure of both the man and the woman." Initially, Sam was careful and gentle, using a condom and entering her only when she was excited and wet.

One evening in the park, as she was unbuttoning her sweater, Sam pulled Clarissa's chin up to meet his face and asked, "Will you marry me?"

Clarissa readily and immediately answered, "Yes, oh yes, that is all I want." Sam threw the condom out the window and declared that night as the first night he would experience real pleasure.

Though she did not wish to admit it, Clarissa was not certain how babies were made. After several weeks she finally got up the nerve to ask Sam, "Are we going to have a child if you do not use that device?"

"Well, it is possible" Sam offered, "but I will always be careful to pull out before any semen enters you. That is what will give us a son." Now Clarissa became very worried. Sam's fluids always entered her and only a small amount was found on the towel they used to cover her seat. And they were not yet married.

A mere three months into their courtship, Sam confessed to his parents, "I must tell you that I have not been out evenings and weekends with my army buddies. I've been visiting and spending time with the girl I am going to marry. Ever since I found her, I have been spending as much time as possible with her." The look of shock on both his mother's and his father's faces gave Sam the pause he needed to add, "In fact, I am going to propose marriage to her tomorrow evening," he boasted.

His mother fell into her rocking chair trying to catch her breath. His father thundered back at him, "You will do no such thing. Why have you been hiding this girl from us? Are you ashamed of her? Who is she? No respectable family would allow such a relationship. We are your parents. We will decide who you will or will not marry. You will bring her here to meet us before you will even consider marriage."

Sam stormed out of the house and sped to the east side of town to see Clarissa. No one was going to tell him what he was going to do with his life, not his mother, not his father, not anyone. He had already proposed marriage. Clarissa had accepted his proposal. Nothing else was required.

**The personal life deeply lived always
expands into truths beyond itself.**

—Anais Nin

Sam

Sam was known to others, especially those in his father's circle, as Sam Jr. He was the son of the well-known businessman, the gregarious and imposing Samuel Martin Disser. Mr. Disser demanded obedience from Sam and from Sam's sister, Grace. Samuel had a quick and fiery temper. It was safer not to confront or contradict him.

From as far back as he could remember, Sam had avoided his father's lectures about conformity to the family rules. His school days and summers were planned for him, he made excellent marks in every class, and he worked in the Disser company to learn the business when school was not in session. Ultimately, Sam was told, he would take over the company. When that would happen was never clear.

Sam's mother, May, was a quiet, frail, and transparent woman. She had difficulty breathing and was told by her physicians to stop having children after the birth of Sam and Grace. May spent the majority of her time indoors, cooking and doing needlepoint. Sam knew his mother was not only weak in health but also weak in spirit. She succumbed to her husband's every demand. Sam never looked to his mother for support in matters of importance.

There were only a few times Sam sought the support and companionship of his younger sister, Grace. As soon as Grace had reached the age when it was obvious how little value she held for Mr. Disser and especially how little worth she could present to the family business, Grace became even more invisible and obscure than her mother. Her gender had no place at The Disser Company. Grace devoted herself to her mother, her job as a secretary at the Revenue Service, and the outside and more physical chores of the Disser home.

Even though Samuel Martin Disser had been the middle child of eleven children, most people declared that he had all the personality. His parents had emigrated from Germany in the mid-nineteenth century. They had first lived in North Liberty, Indiana, and then moved to

Glendale, Ohio, so Casper Disser could start a business of his own in construction. Casper and Anna Maria Disser (née Mider) had their first two children in Indiana, George and Francis. After the move to Ohio, they raised nine more children: John, Maria, Luis, Samuel, Carl, Friedrich, Halharina and Heinrich the twins, and finally Gresenci. To be a standout in the one shy of a dozen Dissers, Samuel was a showman. He gathered other children in the neighborhood to put on plays and variety shows for parents and friends.

Sam Jr. had inherited his father's talent for the theatrical. In high school, Sam was in the musical *Minstrels*. After graduating from high school, Sam had defied his father and, with his best buddy Glenn, become a plumber's apprentice. The work was interesting, and the pay was good. Every night at dinner, Sam faced his father's disapproval and lectures. When America called for volunteers to go to war, Sam saw a chance to get away from home. He enlisted without his parents' knowledge. In the army, Sam continued to entertain and amuse his fellow soldiers. Acting as a "master of ceremonies," Sam convinced other servicemen with various talents to join in weekend shows in the mess hall.

Sam announced his enlistment to his father and mother at the dinner table the evening before his departure for training camp. "Well, it's off to war I go," quipped Sam. While his mother silently wept in her napkin, Sam continued, "Yes, I leave on the morning train bound for

New Jersey with the hope never to return to this doleful and unhappy house. Farewell to all…farewell."

While Sam may have assumed and even dreamed of going overseas to fight in the European Theater, his fate was to never leave New Jersey. During boot camp training, he broke his leg in five places and missed the ship to England. The armed forces deemed it best to reassign Sam to be a cook for the troops who passed through New Jersey for boot camp before departing to fight overseas.

The fact that Sam never experienced combat gave his father yet another reason to be disappointed in his son. Despite all expectations for a war hero or at least a combat soldier, to know that Sam was just a cook for real fighting men was embarrassing. Samuel's brother Friedrich had fought in the Spanish-American War and had come back regaling them with tales of battles won. Samuel denied his wife's request to hang the single star service flag in the window confirming their son Sam was in the armed forces.

When Sam returned home, he felt he had no choice but to give in to his father's plan for his life. Samuel taught his son the art of cement finishing along with the colored men in his employ. Sam was treated the same as the employees, no better and no worse, and received the same pay. His life was meant to be lived at home with his parents and his destiny was to own and run the family business. As the months passed, Mr. Disser reminded Sam of his duty to marry a socially acceptable woman and to produce sons to carry on the family name.

While there were plenty of girls to date in the Dissers' social circle, Sam knew it would be difficult to convince any to agree to his father's prerequisites for a wife and mother. Though they anticipated the eventuality of being a wife and mother, young women of a significant social standing were not interested in Samuel's conditions of living in the Disser home, enduring his rules for submission to his orders, and producing a son and heir to the Disser name as soon as conception was possible.

Between high school and his enlistment, when Sam was working long hours as a plumber's apprentice, there were few opportunities to fraternize with girls his age. When the war began, Sam found company in the arms of a variety of less than reputable women. An epidemic of venereal diseases among soldiers became widespread because of the soldiers' frequent visits to whorehouses.

President Wilson mandated sex education for all US recruits. In required classes, Sam's army corps were shown photos and movies about vaginal diseases and their effect on a man's sex organs. This was effective awareness for the men. Especially useful were the free condoms the US Army distributed. While the purpose was not to condone sex (printed on the condoms was "for prevention of disease only"), every army recruit kept a private stash of condoms in their wallets. This small inventory was for emergency use only, of course.

The soldiers who came home had adapted admirably to the sex education they had received and had every intention of pursuing additional wisdom. With the general availability of condoms and the recent proliferation of cars, premarital sex was common. After the war, women had twice as much sex as women in the turn of the century had had. Prominent physicians and educators wrote openly that sex was not only for reproduction but for pleasure as well. Sigmund Freud confirmed sex as a "natural human behavior" and explained that every human possessed a "biological sex drive."

Sam was trying to resign himself to his fate of living at home and working in the family business. His sole ambition was to find that perfect bride, a young lady who would enjoy his appetite for physical intimacy and who came from a socially acceptable family. He believed all his dreams had come true when he met Clarissa Doppler. She was chaste, adoring, and from one of the leading families of Hyde Park. Yes, Father would have no choice but to be pleased with Clarissa.

> **We know the truth, not only by the reason,
> but by the heart.**
>
> **—Blaise Pascal**

Clarissa

The first meeting with Sam's parents did not go well, not well at all. Mr. Disser intimidated Clarissa with hard-hitting questions about how she and Sam had met. "Where exactly did you meet my son? How long have you been seeing him?" Clarissa was not prepared for his rude questioning and only answered with the truth.

Mrs. Disser sat quietly, stiff and straight, in a wing-back chair. Her spindly legs were covered in a dark paisley shawl. She was not unattractive but was obviously not well. Her chalk-colored face presented a sharp contrast to black hair pinned on top of her head in tight curls. A small mouth was pursed in tiny wrinkles that deepened as her husband interrogated Clarissa.

"What exactly is your heritage? Who are your parents? Where were you born, and where were you raised? Which schools did you attend?" Mr. Disser fired one question after another. Clarissa could barely collect her thoughts to answer before Mr. Disser aimed another question at her.

She answered every question as factually as possible. Clarissa looked to Mrs. Disser and then to Sam for help. At the end of Mr. Disser's interview, both of them were studying the floor. Mr. Disser had worked himself into a lather, fists clenched at his sides, his eyes wide and unblinking.

After returning Clarissa to the Doppler house, Sam came home to his father's vehement disapproval. Mr. Disser stomped his foot. "I forbid it. That's right, I *forbid* you to marry that girl. Besides the difference in your ages, she is not worthy, I repeat, not worthy of the Disser name." Mrs. Disser began to weep.

In his heart, Sam knew his father was right. When he put the questions to Clarissa in the manner he did and she answered as honestly as Sam should have known she would, her story was not as pretty a picture as the one Sam had painted for himself. Sam was twenty-six years old, and Clarissa was a child of sixteen. What Mr. Disser saw as a temporary infatuation Sam felt was the love of his life. "Most important of all," Mr. Disser thundered, "a Disser wife must be a young woman of means, from a decent family. That girl is an orphan and your whore!" Mrs. Disser gasped at her husband's frankness and began sobbing and shaking.

Mr. Disser's vague expectations of Clarissa had been irreparably shattered. She had answered him directly that her mother had died in childbirth leaving her father with three children to care for alone. Openly explaining that her father could not work to support his children without a spouse at home to care for them, he had proposed to one of his late wife's sisters, Marie. She had refused his proposal of marriage because she already had four children of her own.

Clarissa's father had persisted. He was desperate. Marie finally agreed on one condition, "Send your three children to family members until they are old enough for school. Then and only then will I marry you." Clarissa's father tried to coerce every relative known to him and other relations to take on one or all of his three children.

Unbeknownst to Clarissa, no one had wanted the middle child and only boy. Little Willie had been taken to an orphanage in northwest Ohio, never to be seen or heard from again. The two girls, Clarissa and Laura, had been taken by Aunt Louisa and Uncle John when Laura was three years old and Clarissa an infant of six months. The girls were separated a short time later when Laura was sent to live with the Feins.

Clarissa admitted that she was taken in by Aunt Louisa and Uncle John Doppler. On her fourth birthday, Aunt Louisa had directed Clarissa to help with the chores of the Doppler household. Sam's father had needed to hear no more. His mind was made up about Clarissa. She was a stray—no better than a dog that had been kicked to the curb. The Doppler family had obviously taken her into their home to serve them as domestic help. Unfortunately, Mr. Disser's crude assessment was true.

**Each new morn widows howl, orphans cry,
sorrows strike heaven on the face.**

—William Shakespeare

Sam

Sam had reassured Clarissa time and again of his undying love for her. Despite the first meeting with his parents, he was confident. "I know Father and Mother will come to see that I love you as I have loved no other. You will be my wife." Sam declared her childhood and upbringing did not matter. "You are a Doppler—you have that heritage, you do. You were raised in a fine family environment. Believe me, you are more than worthy to be a Disser." Clarissa put her faith and love in Sam's urgings and believed him.

It was the Christmas season, and Sam steeled himself to bring Clarissa to the holiday parties at the Disser home. There were three parties on the calendar: one with the neighbors and community at large, one for Mr. Disser's business clients and their families, and one for Disser family members. The festivities began the first week of December and continued until New Year's Eve.

The Disser property on Harrison Avenue encompassed almost five acres, though the majority of the land was adorned with towering oak and catalpa trees, dating back to the late nineteenth century. The blood red brick of the house and limestone foundation made a severe first impression. A wide-as-the-house stone front porch was supported by blood red brick columns. Every evening of the holiday, Mrs. Disser flooded the front porch with so many candle glasses that the shadows of dancing light gave the austere house an eerie rather than a festive appearance.

Inside the Disser home, there was a similar sense of somberness. A smoke gray tile foyer exposed four square rooms. On the left was a drawing room, which led directly to the dining room. On the right was a library that led to the study. All the rooms on the first floor were wallpapered in a pale grey variety on the same theme, featuring English gentlemen and ladies. High, wooden-beamed ceilings and fireplaces covered with black iron screens emphasized the lack of color and interior features. Lamps set strategically on armchair tables provided the only light in the rooms, except for the silver chandelier in the dining room that presented eleven glass crystals around a center etched globe.

Grace and Mrs. Disser had adorned every interior surface with holly branches and had decorated the Christmas tree in the drawing room with the same, adding only a few small red bows for distinction.

Clarissa was melancholy throughout the entire holiday. She attributed it to the chill inside the Disser house from the winter drafts that blew in with the arrival and departure of every guest, as well as the heavy foods that were served. It could even have been due in part to the indifference she felt with each cold reception from Sam's parents, his sister Grace, or the family and friends who turned and walked away without engaging in casual conversation when Sam introduced her.

Even though Sam introduced her as Clarissa Doppler, everyone took their cue from Mr. and Mrs. Disser and recognized that this was not the match Sam's parents had dreamed of. Clarissa and Sam had held such high hopes that they would find at least a few allies or convince Sam's parents to take the time to know her and to love her. Not one of the invited guests or relatives, not even one, had the courage to reach out to the young couple.

Introduction to hard liquor was Sam's explanation for the ensuing headaches. Clarissa had discovered most alcohol did not agree with her belly or her head. Though she tried wine, spiked cider, scotch, and even straight whiskey, none of it tasted particularly good, and each one landed in her stomach with a thud. On New Year's Eve, she stopped after a shot of whiskey and a few sips of champagne at midnight.

Nausea interrupted her housekeeping chores in the Doppler home and her January schoolwork suffered as well. For the first time in her school years, Aunt Louisa received a call the end of January advising of Clarissa's failing grades.

After the Christmas parties, Sam ceased taking Clarissa to his house. Every time she inquired, "Why aren't we going to your home? Isn't it more appropriate for us to continue to visit there?" Sam claimed, "Father is busy at work now that it is a new year, and Mother's health worsens in the winter."

The truth of the matter was that Mr. Disser had banned Clarissa from his home. It had not taken long for family members and friends to discover the truth about Clarissa's background. It was the topic of every conversation. This was not such a big city after all, and the Dissers exclusive social circle could not stop talking about Sam's choice for a bride.

Sam had announced his intentions toward Clarissa at the Dissers' holiday gatherings as often as possible. Clarissa began to sense that it was more in defiance of his father than it was his love for her. "Yes, this is the lovely Clarissa. Have you heard? I have asked her to be my bride. Wonderful news, isn't it?"

The day after Christmas, Mr. Disser had decided he would not be embarrassed or disgraced by his son's infatuation. His decision was final. "I forbid you from ever bringing that girl to this home. She is not welcome here. If you insist on associating with her, you are not welcome in this house either."

So it came as no surprise that, six weeks after the New Year holiday, Sam and Clarissa made their own decision to start a life together. Sam drove them in the Ford Runabout across the bridge from the state of Ohio to the Commonwealth of Kentucky. At the Covington Courthouse, where Clarissa could be legally wed at the age of sixteen, their marriage ceremony was presided over by a justice of the peace. It was Valentine's Day and Clarissa was pregnant.

**Love is blind,
but marriage restores its sight.**

—Georg C. Lichtenberg

Clarissa and Sam

After the brief ceremony, it was time for the newlyweds to start their life as husband and wife. Sam drove his new bride directly to the Disser house. "Father and Mother will not be able to deny our love for one another now that we are married." Sam was defiant in his new role as husband. Clarissa accepted his boldness as truth. She thought to herself, *Perhaps Mr. and Mrs. Disser will now accept me and our marriage. Surely they will be thrilled that Sam and I are legally wed.*

"It should be a joyous occasion, right?" Clarissa asked with a shaky voice. "Your father should be pleased now that I am your wife and that he will soon have a grandson." She smiled tentatively at Sam. His measured smile in return gave her little reassurance.

On their arrival, Sam and Clarissa noticed a car in the driveway and could see the silhouette of a visitor in the Dissers' drawing room. It was a previous schoolmate of Sam's, a pretty redhead named Annie. She looked like a model from one of those fashion magazines Clarissa had seen in a store window on her walks to and from school.

Annie's personality was engaging. She was heard laughing at one of Mr. Disser's jokes when Sam and Clarissa came into the drawing room. Annie had been a friend of Sam's since they were in grade school. She had stopped by to tell Mr. and Mrs. Disser about her new job as a legal secretary. They had been congratulating her when Sam and Clarissa were seen walking to the front door.

Sam announced himself to his parents' guest. "Annie! How good it is to see you."

As Annie turned to embrace Sam, she noticed Clarissa and reached past him to embrace her instead. "So this is the beauty I have been hearing so much about! Hello, my name is Annie." Clarissa was taken aback by Annie's hug.

Trying to make up for the conversation they had missed, Annie explained, "I did not get to attend any holiday parties thanks to final exams. It would be great for all of us to get together." Annie was thrilled to see Sam and intrigued by the rumors of his infatuation with Clarissa.

Sam seized the opportunity to declare their new status. "You should receive an invitation very soon to a wedding reception. Clarissa is my wife." Stunned by the news, Annie congratulated the couple with yet another embrace of Clarissa.

"Why, you really did steal the ole boy's heart, didn't you? Here I am going on about my exams and I didn't even give you two a chance to tell me your wonderful news." As Annie turned to smile at Sam's parents, it was obvious they were in shock.

As quickly as she had dropped by to see the Dissers, Annie just as abruptly congratulated the newlyweds again. Walking toward the foyer, she insisted, "I do have a previous engagement for which I will be late if I don't hurry." Hugging first Clarissa and then Sam, Annie promised, "I will stop by for a visit again soon. Good-bye!" With Mr. Disser standing stiffly at the window and Mrs. Disser sitting stock-still in her chair, Annie retreated out the front door.

Once the massive outer door clicked closed, Mrs. Disser broke down in hysterical crying, hiding her face in her handkerchief. Mr. Disser exploded. Sam had seen the color creeping up his neck even as Annie had announced her departure. Now there was a swollen red face to match his angry, bellowing voice. He spit at Clarissa, "You are not a suitable wife for my son. You are not a suitable daughter-in-law. You have no place in this family or in this house. You will never be a Disser. You will never have my family name or a place in this family!"

He turned his back on both of them. "Well," Sam yelled at his father's back, equal in his father's anger, "that's not all our news, Father. We are having a baby. Doc Simmons said so last week. The baby is due in September. So let's just get all your unhappiness out in the open at one time!"

Clarissa's tears and shaking would not sway Mr. Disser. She feared for her safety if she were to approach him directly. Standing behind Sam, she pleaded, "Give me a chance. I love Sam. I am worthy of being a part of your family. Please, Mr. Disser, oh please."

In desperation she fell to her knees at Mrs. Disser's feet, begging for her blessing, begging for her understanding. "Please, Mrs. Disser. You are a wife and a mother. Please?" She pleaded over and over again. Mrs. Disser never looked up from her handkerchief. Mr. Disser finally turned from the window to face his son.

In a rage, Samuel railed, "That girl will never be accepted, never be tolerated, and never be your wife. Look at Annie—now there is an example of the woman you should have married. Instead…instead, you have chosen this pitiful servant? She obviously slept with you to find a way out of her miserable situation. Can't you see what a horrible mistake you have made? Did you do this just to defy me? Did you do this to kill your mother?" Samuel's rapid fire, "Why? Why? Why?" finally turned to silence.

Mrs. Disser's anger and disappointment did not diminish despite her unyielding silence. Sam recognized his mother's suffering, and his father's wrath was unlike anything he had ever encountered. He took Clarissa's arm to help her up and led her out of the house.

Grace had been eavesdropping on the family disaster from the top of the stairs. She sympathized with Sam and with Clarissa but knew better than to voice or show her support. Under her breath she mused, "I have never heard Father so angry. Clarissa will not have a chance for happiness in this family." Sighing in resignation, she retraced her steps to her bedroom and shut the door to the family tragedy.

A speedy departure from the Disser home found Sam and Clarissa back on the road. To break the silence between them, Sam announced, "We are going to go to the Doppler house to share our news. At the very least, your uncle John and your aunt Louisa will be happy for us. We deserve a more appropriate reception." Clarissa was panicked. If Uncle John was home it would be a suitable conversation. If he was not at home, there was no telling what Aunt Louisa would say.

Not surprisingly, Mr. Doppler was not at home. He was putting in his usual long hours at the furniture store. Sam and Clarissa sat nervously on the settee in the drawing room and shared their news with Mrs. Doppler. "Mrs. Doppler," Sam began, "We have news, and we know you will join with us in rejoicing."

"And what would that be?" Aunt Louisa gazed purposefully at the blush on Clarissa's face and the nervous grip Sam had on Clarissa's hand.

"Why, we were married this afternoon, at the justice of the peace, a proper ceremony to confirm our love for one another." Sam gained conviction of their decision as he spoke.

Aunt Louisa merely shook her head from side to side. When she spoke, she directed her interrogation at Sam, "You think that I would join with you in rejoicing? You are wrong, young man. It is disgraceful that you have gone behind our backs and, I can only assume, behind your parents' backs as well to take this step." Turning her face and curling her upper lip in disgust at Clarissa, Aunt Louisa demanded, "I want you to gather the few personal items that are truly yours and take your leave from this house. You are a disappointment and a disgrace to this family. I will be glad to be rid of you and rid of the responsibility for you."

She rose from her brocade chair and stepped into the foyer, pointing a finger at the hall leading to the kitchen and the attic stairs. Clarissa rose slowly from the settee, feeling sadness so thick and dense she could barely move her feet in Aunt Louisa's direction. Moments later, Clarissa appeared in the foyer clutching a paper bag of belongings. There was no one there to say good-bye.

As Sam pulled the car away from the curb, Clarissa dared not look back at the Doppler house for fear she would see Aunt Louisa's grinning face in the front window. Hadn't she regularly reminded Clarissa, "If left on your own you would be of no use to anyone. And then where would you be? Out on the street with no home, that's where." And here she was, out on the street with no home.

> Love: a temporary insanity,
> curable by marriage.
>
> —Ambrose Bierce

Clarissa and Sam

In an attempt to take control of the situation and celebrate their marriage, Sam treated his new wife to dinner at Mecklenbourg's restaurant in the central area of the city called Clifton. Sam had frequented the restaurant with friends and enjoyed the authentic German specialties. They laughed when Sam spilled a bit of the sauerbraten on his dark blue suit. They laughed again when Clarissa spilled a bit of cheese sauce on the dress she had worn for the dance contest when they first met.

With nothing for the two of them to change into except for Clarissa's school and work clothes that she had rolled up in a bag and stashed in the Runabout, Sam asked the restaurant if he could use their phone. Hoping Grace would pick up the house phone in the main hall, Sam was relieved when it was indeed Grace who answered.

"Grace, oh thank God it's you. I would like to ask you a favor." Sam was crossing his fingers.

"What is it?" whispered Grace, fearful that her father might be listening from the study.

"Could you bring a change or two of clothing from my room for me, and if it's not too much to ask a change or two of something that no longer fits you for Clarissa?" Sam was hopeful his sister would be of this much help.

"All right, I will. But Sam, you cannot ask me to take sides. If Father finds out I have helped you two, I will never hear the end of his arguments and tongue lashings."

Sam promised, "This is all I will ever ask of you. Oh, Grace. Please help us."

"Very well. Where should I meet you?"

"We just finished dinner at Mecklenbourg's. We will order dessert and wait for you here." Sam was grateful for his sister's support.

When Grace arrived at the restaurant, she stood her distance from the happy couple. "I overheard the fight with Mother and Father at home. I imagine you have no place to stay tonight. So on my way here, I stopped to speak to the manager at the Vernon Manor Hotel. He had some trouble with his taxes last year and I helped him correct his revenue forms. I hoped he would remember me." She was folding and unfolding a piece of the Vernon Manor stationery in her hands. "Here, I took some of the money I keep in my room and booked the wedding suite at the Vernon Manor Hotel for two nights. It is my wedding gift to you. It's all I can do, Sam. You understand, don't you? It's all I can do, for either of you. Father sees no significance in a daughter, in me. If I go against him on this, if I take your side, I will be out on the street." Grace handed her brother the hotel receipt and walked back to her car. She lifted a suitcase from the trunk, set it on the curb, and without looking back at the newlyweds she drove away.

Sam had never felt close to his sister. At that moment, he was grateful for this single gesture of kindness. They did need a place to stay. Quite honestly, Sam had no idea where they were going to spend the night. Tears welled in his eyes as he watched her disappear into the night. Without her seeing, he waved, and without her hearing, he sighed, "Thank you, Grace."

They climbed in the Ford Runabout for the short drive up the hill to the Vernon Manor Hotel. Sam pulled in the drive and under the white pillared portico. When the room key was in his hand, Sam and Clarissa ran up the stairs to the wedding suite. He lifted her up in his arms and opened the door to the suite.

"Oh my goodness!" Clarissa exclaimed. "This is like a dream. It is so beautiful. And so big! Is this really just for us? For two nights?"

Sam spun around trying to take in all the space and splendor. "This is our private and glorious hideaway," he agreed. "The best part is that no one knows we are here. I think we should stow away in this enormous suite until they kick us out!"

The room twinkled with the lights of the city along one wall, which featured windows from the floor to the sixteen-foot ceiling. The walls and carpet were a complement of green and gold patterns of leaves and large petal flowers. Furniture in browns and greens were muted by the cream satin down-filled spread and pillows covering an enormous bed. On the bedside table were a magnum of champagne and a basket of fresh fruit, compliments of the hotel manager.

A spotless cream tile bathroom was larger than any bathroom either of them had ever seen. It had an over-sized claw-footed tub and two marble sinks. A forest green dressing table with mirror and matching stool sat in the corner. Thick cream-colored rugs were situated at the dressing table, tub, and sinks.

Giggling and happy, they ran to bounce on the bed and kick off their shoes. Sam lifted Claire's head off the cream satin bedspread and looked longingly into her green eyes. "I love you," Sam declared.

"I know," Clarissa smiled. Kissing her eyelids and then her cheeks and parting her teeth with his tongue, Sam unzipped the back of her dress. He gently pulled her dress forward off her shoulders and let it fall down her arms. He pulled first one breast and then the other out of her slip and pushed her down onto the pillows. Sam straddled Clarissa's hips and massaged her breasts with his hands until her nipples were swollen. Then he gently pulled on her nipples to make them hard.

Still in the sleeves of her dress, Clarissa's arms were bound at her sides. She struggled enough for Sam to know she was uncomfortable but not enough for him to stop kissing her breasts. When his penis was so large and hard he could not manage the foreplay any longer, Sam pulled the dress down Clarissa's legs, slid her panties to the side of her opening, and guided his way inside her.

Even though Clarissa had experienced Sam on top of her in the Runabout, she had not felt the full weight of him or the strength of his thrusting. She moved with his rhythm to minimize the tearing sensation. When he exploded and fell to her side on the bed she was relieved and exhausted too.

They fell asleep cradled in each other's arms until the early shards of sunlight through the wall of windows startled them to greet the next morning. A knock at their door was a bellman presenting a silver tray holding a sealed message addressed to Clarissa.

Sam tipped the bellman and teased Clarissa with the envelope. He ran around the hotel room while she chased him, grasping for the message. Sam ran to the bed and hid it behind his back. When Clarissa leaped on the bed Sam gathered her in his arms and smothered her with kisses. The message was only temporarily forgotten.

Her dear, sweet Cousin John had heard the news and was surprising them with a wedding reception at the club that very afternoon. It read, "To the newlyweds, my gift of a proper wedding party, to be held this very day at the Hyde Park Country Club promptly at 1:00 p.m." Clarissa was frantic. What would she wear? What should they expect? Who would be attending?

Clarissa quickly bathed and resisted all attempts by Sam to join her in the tub. She washed and towel dried her hair, brushed it through, and applied what makeup she had in her purse. Sam relented to a bath alone, and they both agreed to make do with the clothes Grace had brought to them the night before. They were casual clothes, sweater and slacks for Sam, and one of Grace's work dresses for Clarissa.

The party was filled with Sam's friends and John's friends. They greeted the newlyweds at the door to the large reception hall with congratulations and best wishes. It was a sincere and delightful celebration.

John had received the news of their marriage through Aunt Louisa's hysterical sobbing about "losing her baby girl" when he returned home Saturday afternoon from work. He had driven downtown to the furniture store to tell his father the news that Sam and Clarissa were married. "Of course Father is concerned for your future and your happiness, as am I," John said, wrapping his arm around her shoulder in concern. "This reception was Father's idea, and the club is going all out for you at his request. So let's enjoy this perfectly joyful occasion!" John raised his glass of champagne and shouted, "A toast, a toast, to the bride and groom!"

The previous evening, the club had held a Valentine's Day dance. For today's reception, crisp white linens were snapped onto every table and the Valentine's Day centerpieces were refreshed. Lovely red berry candle rings held red felt hearts of varying sizes circling fluted vases filled with blossoming pink roses. The typical afternoon finger sandwiches, fresh fruit, cheese and crackers, fresh vegetables with dip, an olive tray, petit-fours, and cookies were laid out on long buffet tables on the side of the room. Maggie had arranged for a lovely three-tier carrot cake with cream cheese icing, a specialty of the club's chef, with a circle of pink roses on the top layer featuring petal designs in the cream cheese icing.

Wine and champagne flowed. Conversations were light and lively about the newlyweds and the bright future that lay ahead for them. All the guests assured Sam and Clarissa they were the perfect match. The outside world and all its concerns melted away for a few hours.

As guest after guest took their leave, Annie came to Sam and Clarissa to inquire, "Where do you two plan to live?"

Sam stammered in reply, "I honestly don't know."

Annie was somewhat taken aback and quickly offered, "Why don't you bring Clarissa to my apartment in the morning on your way to work? She can spend the day there looking through the morning's newspaper at ads and walking around my neighborhood for a place to rent. I'm not that far from the hotel, and it's a nice area. Besides, I'd love to have you two close by. What do you say?"

Clarissa tugged at Sam's sleeve, "Oh, yes! That's a perfectly wonderful idea, Annie. Thank you!" What a relief that finally, after all their efforts to find a friend, not just Sam but Clarissa had someone's care.

Sam smiled and patted Clarissa's hand on his sleeve. "That sounds like a plan. Thank you, Annie."

**The woman cries before the wedding and
the man after.**

—Polish Proverb

Sam

The weekend had been like no holiday Sam had ever known. Sunday was consumed by the impromptu wedding celebration at the Hyde Park Country Club. How John had pulled together a reception with so little notice was a mystery to both Sam and Clarissa.

When they returned to the hotel Sunday evening, they were giddy as schoolchildren and made love slowly and sweetly. Clarissa fell into a deep sleep. Sam, agonizing over what he would face the next morning at his father's company, laid awake looking out at the city skyline until the telephone rang, reminding him it was time to get up.

Earlier than usual on Monday morning, Sam was headed into work. He had first driven Clarissa to Annie's apartment. Annie did not have to report to work downtown until nine o'clock. She was preparing toast and eggs for herself and her new friend. Clarissa promised Sam, "I will find an appropriate and inexpensive place for us." He kissed her on the forehead and walked back to the car.

In the workers' bathroom, Sam had already changed into a spare set of work clothes and was bent over, changing into his work boots. He heard familiar footsteps and recognized his father's size twelve shoes. "Just where is it that you intend the two of you to live?" Mr. Disser growled.

Without looking up, Sam answered, "Clarissa is looking for a place for us to rent."

Still seething at his son's defiance, Mr. Disser grabbed Sam's arm and pulled him upright to look him in the face. "No son of mine will live outside the Disser home. I am not paying for such luxury. You and your tramp will live in the Disser house…my house. There will be no renting on your salary, on my hard-earned money." Mr. Disser stormed away and slammed the door.

That evening, Clarissa and Sam walked, hand in hand, up to the front door of the Disser house. Sam's mother opened the door and silently led them up three flights of stairs to the top floor. The first living quarters for the newlyweds was to be the Disser attic...yet another attic for Clarissa.

Being content with an attic ought not to mean being unable to move from it and resigned to living in it...

—Gilbert K. Chesterton

Clarissa

As they stood together surveying their new accommodations, Clarissa offered as boldly as she could through sniffling and tears, "I am determined to be a part of your family. I can help your mother and Grace. Why, with no rent to pay, we will save money for our own apartment in no time at all." Sam was silent. Dejected and depressed, his shoulders slumped forward as he quietly moved discarded furniture to the far end of the attic where there was no window. When he descended the attic stairs and closed the door, Clarissa felt her heart pounding from her chest clear up to her throat. She was abandoned.

Sam returned several times to the attic. With Grace's help to maneuver the furnishings, he brought his twin beds, mattresses, dresser drawers, and dressers from his bedroom. Next there were lamps, throw rugs, and linens. Clarissa stood against the door watching Sam's pride and confidence extinguish with each transfer of his old life to his new life. At last the room was filled with essentials. Grace touched Clarissa's folded hands and reminded her, "I am not on your side. Not now, not ever." As a way of explanation, she offered, "You have no idea the extent of Father's influence in this city. I will not go against his wishes. If I do, he has threatened to put me out on the street, disowned and abandoned."

When they came downstairs for dinner, Mr. Disser was already seated at the head of the table. He chose to ignore them both. Mrs. Disser was seated at the opposite end of the table from Mr. Disser. Grace sat opposite Sam and Clarissa.

Mrs. Disser interrupted the silence and directed her comments at Clarissa, "I want to explain to you your role in this house. You are to be responsible for all the house-work, the washing and ironing, and the kitchen chores. When Sam and Mr. Disser leave for work in the morning, you will begin by cleaning the house, followed by doing the washing and ironing. After the evening meal, you will wash the dishes, pots, and pans, and then you will scrub the kitchen floor. Is that clear?"

Clarissa locked her eyes on her hands that were folded in her lap, willing them to stop shaking. She waited for Sam to object. He did not respond. There was nothing she could think of to say. Clarissa nodded in understanding but not in agreement. When everyone was finished eating, Sam retreated sullenly to the attic. Clarissa cleared the table and washed the dishes, pots, and pans. When the kitchen floor was spotless, she ascended the stairs to the attic. Clarissa crawled into the remaining twin bed and listened to Sam's labored breathing until she had cried herself to sleep.

If her life was to remain the same as it had always been, Clarissa was more committed than she thought possible that her child would be no one's servant. She had a husband and would soon have a child. She cherished this new life growing inside of her, a little person who belonged to her and would for all time. "Oh, little one, so pure and sweet, rest and grow, from week to week. The day will come, when you will be, a ribbon to bind us, as a family." She hummed the tune and repeated the words she had learned from who knew where—she could not remember.

It is one thing to show a man that he is in error, and another to put him in possession of truth.

—John Locke

Sam

The weeks were dragging by, and the summer heat was wearing on both Sam and Clarissa. One evening, he mused to himself, "Perhaps Father is right. Clarissa has no idea what it means to work for a living wage." Then out loud he shared some of what he was thinking, "Clarissa, you can't imagine what it's like out there in the real world. We have to fight for every contract we get now. The work doesn't just come to us anymore."

Clarissa countered, "And you cannot imagine what it is like to be confined to this house, day in and day out, in the heat and the silence. I wish you would support me in front of your family, with your father. Everyone in this family treats me like a servant."

Sam gave up. Clarissa would never be able to understand what life was like with his father or the horrible treatment he had to endure every day because of his father's disappointment in him. To make matters worse the decline of the economy drove Samuel to make very difficult decisions for the family business. Sam could see the impact not only on his father but also on the company workers and on the city. Most days, Mr. Disser was tasked with deciding which laborers to keep and which ones to fire.

Mr. Disser had experienced a sixty percent decline in business since the first of the year that Sam and Clarissa were married. The economic stress on the company was borne on his shoulders alone. Corruption and pay-offs were becoming the norm in construction contracts. Having the additional mouths to feed, with Sam and Clarissa in the house and a baby on the way, only added to his financial pressures and to the sources of his frustration. He reminded Sam of his distress every chance he could.

"You know you have burdened your mother and me for life with your decision to marry and have a child. The situation you've got yourself in compels your mother and me to require both your labor and hers, for who knows how long."

Sam nodded in increasing agreement and regret. "Yes, Father, I know."

Late in the summer, Mr. Disser reduced staff to less than a full-time work force. He resorted to hiring construction laborers only as he needed them for the projects of the day or week. Sam was his driver on the daily route to the bowels of the city, where colored men lined up on the street corner every morning to be selected for work.

It didn't matter if the contract called for a partial schedule or reduced hours, men who wanted to work were lined up along Vine Street downtown to barter for jobs. A job, an income, was a badge of honor and pride to these men. Those who had expertise in the building trades were the most sought after by the construction companies. Mr. Disser tried to arrive on Vine Street as early in the morning as possible and paid as high a wage as he dared in an attempt to preserve his company's hard-fought reputation.

"Hey there, young man, do you want to come work for me?" Mr. Disser would call out to a man Sam could barely see in the dark of the predawn morning. His father grabbed his arm whenever he wanted Sam to slow down and then he squeezed his grip when he wanted him to stop.

Mr. Disser recognized a man standing in line who had worked hard and long hours for him before and made him an offer. "Yessir, Mr. Disser sir. I need me leastways uh full day. And I need to brings my son wid me too," the man bargained.

"You have yourself a deal. Jump on in the back of the truck here and we'll be on our way shortly," Mr. Disser agreed. The process would continue for a short while until father and son had the labor for the day.

As the economy worsened, Mr. Disser was forced to sign contracts with anyone having the financial means to keep his company solvent. Unemployment had risen from hundreds of thousands to millions, and yet Mr. Disser continued to be able to attract and employ a core group of skilled tradesmen. Unfortunately, he found himself making business deals with men of questionable means.

Sam did not reveal to Clarissa the nature of the contracts his father accepted. It was none of her business, and she probably would not understand the reasons why it had to be done. He did not want her to know about the partnerships they were forming with gamblers, gangsters, and thieves.

Besides, he was beginning to enjoy some of the nights out drinking and socializing to keep the family business solvent. His father sent him out on these evenings for two reasons. One, he was no longer interested in the nightlife and knew that Sam would enjoy making the deals that would keep the company in business. It was his future, after all, if the business stayed afloat. Two, the nights out were driving a wedge between the couple in the attic. Mr. Disser was determined to do what he could to end the marriage.

"I don't like it when you go out for these dinners," Clarissa protested. "You always come back smelling like beer and you are rude and loud. Why can't your father go?"

Sam roared, "Because I am the man of this little family of ours, and I say I am going. Besides, I do a better job of closing the deals with these men than he does."

No, Clarissa needed to remain as much in the background as he did growing up in the Disser house. Women were meant to be seen and bedded—not heard. Sam turned on her, "Provide your fair share and more if need be. That's how it's always been in this house, and that's how it always will be. You need to accept it, even if it means more chores for you. Besides, doing chores is the life you've always known, so you should be good at it. What else could you ever do to contribute to this family?"

Smarting from his words, Clarissa held back the tears as he left the attic for another night out. Didn't he know she was doing the best she could to make a life for them and for their child? His words had pierced her heart. She had merely traded a life of obedience and labor from the Doppler home to the Disser home.

I care for myself. The more solitary, the more friendless, the more unsustained I am, the more I will respect myself.

—*Jane Eyre*, **by Charlotte Bronte**

Clarissa

Without a single book to be found in the Dissers' attic, Clarissa cherished her little white Bible, stored safely in its black linen box. While Mrs. Disser napped in her chair every afternoon, Clarissa was able to sneak up to the attic and read random and favorite Bible verses out loud, a solitary conversation with the baby growing inside her.

She sang the hymns she remembered from church to soothe the baby when it kicked. When Clarissa could not remember the exact words, she made up words that sounded suitable. She ran her finger over the beautiful gold edges of the pages of the Bible. Each time she read a Bible verse, she looked back in fond memory on the dedication written by Mrs. Laine. It was then that she decided what to do next.

In a bold move of defiance, Clarissa made the decision to change her first name. Mr. Disser had taken great delight in hissing the *iss* and making the *a* at the end of her name sound like "ugh." She was tired of her very name being part of his torment. Sam had dismissed her pleas for his support as insignificant and childish. He had suggested she just ignore his father's irritating way of pronouncing her name.

The first chance she had to escape the Disser property, Clarissa conspired with the family's part-time gardener and her only friend, Ralph Noese. On the ruse of a disease that might be threatening the catalpa trees, Clarissa and Ralph planned a trip to the local nursery in his truck. After a short detour to the nursery, they headed to their true destination, city hall.

Clarissa inquired at the information desk, "How do I go about changing my first name?"

The clerk replied, "Why, that is quite easy and costs only twenty-five cents. Go over to that table and complete this form. Then bring it back to me with your payment." Quick as she could, Clarissa filled out the single sheet and drew a dollar from her pocket. This was the first deduction from her long-ago dance contest money, and it was worth the expense. From that moment forward, Clarissa would be known as and called, simply, Claire. It was a small victory, but a victory nonetheless. She felt a sense of independence and strength in her own decision to make a change.

At dinner that evening, Claire announced, "Today I went to city hall and legally changed my name." Sam raised one eyebrow, looked at her briefly, and then turned back to his dinner. No one replied. No one dared to reply. "From this day forward, I am to be called Claire," she defiantly repeated, "Claire—yes, Claire—which in French means famous." Again no one spoke. Everyone continued eating their dinner.

If to no one else, Claire would be Claire—famous— to her child. Claire would be a mother who would give everything to her baby. She would love and cherish and kiss and coo and talk to that baby all day every day. No one could say or do anything that would take her love and devotion from her child.

With her newfound courage and defiance, Claire made a valiant effort to brighten their little hovel in the attic. Even though the form she read at city hall said she was officially counted as a member of a parental household, she and Sam were a married couple, they were adults. Claire took remnants of fabric from the cellar, washed and pressed them, and sewed curtains for the attic window on

Mrs. Disser's pedal sewing machine in the sun room while she was napping. She took other remnants of fabric and made scarves to brighten the tops of their two mahogany dressers. When Sam did not notice her efforts, she sewed trim on their sheets and pillowcases.

Sam did not care about Claire's interest in fabric or decorating. The men at work and the customers he had dinner with reminded him a wife is just a wife. Every man had one. A son, now that was something the men he knew talked about with pride. Sam took solace in the fact that he would soon be crowing about his own son. A son was required. Only a son would satisfy Samuel's demand for an heir.

More and more, Sam had been hearing about the economic trials of men who were struggling to make house payments, to put food on the table, and to clothe their families. Claire despised living in the Disser home and so did Sam. But he had to admit they had a roof over their heads and food to eat. With a son on the way and his own contributions to try and keep the company solvent, Sam held on to a dim hope for the future.

How long would Mother and Father live anyway? Hopefully they would not survive too much longer.

Claire knew the basic truth even if Sam did not give her credit for having any sense about the world. Sam's income and future, his very life, was dependent upon his father's generosity. His wage had nothing at all to do with the amount of time or effort he spent working. Sam's salary was the same as it always had been and would remain the same as long as his father was alive.

Their lack of a consistent or sufficient household income to live on provided an immodest and insecure existence for Sam and Claire. With Sam's support and presence disappearing, Claire had difficulty imagining a different future for them. Their clothing, the furnishings, and the food they ate was charity from the Disser household. Mrs. Disser frequently reminded Claire, "Everything you have, dear, is on loan to you and Sam. You must understand that and accept that."

When Claire needed maternity clothes, Mrs. Disser presented her own garments from a cedar chest in the cellar. Replacement work clothes, boots, and undergarments for Sam and food for both him and Claire were provided according to a budget prepared by Mr. Disser. The amounts were calculated by Mr. Disser and deducted from Sam's weekly pay.

Sam's father insisted on receipts for any personal items that were charged to the household account, and that, too, came out of Sam's salary. Regardless of need or frugality, Mr. Disser exacted from his son every penny of his wage. There was never any money left over, no opportunity for savings or expenses beyond Mr. Disser's approval and stipend.

Regrettably, they were also dependent on family for friendship. Despite Mr. Disser's standing in the community, he had refused social gatherings and denied any requests by Sam, Grace, or Mrs. Disser to bring or invite guests to the Disser home. Birthdays and holidays were treated the same as any other day, the meal planning and menu was not special or unique, and no mention was made of including other family members who lived in the city.

Sam's father declared to anyone who would listen that the family had been disgraced when Sam married "that girl." Whenever the opportunity presented itself, Mr. Disser would repeat, "After the war, Sam could not contain his arousals and poked the first schoolgirl he saw. Unfortunately for us, she was a servant, no better than a gutter whore, and she tricked him into being the father of her bastard baby. Let's wait and see who this child looks like before we decide it is any descendant of mine."

Mr. Disser's anger at the economic depression and his disappointment in Sam's marriage to Claire distanced neighbors and friends. No one came to make a social call or sent invitations to parties or community events. Everyone in the Disser family was sentenced to a life of isolation. Claire was of course the primary cause of everyone's suffering. Cousin John had made repeated attempts to call on Claire, to call on the Disser family, but he was turned away at the front door each time and told never to return.

More devastating than any dependence on the Dissers was the lack of someone to talk to. Claire yearned for companionship. Sam was either working long hours or working and then going to dinners with customers. Mr. Disser had been so relentless in his disdain for Claire that Mrs. Disser dared not initiate a relationship. She turned her back on Claire whenever they were in the same room together.

Grace worked each weekday as a secretary at the Internal Revenue Service, headquartered downtown. Even when she was home at night and on weekends, Grace sequestered herself in her room. As the pregnancy progressed, Claire became more emotional and weepy. She clung to Sam as soon as he returned to the attic after work, begging him to spend time with her, to talk to her, to tell her about his day. Sam was annoyed. "I have Father pulling at me all day to do this and do that and then I have you pulling at me all night to talk? What do you want me to say? There is nothing to share. All my dealings are about business. What could we possibly talk about?"

Even when Sam did not have a dinner meeting, he arrived home hours after his father, required to check the construction sites in place of his father after the laborers had departed for the day, accounting for tools and equipment and securing each location for the evening. This made him especially late for dinner. When Sam was not home for supper at seven o'clock sharp, an argument ensued.

"You cannot even check a few sites and lock up by a reasonable hour?" Mr. Disser was exasperated with his son, "I give you the simplest tasks, and you continually disappoint me."

Sam was depressed and tired most evenings. He confessed to Claire, "I hate my father, do you hear me? I hate him. I hate construction work, and most of all I hate living in this attic. It is as if he has me on a chain. And the chain is tied around my throat, choking the life out of me."

Sam's dark moods dampened the only time the newlyweds had together. Claire tried her best to console him. "We have each other. When the economy gets better, you will find a way for us to leave and have a place of our own."

Sam threw back his head and howled. "Leave? I feel his clutches clawing through to my bones. He knows everyone in this city, the good men and the bad, and every one of their dark and dirty little secrets. Do you think we can ever leave this house?" Thrashing around the attic, Sam was at his wits' end. "I want to be out of this family. I want to be out of this city. I want to be out of this marriage! I'm caged in this attic like an animal. I have no life of my own. Don't you see, Claire? This is all my life will ever be. This is all *our* life will ever be. This, this hideous existence—and one work site after another—is it for me. This is it. I can't bear it. You hear me? I hate this life. And I hate you."

He took the stairs so fast he missed a few of the steps but kept going until he had run out the front door. Claire's heart was pounding so loudly and so fast she thought it would leap out of her chest. Pacing the attic, she kept wringing her hands and praying, "God, please keep him safe. Please bring him back to me. We have to be a couple. Without Sam, I have no one, the baby has no one. Oh Lord, please help us. Please, oh please help." She fell to her knees at the window to watch for Sam's return.

When Sam did come back to the attic, it was almost dawn. He found Claire asleep on the floor beneath the window. He picked her up and laid her in her twin bed. Without speaking, he fell into his own bed facing the wall and fell asleep. A heavy resignation settled in Claire's soul. Sam was right. This was their life.

She rolled onto her side to stare out the window at a hazy sky of pink and gray until sleep folded her into restless dreams. Babies, too many to count, were crawling around on the attic floor. Claire was wiping up behind them. Mr. Disser was standing in the doorway scowling and pointing at a drunken Sam, who was vomiting beer out of the attic window.

The couple's miserable existence weighed on them for weeks. Clarissa's work schedule continued until two days before she gave birth. Her full days of chores resumed three days after the birth.

**We seldom find people ungrateful so long
as it is thought we can serve them.**

—Francois de la Rochefoucauld

Mr. Disser

Without money for gas in the car to take those once-treasured drives into the country, Sam's pride and joy had languished in the old garage behind the garden wall. One Saturday morning at breakfast, Mr. Disser announced, "Sam, I sold your Ford Runabout to pay for the doctor and the hospital bills for the baby." At the sight of Sam's reddening face, Mr. Disser quickly added, "It is too late for argument. The sale is done, the car is gone, and the money is mine."

Sam protested anyway, his anger overflowing at his father: "You…you have no right to sell what is mine. I bought that car with *my* money, *my* money, do you hear? That was my money from my service in the army. How dare you!"

"How dare I? *How dare I?*" thundered Mr. Disser, pushing his chair away from the table. "It is not for you to dare me. You owe me everything you have and everything you ever will have." His voice reverberating through the foyer, Mr. Disser stormed out the front door.

When the time came for the baby to be born, Mr. Disser refused to drive Claire or to give Sam the keys to his car to drive her to the hospital. Mr. Disser called Doc Simmons to recommend a midwife to attend to the birth. The Disser family was not going to accept the expense of a hospital or a doctor, or to face further ridicule with a public announcement of a bastard child in the city's newspapers.

"Take her to the spare room," Mr. Disser directed his wife. Mrs. Disser ushered Claire to the unused guest bedroom at the back of the second floor. Eighteen hours after her first contraction, Claire gave birth to a beautiful baby girl. Sam and she had not discussed names for a girl, only for a boy.

The greatest enemy of any one of our truths may be the rest of our truths.

—William James

Sam

When Claire's labor pains had begun in earnest, Sam's father had taken him downstairs to the drawing room at the front of the house. The drawing room was as far away as possible from the room being used for the birth. He began to lecture Sam on the risks he was continuing to take. "This woman has brought you nothing but hardship. The responsibility of a child is going to bind you for life, strangle you." Mr. Disser warned his son, "This must be the only child."

With this opportunity to convince his son to restrict his family to just a wife and child, Mr. Disser conceded. "I will forgive you this one *mistake* and never speak of it again, but there must be no more children. Times are tough. I cannot agree to any more mouths to feed or put up with any more of your foolishness. Claire has no heritage and no claim to Doppler money. She is useless to this family."

As he endured his father's speech, Sam assumed that not only the midwife but his mother and possibly even Grace were at Claire's bedside. Though he heard every word his father was saying and recognized the weight of the truth, he was anxious to learn the sex of the baby. He was desperate to confirm that he had a son. Surely Claire was in responsible hands.

Taking his son's silence as listening, Mr. Disser continued lecturing about responsibility. Sam lost himself in memories of the stories his aunts had willingly shared with him about the births in his mother's family, especially about the birth of his mother, also by a midwife. She had been born "upside down" they told him, and had come out screaming and yelling. Sam could not believe it, particularly since the woman he knew as his mother spoke only in hushed tones.

The fact that his mother May (née Edwards) had three older sisters was a revelation to most, who believed May to be an only child. That May's fourth and youngest sibling was a boy, who survived living with four girls in a three-room house, was quite a story in itself. May had lived most of her life in Blue Jay, Ohio, with her sisters Hannah, Jenny, and Ida; her brother, Sam; and her mother and father.

Before they settled in Blue Jay, the family had lived a few hundred miles west of Chicago. The land was untamed prairie. Most of the year, storms would form farther west. The Edwards family could see clouds and rain approaching for miles before they reached their farm. Mr. Edwards dug a dirt storm cellar several yards from the house. There the family would try to rest and remain calm until the wind, hail, and rain had passed. Then they would emerge, covered in a pale brown dust, to see how much damage had been done to the crops and to check on the livestock.

Severe weather finally became too much for the farm and the family's survival in Illinois. The Edwardses traveled to Ohio and settled in the small town of Blue Jay, a hilltop community overlooking the Great Miami River. There they operated the one and only tollgate on State Route 52. The state route was a single road carved in the earth parallel to the Ohio River, giving flat and easy access to people traveling to the western territories. Because of the nature of the business, the family was required to provide passage at all hours of the day and night.

The toll was ten cents per person, horses were five cents, and wagons two cents. Cattle were one penny a head. One day, the Ringling Circus came through and Mr. Edwards had to calculate toll fees for the cages containing wild animals. The initiation of the toll gate by the Edwards family was during the Civil War. When a union soldier brought news that Morgan's Raiders were coming, Mr. Edwards gathered the family and hid them in what is now known as the Miami Whitewater Forest. Shortly after that, Mr. Edwards disappeared. He had agreed to accompany a frequent traveler who promised large profits selling coffee to states south of the Ohio River. Mr. Edwards was never heard from again.

Mrs. Edwards and the children continued to man the toll gate and make a living, waiting on Mr. Edwards until the years drifted away and with them all hope of his return. To while away the quiet hours, Mrs. Edwards homeschooled the children. Each of the girls refined talents of their own choosing. Sam spent his leisure time in the woods and along the river, hunting and fishing.

May took up the guitar and sang. She could sew a perfect seam, designing and making all of her clothes. Candy-making was one of her pleasures. She made several flavors of cream candy, which she dipped in chocolate and sold in wax wrappers to travelers. As the years progressed, May's breathing became more labored, either from allergies or asthma. Most of her time was spent in the toll office or in the house. Her sister Hannah kept her company.

Hannah was the exact opposite of May. She was tall and big-boned, not fat but large like her father, with a lovely round face and deep-set hazel eyes. Hannah had special talents as an artist. Her paintings and crafts caught the attention of many travelers, who purchased one-of-a-kind items that she displayed in the toll office. Her most memorable creations were unshelled peanuts on which she painted human faces. Once the characters were defined, Hannah added pipe stem arms and legs covered in multicolored crepe paper clothes.

As adults, the Edwards sisters visited May at the Disser home every year for the Fourth of July celebration, along with their spouses and children. Their brother, Sam, never came to celebrate the holiday. Hannah extended her time at the Disser home for the entire month of July. She became a once-a-year companion for May, sometimes staying more than a month. Sam was always glad to see the spark in his mother's eyes when Hannah arrived.

Aunt Hannah's summer visit when Claire was pregnant was a special treat for both of them. She welcomed Claire to the family and began an easy friendship with her from the first moment they met. The camaraderie between Aunt Hannah and Claire softened May's feelings for Claire, except when Mr. Disser was present. Sam was pleased to hear laughter in the Disser home once more.

His mother and Aunt Hannah shared stories of their children's births with Claire, in more detail than Sam could have imagined. All he cared about was a son. A son was what he expected. A son was to be hailed as heir to the Disser name and family business. The birth of a grandson was the single thread of hope that gave Mr. Disser a positive topic of conversation with Sam and a future worth planning.

All truths are easy to understand once they are discovered; the point is to discover them.

—Galileo

Claire and Sam

When the midwife arrived at the parlor door to announce the birth, Sam shook himself from his daydreaming and ran down the hall and up the stairs to the guest bedroom, where he could hear subtle baby cries. Claire was crying. "Where have you been? I have been here all alone."

Sam protested, "I thought surely Mother or Grace would be with you. Where are they?"

Claire sobbed, "They have not been here. No one has been here."

Sam assured her, "I had no way of knowing you were alone." Oh, how she loved him. Claire knew this baby was going to bring all the happiness she had dreamed of. Clinging to his apologies, she wrapped her arm around his neck. He wiped away her tears of forgiveness.

Claire held the newborn out to Sam. "Here, darling, hold your beautiful daughter." Sam stood straight up and without thinking questioned, "A daughter? I thought we were having a son. We only chose a name for a son."

Frightened by his withdrawal from her, Claire embraced her baby against her breast. "But we never knew for certain—no one can. I know you hoped for a son. Perhaps our next child will be a son." Sam bent down and tried his best to hide his disappointment. His father's words started spinning in his head.

"Let's wait a while to talk about another child," Sam mumbled as he reached out to take his new daughter in his arms.

"A baby, our baby. Oh, Sam, we are a family now. Isn't this wonderful? Life has changed for us. Isn't it amazing that we are parents? This is exciting. Oh, Sam, are you excited?" Claire was bubbling over with emotion for their first child, gurgling and glowing in his arms.

Sam replied, "I am overwhelmed...simply overwhelmed."

"I have already chosen a name for her. She will be called Janet." Claire was pleased with her Bible knowledge. "The name Janet in Hebrew means 'God is gracious.'"

"Well, then," Sam countered, "let's pray for His grace on all of us."

I think being a Mother is the cruelest thing in the world.

—Nella Larsen

Grace and May

Two days after Janet's birth, Mr. Disser instructed Mrs. Disser to return Claire to the household chores. Mr. Disser faced Claire at supper and said, "I have told my wife to return you to the work of the house in the morning. This will require that Janet's daily care and attention be taken on by Mrs. Disser. I do hope you realize the burden and the trouble you have given to this family and to my wife with this unnecessary child."

"That is not fair!" Claire mumbled to her lap between tears and sobbing. "She is my child—our child. You cannot dictate our lives." Clarissa reached for Sam's hand in support. Looking up to see his father rise from the table and lean over to confront Claire if she said another word, Sam withdrew his hand and left the table.

Claire left the table also, taking baby Janet with her out the back door and into the backyard to sit on the wrought-iron bench in the garden. She would not care who was washing the dishes, and pots and pans, or scrubbing the kitchen floor. The fresh evening air and the refusal of chores until the morning was the most defiance she could muster on her own.

Straining to swallow the contempt for Mr. Disser that was burning in her throat, Claire handed her baby over to Mrs. Disser when Sam and his father left the house to go to work the next morning. She could swear she detected a slight smile on Mrs. Disser's face. Did Mrs. Disser feel some triumph over her, a retribution for having to endure her presence? Her marriage to Sam?

Quiet and austere as she was with adults, Mrs. Disser became carefree when it came to caring for Janet. She pulled all of Grace's baby clothes out of the cellar for Claire to wash and press. Mrs. Disser herself washed and presented Grace's baby toys to Janet.

In the mornings, she played with Janet in the sun room at the back of the house, overlooking the garden. Claire could hear Mrs. Disser talking to Janet in a baby voice, cooing, and making the sounds of each animal as it was introduced in the baby books.

Afternoons were spent in Mrs. Disser's room reading and taking naps. Claire protested, "I can care for Janet myself between chores. I need to see her. I need to spend time with my baby." Despite her objections, the decision had been mandated by Mr. Disser. Mrs. Disser was adamant about her allegiance to Janet's care.

Acknowledging her husband's decision, Mrs. Disser took the direction to the extreme and was silent with Claire. As if she wanted to inflict as much punishment as possible, Mrs. Disser did not share even a bit of what each day's events held with Janet.

To nurse her baby, Claire had to knock on the door of the sunroom or Mrs. Disser's bedroom and request permission to enter. Then she would spend this most private time while Mrs. Disser stared at her, waiting to retrieve Janet for herself.

To give Mrs. Disser a reprieve, Grace took responsibility for Janet in the evenings. That allowed her mother to prepare the evening meal. Previous to this new nurturing role, life at home for Grace had consisted only of assisting

Mrs. Disser with the evening and weekend cooking and baking. Now she was also a caretaker for Janet.

A woman who had never even held a baby, much less cared for a baby, Grace also took to this new role with pleasure and excitement. Each night, Janet was swept away by Grace before dinner so Claire could help Mrs. Disser put the meal in serving dishes and serve the family. Then Grace sequestered Janet again in her bedroom until Claire could wash the dishes and scrub the kitchen floor.

After almost two years in the Disser home, Sam and Claire were despondent. Claire was more unwelcome with each day that passed because of her relentless pleas to Mrs. Disser and Grace for time with Janet. Grace and Mrs. Disser were becoming increasingly attached to Janet. At times, Claire had difficulty removing Janet from the two of them to retire upstairs in the evening. Sam was tired of the arguing and tired of Claire's complaining every night when they had their only time alone in the attic. He was just plain tired.

Mr. Disser found the conflict between the women in his home had become unbearable. He complained, "This bickering has to stop. I cannot stand to hear the chicken-squawking that goes on in this house. That child is just a child. There is a time and a place for each of you to be with that child." The living situation with Sam, Claire, and Janet was intolerable. Sam stayed out of the fracas, arms folded, watching the veins in his father's neck expand. He had nothing left to say to his father about anything at all.

Work had actually improved for Sam. Despite the difficult economic times, two construction opportunities were in the offing thanks to deals that Sam had made over evenings out with influential businessmen. The company was on the brink of contracts with men of significant wealth.

One confirmed construction contract was with Mr. "Boss" Cox for a racetrack on the east side of Cincinnati. Mr. Cox demanded not only that The Disser Company handle the project but that Sam be named the foreman on the project site. Because of the size of the job and the lack of anyone who had the required experience and had Mr. Disser's trust, Mr. Disser agreed with Mr. Cox and promoted Sam to the position of site foreman. He put him in charge of the construction site, the project expenses, and timing, as well as the workers.

The racetrack project was next to the Coney Island amusement park that The Disser Company had constructed a few years before. Boss Cox had recently purchased the amusement park and the adjacent acreage for the racetrack. With the two properties now combined, the amusement park and the racetrack would cover more than two thousand acres.

Mr. Cox had chosen 'River Downs' as the name for the racetrack, to echo the famous Churchill Downs in

Louisville, Kentucky, just three hours' drive to the south and west. As the southernmost boundary for both Coney Island and River Downs was the Ohio River, tourists and locals could ride the riverboats for half an hour from downtown Cincinnati or a leisurely two and a half hours from Louisville.

Sam and his father drove out to survey the River Downs project from the east property line of Coney Island. Walking back to Mr. Disser's car, the conversation turned, as it almost always did, to the escalating disagreements between the Disser women over time spent with Janet.

At the entrance to Coney Island, Mr. Disser turned and pointed at a white frame house on a road that stretched north from the amusement park entrance. It was the only residence Sam had noticed in the area. "See that house, Son? It's been vacant for almost a year. Mr. Cox has instructed that it is to be your residence while you are on this project. Tomorrow morning, pack up your things and get Claire and Janet out of my house. You three live there, and I will deduct the rent for the house from your salary. I am tired of the discontent in my home. You need to get out."

His father had meant for this revelation to be an insult to Sam. Instead, Sam was triumphant. At last he had achieved not only a work project of his own but a place of his own as well. Despite his father's scowl, Sam could not hide his elation. He dared not thank his father or shake his hand for fear the decision and direction would be withdrawn. As Sam turned to walk to his father's car, he felt a grin spread over his face from ear to ear.

He couldn't wait to tell Claire and to pack and move out of the family home. Sam bounded up the stairs to find Claire cleaning Grace's bedroom. He swept her off her feet and whispered the news in her ear. Their celebratory embrace and kisses were interrupted by the mournful sounds of wailing from the drawing room. Mr. Disser had told his wife he had directed Sam to move himself and Claire and Janet out of the house.

May was at her husband's feet, sobbing and begging that Janet be left behind. "Give her to me. I want her. I need her. I cannot live my days without Janet. Please, Samuel, please!"

Mr. Disser was steadfast. "It is good riddance to the three of them. Sam has a project of his own. Let's see what he makes of it. As for the whore and her pitiful child, I am relieved to say good-bye."

Every act of rebellion expresses nostalgia
for innocence and an appeal to the essence
of being.

—Albert Camus

Claire

Claire could not believe their good fortune. She could barely collect her thoughts enough to consider what it would mean to leave the Disser home. "Can it be true? Are we really leaving to have a life on our own?" Claire was incredulous. Sam could only stand back to smile at her, dance a little jig around her, and kiss her over and over again. He was ecstatic.

The next day dawned as a sunny and crisp October Saturday. Claire and Sam gathered their belongings and packed. With great delight, Claire dumped the contents of boxes of Disser family whatnots on the floor at the other end of the attic. She folded everything except what would not fit in a box, and Sam taped the top flaps shut. When she could see only two bare beds and empty dresser drawers, Claire ran down the stairs to collect Janet and to call for Sam to bring the boxes downstairs.

Janet was in her crib in the sunroom. Mrs. Disser and Grace were nowhere in sight. Claire swept Janet out of the crib and grasped her to her chest. Sam came through the door. "The truck is waiting for us. Go ahead and get in the front seat. Gus and I will load the boxes. Yes, and the crib too."

Mr. Disser had arranged for one of the construction trucks to move the couple and Janet to their first home. Neither Sam nor Claire knew what state this rented house would be in when they arrived, nor did they care. They were on a course to have a life on their own, and that was all that mattered.

As soon as they laid eyes on the rented house, they knew they were faced with extensive repair and cleaning. It was a small white frame house, a square of four rooms, all accessible from a narrow hallway. The windows and doors were not operable without considerable force. The back door and five of the eight windows had been nailed shut. The front door was missing a top hinge and a lock. Inside the house there was dust and grime from floor to ceiling.

Sam turned immediately to Claire, assuring her, "I can fix whatever is broken. We will be fine."

Claire took a deep breath and proclaimed, "Why this is nothing soap and water and elbow grease won't clean."

"Then let's get started." declared Sam.

"Yes, indeed, let's make it ours, our home," agreed Claire.

Someone had left a few pieces of well-used and worn furniture. Two dark green overstuffed chairs covered with a grimy sheet that had once been white and a small table were in the front room, a scratched table with only three legs was in the dining room, and a large pine bed supported by boards of varying shapes and sizes was in the bedroom. There were no curtains, no bed linens, and no pots and pans or dishes in the kitchen.

Sam remembered his father had seen the place with Mr. Cox when they were finalizing the racetrack project. What should he have expected but another slap in the face from his father? This place was a mess. It was uninhabitable. They would surely freeze in this place in cold weather. Sam knew he must ask Gus to take him home to ask his mother—beg her if he had to—for any spare essentials she may have so they could at least sleep and eat.

Gus was standing in the doorway shaking his head. Even though he dared never to contradict Mr. Disser, this was more than he could stand. Not only Gus but all the colored workers had witnessed first-hand Mr. Disser's treatment of Sam every day. He seemed to take pleasure in demeaning and humiliating Sam as much as possible.

As one of the most seasoned employees of The Disser Company, Gus felt he knew Sam well enough to make a personal offer. "Sam, son, we dunnever have much, but wha'ever my fambly can spares is your'un." Gus patted Sam on the back, walked down the hall, and drove away.

Fortunately, Claire had packed rags, soap, and a bucket. Sam had retrieved a broom and a few basic tools from the construction truck. They stood in the front doorway and watched Gus pulling out of the drive. "We can clean and fix, but then what?" Claire inquired. "We have no linens or curtains and not a single kitchen utensil, pot, or pan, and nothing to eat." Sam had no idea what to do.

No more than two hours later, Gus and some people Claire and Sam assumed to be his relations and friends showed up with more necessities and cooked food than Claire and Sam had ever seen. There were lamps and scatter rugs, mismatched dishes and pots and pans, linens for the bed, curtains for the windows, straight-back wooden chairs of a variety of shapes and styles, a lock for the door, tools and nails, as well as children's clothes and women's clothes.

Colored people poured into the house, grinning and hugging Claire. When the three-legged table was repaired, the cooked food was set out beside a stack of dishes, utensils, and napkins of every color and size. People ate what they wanted, when they wanted. The women cleaned and sang alongside Claire. One of the elderly colored ladies held little Janet in her arms singing hymns in a glorious voice. Sam joined Gus and the rest of the colored men repairing the doors and windows.

By nightfall, the rented house was clean, snug, and filled with love. It was a fitting start to begin their lives on their own. Even though they were exhausted from the day's activities, Sam and Claire felt a joy they had never known. "What a relief it is to be out of that stuffy, old, horrible, dark, and gloomy house!" Sam declared at the top of his voice.

"It is a blessing, an answer to prayer! We have a home, Sam. A home." Claire was ecstatic.

For the first time, Claire was unrestricted in her love for her child and for her husband. The hymns she had sung to her baby came out loud and clear, one after another. Sam joined in her singing, but his were the songs of barrooms and war ditties. It did not matter that their voices were not in harmony—their hearts were light with freedom.

What Claire did not remember from her school lessons was that Coney Island was located in what was considered the country. It was accessible by those who had automobiles or traveled down the Ohio River by boat. Their little rented house was very far from the city, remote and isolated. The only personal contact she was going to have would be little Janet and Sam.

As the weekend flew by and Monday morning approached, Sam could keep his secret no longer. He had hoped either his father would change his mind or he would be able to change it for him. But Mr. Disser was unwavering in a stipulation for the promotion and for the move. Mr. Disser would be visiting the racetrack construction site every day to review the progress of the project. And every day, he would be driving Sam home to the rented house to eat lunch.

Claire was hysterical when Sam divulged Mr. Disser's demand for lunch. She did not know the first thing about cooking. Aunt Louisa and then Mrs. Disser had had command of their kitchens. Claire did not even know how to boil water. There was no food in the house except the meager leftovers from what the colored people had brought to them as part of their housewarming hospitality.

Sam promised, "I will tell Father we do not have groceries. In fact, we do not have the means to buy groceries in this isolation. He will just have to postpone his expectations."

Claire was not persuaded. She reminded Sam, "Even if we delay your father until we have groceries, I still do not know how to cook! Please, Sam, promise me you will discreetly ask Gus if someone can come to the house to teach me," Claire implored. "Groceries will be of no use if I cannot cook. You, you can cook, right? Could you teach me? Or, better yet, could you come home before your father, before the midday meal and help me?" She was frantic.

Claire was in shock. Just when she had begun to envision a life without him, Mr. Disser was back in their lives. He was back in their lives not on occasion but every day. She swallowed hard and closed her eyes, muttering to herself, "This rented house, this life in the country, is better than anything we've had. I will make this work; I must make this work."

As Sam stood at the front door to leave for his first full day on the racetrack project, he repeated his promise to tell his father there would be no lunch. Claire prompted him, "Not today and not this week. Please find someone to help me learn cooking. Oh please, Sam, please." He nodded and kissed her on the forehead.

Claire had no sense of how much time had passed and was in the midst of scrubbing the kitchen floor while Janet was napping when she heard the front door screech open. As she craned her head around the side of the oven and peered down the hall, she could see Sam and his father standing in the hallway. A wave of hot panic flushed through her from her toes to the top of her head.

Mr. Disser shouted down the hall at Claire, "I give you this chance, and look at this place. It is a mishmash of crap. You expect my son to live like this? It's a gypsy hovel." In truth, Mr. Disser was dismayed that there was furniture and provisions. He was certain the day he and Mr. Cox had seen it the place had been desolate. Who had shown them favor? Who had given them support?

By the time he entered the kitchen, he was furious, "Where is my lunch? There is no food for me to eat? How much disappointment am I supposed to tolerate from you? Well," he threatened, shaking his fist in Claire's face, "I've fired men who are better workers than your husband, and I've kicked their tramps out on the street. I can do the same to you! You're a failure, a disgrace, useless, good-for-nothing. Tricked my son into marrying you, didn't you? Now you think you've got him in a trap, stuck with a miserable wife and bastard child. Well, I have news for you. Yes, I have news for you."

Mr. Disser pushed his son out the front door and poked him in the back until he climbed back into the car, and then gravel flew as he sped down the driveway and back to the racetrack project. Claire fell in a heap beside Janet's crib. She was shaking all over, sobbing. There was no one to turn to for solace or help.

That night, Sam came home late. He tried to explain to Claire that he had attempted to convince his father not to come to the house for lunch. But his father had reminded him, "You know the Disser rule, a promise is a promise."

After work Gus had helped Sam find a grocer several miles away, and Sam had brought home with him basic groceries and handwritten instructions from the grocer's wife as to what to fix and what foods went with other foods. The only problem was that Claire still didn't know how to prepare anything.

Day after day, she failed miserably in trying to meet Mr. Disser's lunch expectations. More than a few times a week, Mr. Disser would spit food out of his mouth, yelling, "This is not food! This is inedible. You are an idiot. Any woman can cook, for God's sake."

More than once, he ripped the oilcloth off the table in anger, pulling the dishes to the floor and breaking a piece or two of the mismatched plates that had been donated to them. He left food splattered on the walls, the window, and the floor. Sam offered no defense. He walked out the door in silence behind his father. Despite his efforts at night, Claire was not learning quickly enough from Sam the basics of preparing a meal.

Claire experimented, tried, and failed at her own cooking. Without instruction or anyone to teach her when she was preparing meals, she either undercooked or burned most of the staples from the grocer. As the grocer's bills escalated due to so many failed attempts at cooking, Mr. Disser's fury escalated at the same rate.

Mr. Disser and Claire engaged in shouting matches every weekday at lunchtime. The bickering and yelling left Sam shaken. He was inept as a mediator. While Claire had every right to be upset that his father did not even give her cooking a chance, his father's patience was thinning without an edible meal, day after day after day. Mr. Disser was, after all, paying all the bills and making all they possessed possible. Sam played with Janet at lunch time in the yard when the weather was nice and in the car when the weather was inclement. Father and daughter left Claire and Mr. Disser to yell at one another and continue to disagree.

Now in their third year of marriage and after several miscarriages, Claire was starting the fourth month of a new pregnancy. She was thrilled. This would mean a playmate for Janet, and it would finally mean a son for Sam. "This is so exciting," she crowed to Sam, "you will have a son and your father will finally have an heir."

Sam was not sure another child was such a good idea. He had not had the courage to tell his father that Claire was pregnant with their second child. But he was certain his father knew the news without the telling because of the recent changes in Claire's shape and the glow on her face.

Mr. Disser became more brazen in the insults he hurled at Sam. "You are stupid beyond measure. This project is one full month behind schedule, and you have no valid reasons for the delay. Are you so intent on poking that whore that you have no blood flow to your brain? I told you, no more children, no more mouths that I have to feed. You think I don't know she's pregnant?"

The second construction project had not been awarded to The Disser Company. Sam and his father had been forced to fire their workers and were doing all the physical labor for the racetrack project. Mr. Disser was tired and discouraged and defiant.

Suddenly, at the beginning of her sixth month, Claire's belly swelled and was tender. She could not keep down any food, no matter what she tried to eat. And Claire was experiencing repeated spikes of fever.

After examining her, Doc Simmons announced to Sam and his father, "Claire must be confined to bed rest for the remainder of her pregnancy. She is very ill, and that illness will transfer to the child if care is not taken. In fact, the lives of both she and the baby are in jeopardy. I will return periodically to check her progress." He departed without allowing Mr. Disser to voice any objections to his diagnosis or the cost of his visits to see Claire.

Sam's father was outraged. "Am I not supposed to eat every day when I come out here to have to sweat and toil and to make sure nothing else goes wrong?" he yelled at Sam. "This is ridiculous. I have to compensate for your incompetence, and now I have to suffer because she is an unfit wife and mother? This is inconvenient, even if the meals are inedible. There is no place to eat this far out of the city. And you are going to face the responsibility of another child when I specifically told you no more. I am struggling every day to pay the bills. Now you have added to my financial burdens. You two will pay for this."

He would accept no further disrespect. Mr. Disser was determined to eliminate this aggravation. "No. I cannot and will not tolerate any more of Sam's mistakes," he committed to himself. Even before he had dropped Sam off at the racetrack Mr. Disser had made up his mind how best to put an end to Sam's marriage.

Instead of returning to the office, Mr. Disser drove from the racetrack site directly home, even though it was early afternoon. Mrs. Disser was startled at the sound and sight of his car in the driveway in the middle of the day. Then she saw how agitated he was as he came up the front walk.

She opened the front door to his declaration: "Janet will live here with us. I am going to go and get her now. You will be coming with me." Mrs. Disser was both confused and elated at the same time. She could barely contain her excitement. "Well, go on, woman. Don't just stand there with your mouth open. Get yourself together and bring whatever you need."

Pacing the foyer, Mr. Disser was pleased with his plan. "This will put an end to Sam's miserable state. And I will be the one he can thank when he comes to his senses. If that girl is confined to bed rest, then the only fair solution is to take Janet. How can she protest? If she puts up any resistance at all, she might hurt herself and the baby. If we get out there quickly enough, we will return home before Sam hears a word of it. Besides, what could Sam do? Nothing. He wouldn't dare."

Claire and Janet were awakened from their afternoon nap by the thundering footsteps of an angry Mr. Disser coming down the hall. She was raising herself up from her pillows when he grabbed Janet from her arms. "From now on, you will have only yourself to care for," he smirked and walked out of the house. Janet wrapped her arms around his neck, half asleep and half awake.

Screaming at him and clawing the air after him, Claire rolled off the side of the bed. She dragged herself down the hall. Claire's weight against the door was too much to hold her up. She fell out on to the front stoop on her side, shrieking and reaching for Janet. "What are you doing? Give her back to me. You can't take her! You can't take my child! What are you doing? Help! Help! Someone help me!"

Mrs. Disser looked out of the car's passenger window in time to see Claire's tear-streaked face and outstretched arms on the front step. Sympathy made her turn away from the scene. Joy overcame her as Mr. Disser placed Janet in her lap.

The car sped in the opposite direction from her mother's screams and cries for help until Janet was occupied with Mrs. Disser's hugs and kisses. Far behind them on the front step of the little rented house, Claire was still screaming, her body racked with sobbing and pain. Her hysteria subsided as she gasped for breath. When Sam arrived home, he saw Claire lying in the front doorway, unconscious.

Doc Simmons was grave in his diagnosis. "Sam, I don't know if she will live through the night. She is dehydrated, exhausted, and delirious at the loss of Janet. What on earth is your father trying to do to this poor girl? All you can do now is to give her sips of water and as much clear broth as she will accept."

From the day that Janet was taken away and every day after, Claire was inconsolable. She railed at Sam, "Your father has stolen Janet. Stolen her, do you hear? He has taken my child away from me! How could he do such a thing? He is a monster, a madman. And you! What kind of man are you to allow this to happen? To me? To us? Aren't we a family? Your family? Get her back. Get Janet back. Take her back. Bring her back to me."

She pulled at his shirt, she pushed at his chest, and she slapped his face. Sam was silent. He dared not admit that his mother and father were right to take Janet. Not in the cruel way in which they schemed and stole her. Doc Simmons had confirmed Claire was not able to support herself, much less their daughter, in her condition. Neither could he. He had to work. It was their only means of survival. Everything in life was dependent on his father.

At first she shook her head and pursed her lips whenever Sam came near to give her water or to try to feed her. She spent several days in bed sobbing and praying for Janet's return. Praying and reading the Bible strengthened her resolve and her will to live. Claire made up her mind to become strong again, strong enough to birth the baby growing inside of her and to take back what was rightfully hers—her Janet, her husband, her family.

Doc Simmons was pleased with Claire's progress. He made it a point to stop by to see her every day. As she approached the last weeks of her pregnancy Doc Simmons witnessed the return of her strength and resolve. Despite her progress, he knew what he had to do.

> **In nothing do men more nearly approach
> the gods than in giving health to men.**
>
> —Cicero

Doc Simmons

Samuel Disser was a punctual and predictable man. Doc Simmons knocked on the front door of the Disser home at the exact time he knew Samuel would be retiring to the library with the daily paper before sitting down to his evening meal. Samuel opened the door and was confused. "Hello, Doc. You must know that no one here is in need of your services."

"Quite the contrary, Samuel, quite the contrary," Doc replied as he stepped past him and into the foyer.

Samuel shut the door and quipped, "I don't expect this is a social call, is it?"

"No, Samuel, it is not. We need privacy. I have a few things to say to you." Doc took off his hat and made himself comfortable on the settee in the drawing room. Mr. Disser slid shut the pocket doors to the foyer and to the library and settled himself in the high back chair closest to the settee. "I know you are not my patient. In fact, I know you are not any doctor's patient," Doc began. "However, as a physician who is sworn to treat and heal, I am here to tell you that you are an evil and despicable man." In typical fashion, Samuel's indignation drew him up to his full height as he stood to show Doc to the door. Doc was resolute. He made no move to get up or to leave. Samuel stood at the pocket door to the foyer, unsure how to remove Doc from his home.

Determined to speak his professional and personal opinion after having seen Samuel's horrendous treatment of Claire, Doc was not going to leave until his message was clear. He ignored Samuel's displeasure as he began to pace and snort. Doc remained seated and continued, "Have you given any thought as to how your actions have affected Claire? You may wish to punish your son for his actions, for your disappointments in him, but does it cause you even the slightest concern that you are destroying Claire's health and well-being in the process?"

"You...you have no business coming into my home and telling me how to address my family issues." Samuel stood over Doc shaking his fist in his face. "This is my family; do you hear me? I am the head of this household, of The Disser Company—the fact is that these people eat and sleep thanks to my sweat and toil."

Doc raised himself slowly from his seat, hoping concentration on this simple activity would stem the anger he felt rising in his chest. Believing Doc was preparing to leave his house, Samuel turned his back and rested his fists on the mantle. Doc took a deep breath and reminded Samuel, "It is history that Sam and Claire fell in love, that they married without your blessing or consent, and that they had a baby. Are you so cruel and detestable that, even when you have tormented Claire with the role of a servant, you continue to look for ways to break her heart and her spirit?"

Ignoring him and trying to shut out all he was saying, Samuel kept his back turned to Doc and his fists clenched. Did this stupid physician not have eyes to see he was poised and ready to deliver a blow? Doc walked right up behind Samuel and, almost whispering, stated, "Your commercial and person tyranny *will not* continue. I am going to see to it."

Turning to face Doc Simmons, Samuel pointed a finger and began to shake it. He opened his mouth to order the doctor out of his home, but Doc surprised him by yelling, "I am not afraid of you, Samuel Disser! I have *nothing* to fear from you."

Samuel dropped his arm and took one step toward Doc. Without moving a muscle, Doc Simmons continued in a normal voice, "The Chamber of Commerce meets this evening at eight o'clock. I have written all that you have committed in a letter demanding your company's dismissal from Chamber membership. The mere fact that you and May have kidnapped little Janet from her own mother shows there may be no end to your disgusting plans for that poor woman or for your own son."

As Doc walked to the pocket door to leave, he turned back to address Samuel one last time. "To be honest, Samuel, it frightens me that I can foresee your continuing to harm and destroy Claire. Let me be clear that taking Janet is to be the last pain and suffering you cause. If you continue to wield your evil against Claire, I will see to it that your company receives no bids in the future and your business will be forced to close." Doc donned his hat and showed himself out.

Samuel stared in shock and disbelief as Doc opened the pocket door and left. May quietly and quickly approached the drawing room to ask for details of the conversation. Samuel brushed her aside, walking down the hall and out the back door. May stood still until she heard the familiar sound of the back door closing. When she dared take the same walk down the hall to peer out the kitchen window, she spotted Samuel seated on the wrought-iron bench in the garden.

Grace and May and Janet ate dinner in silence, not knowing whether or not to anticipate Samuel's presence. Grace cleared the table and washed the dishes while May took Janet upstairs to prepare for bed. When Janet was tucked in bed for the night, May retired to her room to change into her nightclothes. She looked out the window at Samuel's still silhouette in the garden.

With girlish delight, May tiptoed back to Janet's bedroom. Without regard for her husband's agitations, whatever they may be, May was delighted this precious grandchild was home with family where she should be. Hearing Janet's steady breathing of deep sleep, May climbed under the comforter beside the child and fell fast asleep.

Doc Simmons drove to the Chamber of Commerce meeting downtown. After exchanging pleasantries with the members in attendance, he approached the Chamber's secretary and requested an addition to the evening's agenda.

At the end of the regular business, the president turned the meeting over to Doc. As he stood to speak, Doc was reminded of the Bible verse in Ephesians, "Do not let any unwholesome talk come out of your mouth, but only what is helpful for building others up according to their needs, that it may benefit those who listen."

Pausing for a moment, Doc bowed his head and then lifted his chin to scan the room. "Dear members and friends," he began, "I am concerned for a fellow business-man in our city. He has experienced a serious decline in construction contracts and is struggling in many ways. I have spoken with him just this evening, and he would not ask for himself, but I will ask on his behalf, that his company be withdrawn from membership. Let us agree to a letter of termination to be sent to him as soon as possible. And let us include Samuel Disser Sr. in our closing prayer this evening."

Understanding that this was the extent to which Doc would share confidential information, the president of the Chamber of Commerce declared The Disser Company should be dismissed from membership. The secretary called for a motion and a second to the motion. The vote was unanimous. The Disser Company dismissal was confirmed.

Chamber members solemnly bowed their heads. Doc Simmons led the group in a heartfelt appeal to our Lord and Savior Jesus Christ for mercy on the city of Cincinnati, its inhabitants, and grace for Samuel Disser Sr. to dissolve all business interests in anticipation of retirement.

May it be so.

"Hush, hush," said the moon. "Turn out the light…someone new sleeps with us tonight!"

—Anonymous

Claire

When the time came for their much-anticipated son to be born, Claire pleaded with Sam, "Stay home from work today. Stay by my side. Please, Sam, I don't want to go through this alone." He refused, not wishing to miss work and give more fuel for his father's disappointments. Gus brought the midwife Doc Simmons had suggested as well as some donated baby clothes and diapers.

The evening of June 9, 1927, Mr. Disser called Doc Simmons. "You need to go and see Claire. Tell me the sex of the child when it is born. And send me the bill." Doc Simmons would not admit that he had already made a visit in the late afternoon. The midwife was confident the birth would take place the following day.

Before noon on June 10, a baby girl was born, weighing just six pounds. At the end of his work day, Sam sprinted up the walk at the sound of a baby crying. He burst through the front door and saw a beaming midwife holding the new bundle of joy in her arms. Without looking in the blanket he asked, "What is it?" certain it was a son. This child simply had to be a son.

The midwife replied, "Why, sir, you have yourself another beautiful baby girl." The anticipation fell away from his face. Sam turned and walked out the door without a word. In confusion and uncertainty, the midwife returned to the bedroom with the baby, saying to Claire, "I think you will need me to stay with you for one more night."

"Was that my husband? Was that Sam?" Claire knew she had heard the company truck in the driveway.

"Yes, ma'am, it was. But he's gone."

Claire didn't know what to think. "Did you show him our new daughter? Did he see his new child?"

The midwife hesitated. "Well, ma'am, well he did. Well, he didn't actually see her. He asked what it was. That's all. He asked what it was. When I said it was a baby girl, he up and left."

Refusing to be despondent, Claire was instead angry, very angry. "He did what? He left because he has another daughter? A beautiful baby girl? After all I have been through he couldn't so much as come to see me? He left me and a new baby? Walked out? What kind of a man does such a thing? Have you ever in your life known of such a thing?" Her voice was getting louder and shrill.

The midwife shook her head back and forth, holding the baby as close as she could to her chest to shield the child from Claire's screams. "Please, ma'am, oh please do not upset yourself so. Maybe he's just scared. Two children now are more responsibility."

Claire threw back her head and fell against the pillows, "Responsibility? That man has never accepted any responsibility. He's a coward and a boy." She turned her face to bury her head in the pillows. The midwife took the baby into the kitchen to sit and wait until the sobbing ceased.

An hour or so passed before there were no sounds from the bedroom. The midwife tried to walk quietly back down the hall, only to see that Claire was not sleeping but was holding out her arms to take the baby. She lied, "I am fine. I need to hold and nurse my baby." The midwife breathed a sigh of relief, and the baby cooed.

Claire looked down at her new little life and said, "We will survive. Disser women are survivors." At that moment, she chose her baby's name. Her second child would be called Shirley. Shirley was the name of the elderly colored woman who held and sang hymns to Janet. From that woman came glorious praises of God's love, and in Claire's arms came a mother's love. Woven together, this child would be loved from above and on earth.

**To be in your child's memories tomorrow,
be in his life today.**

—Anonymous

Sam

Rather than pretend to be pleased with the birth of another girl, Sam drove to his parents' home. He needed time, maybe just one night alone without the emotion and madness that had consumed Claire.

Mr. Disser met his son's news of a baby girl with a knowing nod and an "I told you so. That woman is nothing but trouble, able to conceive nothing but girls. Will there be no son to carry on the Disser name? I can only imagine your disappointment. Perhaps now you can understand how concerned your mother and I have been for you."

Mrs. Disser could not believe her ears. Her husband was right. Sam had recognized his mistakes and had come back to them. In support of her son's homecoming, Mrs. Disser came into the hallway to embrace him. She called for Janet. "Come and see. Your father is here. He is here to see you, to be with you." Janet hid behind Mrs. Disser's long skirt and held on tightly to her grandmother's hand.

Sam ate a few bites of dinner with his father and mother. Grace had taken her dinner up to her room to avoid taking part in any discussion. When Sam could stomach no more food, he asked to be excused. Mrs. Disser gently put her hand over his. "Sam, we had Gus move the furniture from the attic back to your room. I have fresh linens on the bed." *So,* Sam mused to himself, *they've been anticipating this day. I disappointed them and now I have disappointed myself. I wonder which is worse.*

Sam crawled under the covers and watched the sky turn from dark to light. He felt empty and ashamed. During dinner his father had spoken aloud to no one in particular that he would make all necessary arrangements for the support of Claire and the new baby. With full confidence his father would clean up the mess that had been his life with Claire, he arose the next morning to eat breakfast with his family and go to work with his father.

> **A divorce is like an amputation: you survive it, but there's less of you.**
>
> **—Margaret Atwood**

Mr. Disser

Sam's father had made up his mind what terms he wanted the judge, a close personal friend, to decree. There was no question that Mr. Disser had the house and family to protect and care for Janet, and Shirley for that matter. To appease his wife's attachment to the child and to ease his son's obvious guilt, custody of Janet would suffice based on a perfect compromise. The court would affirm the Disser family support of the older, more demanding child, while giving custody of the younger and more dependent child to her mother.

Samuel had already been in contact with John Doppler. After years of being refused access of any kind with Claire, John was anxious to be a part of her life again and offer whatever support she needed. Mr. Disser knew John Doppler would never allow Claire to suffer. He was a man of means and could support both she and the youngest child's needs for as long as was necessary. He earned sufficient wages to maintain John Sr. and Aunt Louisa in a nursing home and pay for his own large home in Hyde Park. In Mr. Disser's mind, there was no question this "split" of the family was the ideal solution.

Mr. Disser discussed his rationale with his friend in the judge's chambers early Saturday morning over coffee and May's homemade caramel cake. The judge deemed that the specifics of the proposed separation were reasonable. On Monday, he instructed one of the court clerks to draw up the required documentation and personally deliver a copy to John Doppler Jr.

> I love people. I love my family, my children…but inside myself is a place where I live all alone and that's where you renew your springs that never dry up.
>
> —Pearl S. Buck

Claire

After two days of never hearing or receiving so much as a visit from Sam, the mid-wife made arrangements for a ride for Claire and the baby with a Coney Island worker into downtown Cincinnati. The workman had strict instructions to take Claire directly to the courthouse. With a letter of guarantee from Doc Simmons for payment of required fees, Claire filed for divorce, claiming desertion and demanding the return of Janet to her care.

Grateful for the workman's time and costs to transport her into downtown and back to the rented house again, she was told it was all due to Doc Simmons' generosity. On the return trip the workman's silence and the rhythmic rumble of his truck on the roads lulled baby Shirley to sleep and gave Claire the solitude and calm she desperately needed.

Three days later, one of Mr. Cox's men came to the rented house to tell Claire a hearing had been assigned for that afternoon. He introduced himself as Michael and told Claire he had been instructed to return after lunch to take she and baby Shirley to court. She had no idea what to expect. Claire wanted her daughters to be with her, especially if Sam wanted no part of them.

She was relieved and ecstatic to see her beloved cousin John in the courtroom. At the sight of Claire, he swept her up in his arms and repeated his pledge. "I promised you, now, didn't I?" he reminded her with a smile and an arm around her shoulder.

Before Claire could comprehend what was happening in the courtroom, the judge granted a separation and not a divorce to Claire and Sam. He gave custody only of the newborn Shirley to Claire. Sobbing and pleading with the court, with anyone who would listen, Claire begged for both of her daughters. The judge threatened her, and then threatened Cousin John, who echoed Claire's requests, to accept his decision or face charges.

John drove Claire and baby Shirley back to the rented house to collect their meager belongings. They were going to live with John and his wife until Claire could decide what to do. When they pulled in the drive, the front door of the little rented house was standing open. Sitting in the hallway was the baby crib and a box containing Claire's personal items. The rest of the house was stripped and empty.

What if it had not been for her cousin John? Where would she be? Out on the street, just as Aunt Louisa had threatened she would be. He had come to her rescue. John took Claire and baby Shirley to his home until he could make living arrangements for them.

John's wife Edna (everyone called her Henny) made Claire and the baby welcome in their home in Hyde Park. They slept in the guest bedroom, and ate meals with the family, and Claire socialized with their friends. She would always remember Henny's kindness. She would always cherish John's devotion.

Henny was curious about John's younger years in the Doppler home. "Tell me what he was like growing up, and who on earth was Maggie?"

Claire flushed and admitted, "Well, John was my teacher and my confidant from the time I started school. To this day, and certainly now, I don't know what I would have done without his kindness and generosity. As for Maggie, she had the biggest crush on John, but I knew he didn't feel the same for her."

Inside of three months, John had rented a two-bedroom apartment located above a candy store in Oakley, not far from his home in Hyde Park. The apartment housed Claire and baby Shirley in one bedroom and her cousin John's mother Louisa in the second bedroom.

Claire was to care for her Aunt Louisa, who was crippled with arthritis and confined to a wheelchair, in exchange for the apartment and all expenses. Aunt Louisa and Uncle John had been placed in a nursing home on the west side of town several years before. Uncle John was no longer coherent and needed to be in a separate and controlled facility.

Claire welcomed her new role as a full-time caretaker not only for baby Shirley but also for Aunt Louisa. Aunt Louisa was not as pleased with the arrangement. She grunted and spit and tried to grab at Claire with bony fingers that had deformed into claws from arthritis. With grace and patience, Claire bathed and clothed and fed Aunt Louisa. Bent over with arthritis, Aunt Louisa was unable to look up from her bowed head and face Claire eye-to-eye. Claire imagined every moment she was caring for her Aunt Louisa was smiling and thankful for Claire's tenderness.

Claire settled into the apartment and into a routine. Within a week, she set about trying to get custody of Janet. She wanted both her children, both her girls, to be with her forever. The day a new hearing was confirmed, John took Claire to court. The same judge who had declared a separation and custody of the two children was honestly alarmed at the news of Sam's behavior when Shirley was born. "He has never seen this baby?"

Shirley had colic and was crying uncontrollably. Claire stared at the judge and spoke in a trembling voice, "He is no husband, and he is no father. He walked out on us, both of us. He walked out on a newborn baby and me without a word or a care in the world."

The judge rapped his gavel in a repeat of his original decree. "I give custody of the older child, Janet, to Mr. Samuel Disser. He has the means and the intent for support of the older child. I grant custody of the baby to Claire Disser. I direct that John Doppler Jr., as Claire Disser's first cousin and closest living relative, take temporary financial responsibility for both Claire Disser and the baby Shirley."

Claire protested, "You cannot decide based on means. I am their mother! Do you hear? These children, both of them, need their mother! The Dissers are not family. They never have been family. They never will be family!" As she protested, she began to cry, and Shirley cried even harder…and louder. Cousin John stood to wrap his arm around her shoulders and begged the judge to listen to Claire's pleas.

The judge had turned to Claire with one question: "Do you wish to petition for compensation from Mr. Samuel Disser or from his son Mr. Sam Disser for yourself or for yourself and little Shirley?"

Claire's response came through gritted teeth. "I never want anything, ever, from the Disser family—not so much as a penny." Cousin John opened his mouth to speak again but the judge shushed him, stood, and pointing a finger at both Claire and John, declared his decision was final.

For weeks after the hearing, John had tried on Claire's behalf to contact Mr. Disser or Sam in person to reason with them on the issue of Janet's custody. He went to the Disser home and Mrs. Disser slammed the door in his face. John finally visited the construction site at the racetrack where Sam and Samuel had locked the entrance gate.

Claire sent letter after letter to the Disser home addressed to Janet telling her how much she loved her and wanted to be part of her life. Every letter was returned unopened. Her persistence lasted almost a year. Cousin John warned Claire, "You must stop torturing yourself. It will do you no good to pursue reason with these people." He had become very concerned for Claire's health. She was gaunt and almost as frail as his mother.

With little Shirley to nurse and teach, and Aunt Louisa to attend to morning, afternoon, and evening, Claire was giving up hope of having more in her life to care for. She came to realize she was truly blessed with one healthy and beautiful child. Claire turned to her Bible for the first time in more than a year. As if with a message that came directly from him, there was the verse of Jeremiah 29:11, "For I know the plans I have for you, declares the Lord, plans for welfare and not for evil, to give you a future and a hope." Amen to that. Amen.

Days passed as Claire prayed and read her Bible to ask God for a better understanding, and clearer sight of her future and Janet's. She had to acknowledge that John was right. The Disser family would never permit her involvement in Janet's life. The best decision was to recognize that not only Sam but his parents and Grace as well may be the better choice for Janet's upbringing.

Emotionally drained and depressed, Claire was truly unfit to take on another child. Janet deserved stability and proper care. It took what seemed like all the strength she had left for Claire to make a final decision to extinguish thoughts and memories of Janet. She threw the letters she had written to Janet, all returned to her, in the trash bin.

Aglamesis Brothers candy store, housed on the first floor of the building in which they lived, was a remedy for Claire's depression. The Aglamesis brothers themselves treated Claire to samples of their daily chocolate creations. On her birthday, they presented her with an expensive black velvet box containing a sampling of their best and her favorite chocolate candies. The brothers adored Claire and pledged to heal her with their "hope for all that is sweet."

During the following Christmas holidays, raising Shirley and nursing Aunt Louisa, Claire had regained her physical strength and her hope. She returned to church, choosing St. Cecilia because it was just one block east of the apartment. Church members helped her wheel Aunt Louisa down the street and up the parish steps.

Claire prayed for the forgiveness of her sins and confessed her guilt to a priest who accepted her confession even though she was not Catholic. She felt a quiet sense of release. God was not punishing her, and he had never stopped knowing her pain and suffering. Claire was glad she and Sam had married and was just as glad they had parted. Loving him and losing him gave her the strength that comes from surviving quite well without a husband.

Making the decision to have a child—it's momentous. It is to decide forever to have your heart go walking outside your body.

—Elizabeth Stone

Sam

When Shirley was born, Sam's father was furious. "That woman has never wanted anything but to tie you down and bind you with one child after another. She schemed to get into the Disser family. Look what it got you: two daughters and a pitiful excuse for a wife."

Sam was exhausted by his father's constant arguments. This second baby was not the son either he or his father had pined for. How many girls would Claire produce? She had become more and more indignant about Mr. Disser's demands and less and less appreciative of what he had given them. She wanted Sam to prohibit his father from entering their house, to go elsewhere for lunch every day, and to tell him they did not need his money. Claire constantly rebelled against Mr. Disser's presence in their lives.

The truth was that his father was the only one who had everything to give. He held all the cards…New business contracts were awarded to competitors of The Disser Company. Samuel had to let go all the workers and manage the day to day tasks between just he and Sam. To make ends meet Sam had to agree to drive for Doc Simmons and for Boss Cox in the evenings and on the weekends.

Divorce was never a consideration for Sam, much less the alternative of separation. Until his father educated him on the new laws that gave legitimate reasons to end a marriage, Sam had no idea he had a choice, a way out of what his father had continually and consistently convinced him was a mistake.

Mr. Disser offered to Sam, "I will pay the attorney to file for separation from Claire and for custody of Janet. I will pay for Janet's education and her care, which you know will be more than attended to by your mother and Grace." Sam knew he needn't have a care at all in the matter. He and his father could be rid of Claire and her constant haranguing, Sam would move back home and resume his previous, single life. No questions would be asked, and no discussion of Claire would be permitted in the Disser home ever again.

For what seemed a small price to pay, Mr. Disser was able to guarantee, "Your mother and Grace will have exclusive custody of Janet. That way you can focus on rebuilding and taking control of the family business." Sam was given no choice in the matter. He would live at home as a respectful and grateful son.

PART TWO

The Disser Sisters, Our Story

New opinions often appear first as jokes and fancies, then as blasphemies and treason, then as questions open to discussion, and finally as established truths.

—George Bernard Shaw

Janet

Grandmother May and Grandfather Samuel, Aunt Grace, and in the summers Aunt Hannah, were my caretakers and guardians. My father was a mysterious figure who appeared at inconsistent times on weekday evenings and on the weekends without much to say to me. If I asked anyone about my mother, the subject was changed, the question dismissed. At first, Grandmother May would briefly laugh as if it were a silly notion that I even had a mother. Aunt Grace would turn and walk away from me as if there was nothing to discuss. Eventually, I stopped expecting an answer.

On my fourth birthday, my father told me, "You have me, a father, and that is all you need." I thought his remark odd, as the truth was I hardly ever saw him. He lived in the same house but was gone in the mornings by the time I got up and was rarely home on the weekends. When he did appear at dinner time during the week, he was usually sullen. Throughout the meal, he would have little to say except in one-word responses to Grandfather's questions about work. There was nothing for me to ask him. After dinner I would kiss my father goodnight, a requirement from my grandmother, not knowing when or if I would see him again.

The days before school were carefree, unstructured. Grandmother and Aunt Grace were tolerant of my every request. I explored the neighborhood and surrounding areas in solitary walks that lasted for hours. Upon my return to the house, Grandmother May would simply ask if I was hungry. There was never any discipline or punishment, even when I was found in a lie concerning my whereabouts. Grandfather and Grandmother believed in open and honest discussions of whatever wrongdoing I had committed. They never paddled me or sent me to my room.

I had no chores. All the housework and cooking, even the milking and care of our cow Dolly, were the responsibility of Grandmother and Aunt Grace. Dolly was docile and aloof. Her shed at the back of the property was a place of interest for my friends. After several interactions with Dolly, they lost interest in her as well. We had fresh milk and butter, cheese, and custard because of Dolly. All I knew was that Grandmother was an amazing woman to take what came out of that cow's belly and turn it into something delicious.

When there was not much commercial work, Grandfather would bring some of the colored men to the house for odd jobs. Gus was the colored man I knew the best. I would hurry to eat my lunch then run out to the yard, turn a bucket over for a seat beside Gus, and watch him eat his lunch. A tall, thin, and gentle man, Gus always wore brown leather shoes with pearl buttons. One day I got up the nerve to ask him about his unusual shoes. Gus chuckled, "Why I has nice shoes 'cause I's a preacher on Sundays."

Gus answered all my questions about the construction business and colored people, but never about Father or about Grandfather. He confided, "If yo' grandfather works us colored pass six in da ev'ning, he has ta drive us all back ta Liberty Street. They's no colored 'llowed on streetcars after dark. No, little one. No darkies aft's dark." He chuckled deep in his throat and smiled at me with big white teeth that had irregular gaps, top and bottom.

Whenever any of the colored got in trouble, Gus told me Grandfather would be called by the presiding judge to say words for or against the men who were in jail. "Now, if 'n' they's part o' yo' grandfather's crew 'n' are good men, he speaks in da favor and they be released." I came to understand why Grandfather and Father did not get along. Grandfather had a definitive opinion about everything.

Father did not. In fact, I did not think he had a thought of his own. It was obvious he wasn't doing what he wanted to do, because he was so unhappy. Gus told me, "I has it on good 'thority that yo' father is a good plummer. But don't you go on tellin' yo' grandfather. No way, little one. No, yo' grandfather don't no way like dat."

Grandfather told me he was growing older. I thought that was an odd statement to make, because he was not growing at all. In fact, he and Grandmother appeared to be shrinking.

"I'm going to work less now that Sam has nothing on his mind but the business, as he should. It's not the same for me anymore. I don't take pleasure in going to the work site." Grandfather and Father went to work in the morning, but Father dropped Grandfather off at the house for lunch with me and Grandmother May.

Grandfather and I began spending afternoons together in the sun room working puzzles, reading books, and taking naps. He became my friend. Grandfather told me I was a great deal like him, "Ah, my little girl. You are observant and bold, just like me." He described me to friends, neighbors, and family as a gift. He boasted, "She is just like me, this one is, just like me."

One month before my fourth birthday, Grandfather took me to a circus training ground. The training area was a large expanse of flat earth. We reached it by driving east to the Beechmont Levy and then turning south toward the Ohio River. It was "low land," flooded with the rains that elevated the Ohio River each year in the spring, surrounded by lush green and high hills.

An airfield was there, Lunken Field. Lunken Field was named for a friend of Grandfather's, Edmund Lunken, who was in the business of manufacturing steel valves. The City of Cincinnati had assumed operation of the airfield. In addition to commercial flights, Grandfather told me it ran a regular airmail service between Cincinnati and Chicago.

With the exception of a control tower and a few airplane hangars, the property adjacent to Lunken Field was uninhabited, not a single building or house as far as the eye could see. Vividly colored circus tents sprang up in random spots stretching from the southern edge of the airport all the way down to the Ohio River. At the farthest tent from the road, Grandfather introduced me to the elephant trainer, Lucas.

Lucas lifted me up as if I weighed only a few pounds and placed me on a howdah. "Let's see what you think of a ride on a baby elephant," he said, and he turned to smile at Grandfather. Grandfather motioned for me to ride down the middle of the last row of tents. It was unforgettable. I had only seen elephants in books, but now I had the experience of seeing and touching and riding on an elephant. I developed a fondness for elephants that day.

Grandfather was excited too. "Take it all in, Janet. This is an opportunity of a lifetime." I learned from him not to say much but to observe people and circumstances. From the vantage point of the howdah atop the baby elephant, I could see in and around all the circus tents at one time. The panorama was lively, busy, and noisy.

Lucas was a strong man, with a thick accent and large bulging arms. Back at his tent, he lifted me off the howdah. I looked into his eyes and knew I was in love. I asked him, "Do you have any children?"

Lucas laughed as he placed me gently on my feet and answered, "Not that I know of!"

At the end of summer, Grandfather remembered my fascination with the circus elephants. Grandmother May and I rode with him for several hours to the Simmons estate in Augusta, Kentucky. It was a white mansion, so large it had two front doors that swung inward to reveal a massive foyer and soaring staircase. A matching white stable sat behind the house, and the double barn doors were swung wide open on either end for air and light.

Inside the barn were animal heads mounted on every crown board. Doc Simmons's son-in-law Bill was inside the largest stall, bent over a long flat table and hand saw. "What are you doing?" I boldly inquired. He looked up at me and smiled. "I am in the process of constructing umbrella stands from these elephant legs."

I was intrigued. "Grandfather and Father are in the construction business too," I said.

Bill chuckled. "So am I. The materials may be different, but the result is certainly the same as long as the customer is happy."

The legs had come from Ole Lil, a circus elephant who had died of natural causes. Bill was both a taxidermist and safari guide. He gestured at the animal heads looming above us, "I take customers to Africa on safari. I've been trying to convince your grandfather to go on one, but he won't make the trip across the ocean. After the safari, the animals are shipped back here to the States. Then I prepare the trophies for my customers."

I was fascinated by his brief description, not realizing the need to kill the animals for the purpose. Grandfather shared the story of my elephant ride. "Yes," I reported proudly, "we went to the circus grounds and I was able to make friends with a real elephant." Bill sliced a piece of elephant hide off Ole Lil for me to keep. Now I had a trophy of my very own.

In every conceivable manner, the family is link to our past, bridge to our future.

—Alex Haley

Shirley

I am quite proud of my family history. Mother purchased a small journal for me so I could write everything down, in as much detail as possible, from her stories. She confirmed it was recorded in many books in the public library that our family heritage harkens back to Davy Crockett, the great American frontiersman, by way of William Crockett. Genealogy records claim a direct Crockett heir, Andrew Crockett, married Catherine Walker Bell and together they had eleven children. Their tenth child was William Crockett.

William Crockett settled in the Brighton Corners neighborhood of Cincinnati, buying a grocery store and, later in life, an ice cream store. William and his wife Margaret Fein had three children: Laura Ann, William Jr., and a baby girl who was unnamed at the time. She would eventually be called Clarissa. There is no birth record on file for the children, because all were born with the help of midwives.

William's wife Margaret died from hemorrhaging during Clarissa's birth. Her burial site was discovered decades later by her cousins. Her grave was marked, but there was no coffin. Alongside her skeletal remains were the remains of a baby girl. Perhaps Mother had a twin.

Baby Clarissa was adopted by Louisa Doppler, her mother's oldest sister, and her husband John Doppler Sr. They gave Mother the name Clarissa Ruth Doppler. Louisa and John already had three daughters, Clara, Louisa, and Emma, as well as a son, John Jr. All the girls were grown, married, and living not far from their parents. John Jr. was still living at home. He did not marry until late in life, as he had promised he would care for his parents.

At sixteen years of age, Clarissa Doppler married Sam Disser. He was twenty-six years old. Mother said they were married on Christmas Eve but there was no record because the ceremony was officiated by a justice of the peace. She was sad when she recounted that they lived for a few years at the Disser home in Westwood. Sam worked for his father in the cement business and Mother tended to the household chores for the Disser family.

A little girl was born to Mother nine months after my mother was married to Sam. Their first home together was out in the country near Coney Island when Sam's father landed a contract with Boss Cox to build a racetrack in California, Ohio.

It was a rented house located close to the job site. Rent was paid based on an agreement between Sam's father and Boss Cox. At the time, all the property in that area was owned by Mr. Cox. He was a gambler and was eventually run out of town because of bad debts.

When their little girl was three years old, Sam took her to live with his parents. Mother was pregnant with me at the time and very ill. I was born on June 10, 1927. My father never returned to the rented house to see me or to see Mother. Mother's efforts to have my older sister come back to live with us were ignored.

Mother stayed home with me and cared for Aunt Louisa Doppler until I was three years old and able to be cared for by other people. Cousin John found Mother a job as a switchboard operator at the Bell Telephone Company. He gave Mother enough money to start her new life.

He moved Mother and me to an apartment in Madisonville on the bus line and transferred my great aunt Louisa to a nursing home. Great Uncle John had passed away quite some time before this, but no one thought it would be good for Great Aunt Louisa's health to tell her the news.

That was all I could remember to write in my journal. Mother told me to write it all down, as she would never repeat what she had told me. The only other writings I have are the notes that Mother continually received from Cousin John. He wrote to her all the time even though we lived in the same city.

My own writing began when Mother changed herself for her job at the telephone company. She dyed her hair blond and wore it back from her face in a tight and high French twist. She rimmed her eyes in brown pencil and coated her lashes with black mascara. The secondhand shop two doors away from us set aside dresses, blouses with skirts, and high-heeled shoes in Mother's sizes.

Outdated fashion magazines and days-old newspaper articles about dressing and makeup were strewn around the apartment. Mother learned from the other ladies at work how to dress. She listened when the ladies at work engaged in conversations with businessmen so she could address each situation with the same courtesy.

Each evening, Mother would loosen her hair and tie it back from her face with a strip of old fabric that she tied in a bow at the top of her head. She lathered her face with cold cream to remove all traces of makeup, rinsed with cold water, and then smoothed cocoa butter around her eyes and mouth and on her cheeks. The scent of cocoa butter reminds me of standing on the toilet seat and looking at her image in the mirror as she repeated the same practiced motions night after night.

My days were spent in the apartment below ours with the two little old Corcoran sisters. Their apartment was stuffy and dark. Most of the day, they slept in armchairs covered with sheets, their feet up on footstools. I occupied myself on their living room floor with whatever I could find in their bedroom drawers and closets. Ribbons, hats, shoes, picture albums, and jewelry were my toys.

For me to be able to stay with the sisters during the day, Mother cooked breakfast in their kitchen every morning and helped them to wash and dress in cotton shifts and sweaters. She cooked dinner in their kitchen when she came home from work. Mother and I ate whatever was left over from the sisters' breakfast and the same at night for dinner. After we had finished the dinner leftovers in our apartment, Mother would go back downstairs to the sisters' apartment to help them wash and dress for bed.

If you cannot get rid of the family skeleton, you may as well make it dance.

—George Bernard Shaw

Janet

At the age of five, it was time for me to go to school. Grandfather announced, "I will be paying for you to attend Mother of Mercy private Catholic girls' school." Not only did he pay for school, but he also paid fifty dollars a year—quite a lot of money in those days—to have the Mother of Mercy school bus come up the driveway to collect me at the house and deliver me again at the end of the day.

"But I would rather walk to the public school with my friends," I insisted. Grandfather would not hear any argument against his choice of school. "My decision is final. Your grandmother and I have visited both schools. Mother of Mercy is by far the better choice. Consistency and strict training are critical for your education. You will attend Mother of Mercy until graduation." And we weren't even Catholic.

I had very few friends at Mother of Mercy. Most of them lived close to each other and played together after school. The distance from school and classmates made it difficult to make school friends. After school I would change into play clothes and take walks or climb one of the giant catalpa trees in the backyard. From inside the massive leafy branches I was invisible and could eavesdrop on the next-door neighbors, Dot and Bob Wheeler.

They had loud and frequent fights. The arguments were always about money, and the exchange was always the same, "For God's sake, Dot" and "Aw, Bob, leave me alone." After a while, I was able to mimic their voices and most of their conversations. Aunt Grace thought my imitation of the Wheelers was spot on and pretty funny.

Most Saturdays, I could persuade either Grandfather or Aunt Grace to take me to the zoo. Grandfather was reluctant to pay the price of admission, but Aunt Grace was eager to go and didn't mind the cost. We would walk hand-in-hand, investigating the cages of every animal. I insisted we visit the elephants upon our arrival and again before we departed. They were my favorite.

The Zoological Park was owned by the City of Cincinnati, though it was run by a board of park commissioners. The animal enclosures were bordered with displays of bushes and trees and flowers that varied with each season. The walkways and grounds were glorious.

For my seventh birthday, Grandfather, Grandmother, and Aunt Grace took me in the car to Coney Island Amusement Park. During the drive, Aunt Grace sat beside me in the back seat and gave me a history lesson. "This park was built by your grandfather. It is very impressive." She was right. When we arrived, I was overwhelmed. The park included a lake and rides, an enormous public swimming pool, and a dance hall.

Grandfather took one ride with me. It was called the Mystic Chute, where you were placed in a gondola-style boat that sailed around and eventually went down a water slide and came to rest in a shallow pool. We were soaked by the huge wave of water that came into the boat. I screamed, and Grandfather laughed at me. Aunt Grace was goaded by Grandfather into taking me on the Wildcat roller coaster. In the heat of the afternoon, I swam in the Sunlite swimming pool under the watchful eye of Aunt Grace. Grandfather and Grandmother walked to Moonlight Gardens dance hall to see if there were any bands they recognized that were featured on the marquee.

On Sunday mornings, I regularly snuck out the back door and walked three blocks to the Methodist Church. It was the church closest to home and afforded an escape from the oppressively quiet Disser house on Sundays. Grandmother was failing, and Grandfather was constantly worried and complaining about everything. They spent most of the day on Sunday in the sun room, Grandfather and I reading books and Grandmother napping.

Church was joyous, filled with congregational singing. The deep voices of the men in the choir echoed to the edges of the pews. My seat was in the far right corner, four pews from the back doors. I pretended to be part of the family that sat in the same pew, week in and week out. During the minister's sermon, I would scoot closer to their little boy.

Sometimes the sermon would put me to sleep. Other times I thought the minister was speaking directly to me, especially when he talked about the need for faith to overcome "conduct unbecoming." His warnings against lying scared me, not that I ever lied about anything to anyone… at least not on a regular basis.

> Happy families are all alike; every unhappy
> family is unhappy in its own way.
>
> —Leo Tolstoy

Shirley

I don't remember much about my life until I started kindergarten at the age of five. It was during this time that Mother bought a forest-green brocade couch with gold fringe around the bottom. She was pleased, announcing, "This is an investment. I bought it with the little bit of savings we have collected. Even though it's secondhand, I think it's in good condition, don't you, Shirley?"

That couch would be my bed for many years to come. Because Mother's apartments were small, typically with only one bedroom, it served as couch in the living room by day and bed for me at night.

During the summer, Mother had moved us to an apartment in Cheviot to be close to Cousin John's sister Clara. In August, she enrolled me in kindergarten at the Cheviot Schoo!. I was boarded with Aunt Clara from Sunday night through Saturday morning. Mother would claim me Saturday mornings and we would spend all day Saturday and Sunday together.

Aunt Clara was married to Fred Higgins, and they had two sons, Randall Leroy Higgins, born September 27, 1912, and David Higgins (no middle name), born August 19, 1927. A daughter, Helen, lived only a short time after birth.

The four of them lived in a two-bedroom apartment in a four-apartment building in Cheviot. Aunt Clara and Uncle Fred slept in one bedroom, the boys slept in the second bedroom, and I slept on their couch in the living room. It was a large gray tapestry couch. The cushions were stuffed to the seams. As soon as I fell asleep and let go of the front of the seat cushions, I would roll to the back of the couch and remain wedged there until morning.

Aunt Clara was severe looking in her dress and in her demeanor. She was a dark-haired woman who wore plain gray or navy dresses and old-lady tie shoes. She pinned her hair back at the nape of her neck in a bun and spent the day cleaning and tidying, washing and cooking.

Randall and I never played together, because he was never home. Randall was fifteen years older than me, he worked, and he had lots of girlfriends. Uncle Fred was a nice man with thinning brown hair, deep-set eyes, and big calloused hands. He worked all the time and was only in the house for dinner and then disappeared in his woodshop behind the apartment garage.

David was the same age as me, a scrawny kid and not very smart. He bullied me, shoving and tripping me whenever he could. David spent most afternoons and evenings and all of our summers trying to find ways to torment me.

Summers were the worst times. When school was out, I was too young to be alone, and Mother thought it best for me to continue to spend time with family. David, mean and nasty David, was the reason I hated summers. I learned to disappear as soon after breakfast as possible.

> The experience of the race shows that we get our most important education not through books but through our work. We are developed by our daily task, or else demoralized by it, as by nothing else.
>
> —Anna Garlin Spencer

Claire

With male-dominated jobs decreasing, work for women was increasing. As men in the workforce declined, women were employed in a growing number of clerical and domestic jobs. As an unwed mother, Claire had no choice but to go to work. Paid childcare outside the home was expensive. Cousin John persuaded his sister Clara to provide for Shirley's care at a minimal cost.

For Claire, this allowed for Shirley to be supported in a family environment and for her to live a step above abject poverty.

The women Claire worked with understood her situation. In fact, many of the women at the telephone company were in the same situation. However, mothers at the market and in the neighborhood did not understand Claire's situation because they were at home with their children. Despite her best efforts at the telephone company, Claire's wages were low. She could barely afford to keep herself in clothes and food after paying the rent.

Claire knew her existence with Shirley was going to be difficult but decided it was a challenge she must accept. She knew they would be poor. Unemployment had skyrocketed from 9 percent in 1930 to almost 24 percent in 1932. More people were leaving the country than were entering it in an effort to escape the desperation.

Though her wages were insufficient to cover the basic day-to-day expenses, Claire stretched her money as best she could. No matter how thrifty she was, Claire and Shirley were hungry and cold by payday. She had no employment benefits, no health care, and no paid holidays. Claire recognized that her poverty would be an ongoing, constant stress. She focused on how to meet the rent, have a bit of food, and ride the bus each day to work.

As if the struggle to support herself and hang on to Shirley were not enough, magazines and newspapers began to print articles and scientific studies on the effects of maternal employment on children. Certainly, Claire protested to herself, such stories did not consider the effect on children of becoming homeless or losing their mothers? The essence of the articles Claire read was that a mother who worked would forever have a negative impact on her children. Working mothers, it was asserted, must expect "repercussions in the children's emotional, intellectual or moral development and the incidence of juvenile delinquency or school adjustment problems."

Not being able to care for Shirley herself preyed on Claire's conscience. Childcare was not readily available, and Shirley was not old enough to stay at home alone. Claire had to rely on Cousin Clara for her generous boarding of Shirley. She could not pay Cousin Clara what it actually cost for boarding her little girl. Claire paid what she could and thanked Clara, continually and sincerely, for the care of Shirley.

With this arrangement, Claire was only able to spend weekends with Shirley. She was grateful for the quality of care that Shirley received in Cousin Clara's home. Claire knew her daughter was growing up in a true family environment. On a salary of twenty dollars each week, Claire paid twelve dollars a week for her room and breakfast, budgeted three dollars a week for food and for heat, one dollar for the bus, and gave Cousin Clara the remaining four dollars from every paycheck.

In April 1932, the nursing home called Cousin John to confirm that his mother had passed away. Cousin Clara told Claire the news that Saturday when she arrived to pick up Shirley. St. Cecelia in Oakley was kind enough to hold a brief memorial service. Not a tear was shed. At a family gathering after the service at his home in Hyde Park, John announced their impending move to Atlanta, Georgia, to be close to Henny's family.

Empty and without words to express her sense of loss, Claire hugged Henny and wished her the best in their new life as tears spilled out of her eyes and down her cheeks. John tapped her on the shoulder, grabbed both of her hands, twirled her under his arms, and bowed. "I must confess, little one, that I will miss you most of all."

"Oh, John. You are my knight in shining armor."

"I am so sorry I did not find you a prince, little one," John smiled through his tears.

Bowing before him, Claire confessed, "I had no need of a prince, because I had you." Claire hugged his waist and buried her head in his chest. Cradling her face and setting his chin on the crown of her head, he once again professed, "Ah, but you will always have me."

**In each family a story is playing itself out,
and each family's story embodies its hope
and despair.**

—Auguste Napier

Janet

Within eight days of each other in April 1932, on April 1 and on April 9, Grandmother and then Grandfather passed from my life forever. No one knew what to do. Father was silent and stoic. Aunt Grace disappeared into her room after work each evening. I had lost my caring, loving guardians. My time outside of school was spent climbing slowly up and sitting idly back in a catalpa tree.

Grandmother May had had a breathing problem for as long as I could remember. In her later years, her breathing sapped more and more of her energy, but I never heard her complain. The year of her death, she gave in to physical weakness and spent most of her days, and nights, sitting in a big rocking chair in the sun room. Her legs were always cold. Birthday and Christmas gifts had typically been store bought and church quilted blankets and knitted throws to keep her warm.

I sat at the foot of her rocker when I got home from school. One day I rushed in the front door to tell her about my day at school and the rocker was empty. I knew she was gone. Grandfather wandered the house unable to sit or sleep. A little more than one week later his grief and loneliness took him to heaven to be with May.

If Aunt Grace could have evaporated with her mother's spirit, I believe she would have gone willingly. She had always been too thin, almost gaunt, but with a silent strength that evidently made her one of the most dedicated secretaries at the Internal Revenue Service. In the few days Grandfather stumbled about the house, pining for May, Aunt Grace was just as lost. Death stole Grandfather in his bed reaching for May as if she were laid out beside him.

When Grandfather gasped the release of his earthly existence, Aunt Grace finally gave in, crumbling in a lifeless, sobbing heap on the floor. Doc Simmons swept me

out of the room and shut the door behind us. I sat on the
floor in the hallway, watching Doc descend the steps and
quietly shut the front door. My heart wanted to endure
the ache with someone, anyone. There was no one.

Father was at work. Father was always at work. After
the deaths of his parents, Father did not know what to
do about the silent house. He decided not to change anything. Because Grandmother and Grandfather had raised
me, Father did not even know me. It had seemed easiest
for us to be as invisible as possible to each other. We had
nothing in common, and I never knew what to say. I had
learned from Grandfather to know my father only by ob-
serving and listening.

Without a word to me, Father discussed my future
with Aunt Grace. "I choose not to take her out of the only
school she has ever known—don't you agree?" Aunt Grace
nodded in understanding that Father knew of no other
option for me. I was to continue my education at Mother
of Mercy. My two best friends who lived down the street
from us, Anna and Patricia, were to come to the house to
play after school.

I was only nine years old and alone in the house. Anna
and Patricia knew I was by myself, and they felt sorry for
me. Grace came home from work as quickly as she could
to fix dinner. Father arrived after dinner, usually after
dark, just in time for my obligatory kiss goodnight.

Aunt Grace became a confidante and friend. She gradually softened and began to smile when we talked in my room at bedtime. Her laugh came much later, after a year or so. The deep lines around her eyes remained. Grief had engraved a permanent feature that reminded me of our mutual loss.

**Family presents a memory
no one can steal.**

—Anonymous

Shirley

It was Aunt Clara who gave me bits and pieces of my family background. On more than one occasion, she said, "Your father's parents were adamant that he not marry but stay at home and work in the family business. He obviously paid no heed to their instructions."

Aunt Clara mentioned only once or twice that my father had two sisters, a younger sister named Grace, who lived at home, and an older sister named Jennette who died of an accident at age fifteen. She said, "Your mother is forever asking me about your safety, you know. I think she's afraid she may lose you in an accident someday."

Details of Mother's life came from Aunt Clara in snippets, as carefully wrapped treasures like the last pieces of precious chocolate Mother kept in an expensive black velvet box. She usually shared the anecdotes at the dinner table, giving her something to talk about and making her the center of attention.

My cousin David teased me with the information we learned from his mother. He took pleasure in telling the other kids on the street, "Shirley's father never wanted her, and that's why we're stuck with her. He wanted a son, and Shirley ain't no boy."

The only story I remember Aunt Clara telling on multiple occasions was, "Your father and his father worked together building the River Downs racetrack. Every day for lunch, they would go to your parent's little rented house to eat. Now you know I can cook better than most, but your mother can't cook. No, she can't cook worth a darn. What yelling and screaming must have gone on at lunchtime what with your mother trying to feed them food that was not fit to eat." She would go on and on with her own descriptions of how horrible mother's cooking must have been.

What hit me the hardest, though I tried not to show it, was one night at supper when Aunt Clara revealed, "You know, Shirley, I must tell you that you do have a sister."

Uncle Fred hissed, "That's enough, Clara. This child does not need your irritations."

She said nothing more, not a name or an age. She never brought the subject up again and warned me not to mention a word of it to Mother. All she would say, as if it would put an end to my curiosity, was, "Your sister was taken to the Dissers' home before you were born, with no intention of ever being returned to your mother."

I cried every Sunday night when I had to say good-bye to Mother at the door to Aunt Clara's apartment building. The weeks seemed so long without Mother. Aunt Clara never felt like family. My only family was Mother. I longed for her, wondered every day where she was and if she would really come to collect me on Saturday. Would Mother disappear the way my sister had?

Friends and neighbors who came to visit Aunt Clara would ask, "Why is it I never see Shirley?" Since David teased me all the time, I took lots of walks, long walks.

Strangers on the street would ask, "Are you lost, little girl?" and I would reply, "No, I'm on my way home." I would walk until I felt I could stand going back to that apartment. It was my way of handling things.

David cut chunks out of my hair as I slept on the couch in their apartment. He punched me in the stomach when no one was around. His favorite trick was to hide a carpet pole on one of the apartment stairs. He crouched under the stairwell, and when he heard me turn on the landing he lifted the pole to trip me down the last flight of steps. The entry was slate, and the fall would either bust my lip open or bloody my nose.

He hated me, and I hated him. But I had no choice in the matter. I knew it was either stay with Aunt Clara or be homeless. It's a wonder I didn't go crazy. Some people of that day did, you know. I heard about them from the other kids out on the street.

I know the difference now between
dedication and infatuation. That doesn't
mean I don't still get an enormous kick out
of infatuation; the exciting ephemera, the
punch in the stomach, the adrenaline to
the heart.

—Anna Quindlen

Claire

Frank Wilson was the most handsome man Claire had
ever seen. He had movie-star good looks. His blond
hair and blue eyes made women melt and men jealous.
And he was not married. The day he walked into the

telephone company, every girl swooned. He made eye contact with no one until he noticed Claire.

Claire looked up from her switchboard to see Frank staring at her and standing beside her switchboard console. She was used to speaking with customers over the telephone wires but wasn't at all comfortable speaking with customers in person. Frank inquired about telephone service for his company. Claire directed him to the sales office, down the hall and to the right.

The offices of the telephone company were new. The wood floors were maintained to a high sheen. There were certain telltale boards and knowing steps that telegraphed an individual's approach. All the telephone operators were able to decipher the high-heel tap-tap of their supervisor, Miss Katherine, as well as the thumping footfalls of their boss, Mr. Sloan.

It was the increase in whispering and the soft shoe leather swoosh that alerted Claire to Frank's return. In a hushed voice, he inquired, "I see no ring. Does that mean no husband?"

"No husband," Claire replied.

"A boyfriend?" he asked.

"No, no boyfriend," came the response.

"Then I will meet you here Friday night at five o'clock to take you to dinner," he said, and he walked away.

His invitation was the talk of the day. The following morning, there were more opinions than Claire could absorb about what color looked best on her, what to wear, what to talk about, and what restaurant to choose. By Friday, Claire was more nervous than she believed she ever would have been had she not had so many points of view to consider.

Frank took Claire's arm and walked her to the Orchids Restaurant in the Netherland Hotel. A table for two was reserved for them in the far corner, surrounded by tall palm trees in giant purple ceramic pots. Small brass library lamps highlighted original oil paintings hanging from invisible wires affixed to green ceiling trim. Silent staff poured water, and wine, and delivered dinner without question or instruction from Frank.

The food was equal to the restaurant's superior reputation. Claire could not imagine the prices and dared not ask. Conversation centered on Frank's career as an architect, with a few brief questions about Claire's work at the telephone company.

While clicking spoons over a shared crème brûlée, Claire and Frank noticed a string quartet arranging instruments and music stands on the three granite steps at the far end of the restaurant. Frank suggested they linger over a drink at a table closer to the dance floor. When the music began, Frank reached for Claire's hand as an invitation to dance.

It had been so long since she had been on a dance floor. Would she remember what to do? He held her right hand in his left and placed his arm around her waist. Without pause, they both drifted knowingly to the music.

What a pleasant evening. Claire hated for it to end. The walk to his car was brief. He drove her to her apartment in silence. He paused at the curb and was only able to brush her lips with his as Claire dipped her head. "I will see you next week," he promised.

He did see her, every Friday night at five o'clock, they met at the telephone company entrance. Eventually, Claire revealed, "I have a daughter, Shirley. During the week she lives with my Cousin Clara and goes to school with her son."

In dismissal of any concerns she may have had, Frank confessed, "My only desire is for you."

As a pair, Claire and Frank turned heads wherever they went—a beautiful blond couple, a perfect match. Claire started to enjoy life again. She looked forward to every Friday night. Despite the teasing from the ladies at work, she was hopeful Frank would ask her to marry him. Instead, Frank proposed, "Move in with me. It will save you the money for your apartment. Together, we can decide our future."

"My only condition is that I want only you, Claire, not Shirley." Frank put his finger over her lips before she could voice her protest. "Here is my plan. Shirley will live with my parents, in their house. It will be better for Shirley to be part of a real family." Claire agreed. That was her preference for Shirley too. That would always be her first priority. Shirley must have a safe and secure family environment, knowing her mother would be with her forever.

There came a time when the risk to remain tight in the bud was more painful than the risk it took to blossom.

—Anais Nin

Shirley

Mother started dating Frank Wilson when I was halfway through the first grade at Cheviot Elementary School. Frank was a soundless man, tall and thin with thick blond hair and blue eyes. Two months after I was introduced to Frank, my Mother sent me to live with Frank's mother, Madge, and her second husband, Harris Watson. "You are to call Frank's parents Aunt Madge and Uncle Harris," Mother instructed. "They are wonderful people. I know you will like them."

Uncle Harris's mother lived in the house too. She was introduced to me as 'Grand Mother'. Grand Mother was a sizeable woman—round, with rouge on her cheeks in two circles of pink flush. Her laugh was silly, girlish, and I instantly adored her. "Welcome, welcome, precious girl. You shall be my cherished little friend."

Frank moved Mother into his apartment a few miles away. I was not invited to their apartment, but Mother assured me she had moved all our possessions, including the infamous green couch.

The Watson house on Lenox Lane was brand new. I was in heaven. This was definitely not an apartment. The cream stucco façade had dark brown accents and a dark brown roof. The porch was enclosed to eliminate the bother of insects. Several ceiling fans moved the air noiselessly and kept the heat at bay.

Four bedrooms, three bathrooms, living room, dining room, kitchen, and solarium all had shiny oak floors and cream tile fireplaces. Even though I shared a bedroom with Grand Mother, it was the largest bedroom of all. She explained, "This is called a suite, my dear. There is a bedroom and there is a bathroom, for the two of us. The purpose of a suite is to maintain total privacy. We need not share our private times with anyone. Isn't that marvelous?"

Grand Mother's dresser was dark and ornate, with deep drawers that emitted a fresh floral scent with every opening and closing. I could almost fit myself in the largest drawer that was closest to the floor. Grand Mother had cleaned out the bottom two drawers of the massive mahogany dresser for my things. She lined the drawers with pink flowered tissue. We were able to fit all of my clothes on the far left side of the first drawer.

The bedroom was wallpapered in large pink roses. Grand Mother presented me with pink sheets and a pink blanket for my twin bed. My first night at the Watson house, Grand Mother lifted me up onto her high feather bed to read a bedtime story. When I was half asleep, she scooped me up and placed me gently in my bed at the far side of the room. This ritual was repeated every night. In the summers, Grand Mother moved my bed under the corner window so I could look out at the moon and stars.

I made friends with a girl who lived on the street that ran behind the house. A white picket fence covered in vines and a flagstone path canopied with willows was all that kept me from seeing her house. I played with her almost every day. Her name was Tootsie. Tootsie had had infantile paralysis, which left one foot and leg crippled and twisted.

The first Monday of my life with Aunt Madge and Uncle Harris, they walked with me to Avondale School and enrolled me in the second grade. The following week, Tootsie and I announced to our class that we were the only two Christians in Avondale School. Well, that was what we had decided. It was a new word for us, and we were determined to use it.

Tootsie and I talked all the time in class. The teacher moved Tootsie and me to opposite corners at the back of the room. There was a bookcase in the center of the back wall. Tootsie and I scooted our desks inches behind and beside the bookcase to be able to keep on talking. We walked home together, played together after school, and ate dinner at each other's houses at least once a week.

Mother and Frank came to the Watson home most evenings to have dinner with me and Frank's family. My only time with Mother and Frank alone was on the weekends. Frank never spoke directly to me. He would stand on the other side of Mother whenever I was in the room or on a walk with them.

Frank and Mother seemed to have a great time together. They were always laughing, teasing, and sitting as close as possible to each other. Their favorite pastime was joining friends at the Hunt Club to go horseback riding. Mother looked very content and affluent in her jodhpurs and boots. Frank purchased entire riding outfits for her, tailored to fit her exact shape, in varying shades of browns and grays. She was very happy.

I know it was difficult for Mother to divide time on the weekends between Frank and me. Sometimes she would come to the Watsons' house very early on Saturday morning, waking me with a whispered, "Get dressed and come with me on a quick walk, just the two of us." On Sundays, she wore a dress and hat, gloves and heels to go to church. Mother now dressed in matching outfits and looked glamorous. If it was cold, Mother wore the full-length fur coat Frank had given her for Christmas. Grand Mother would choose for me a dress and patent leather shoes, white gloves, and a hair ribbon to match my dress. Mother and I caught the bus to the Episcopal Church on William Howard Taft Road.

The church was built of gray stone and was always cold. Mother never seemed to notice. She would smile and greet everyone as if it were her favorite day of the week. People were drawn to her beauty and to her kindness. Church was a place that seemed to bring her comfort. How she knew the different Bible verses and hymns each week, chosen specifically for the priest's message, was a mystery to me.

We went to church first and then I attended Sunday school. While I was in Sunday school, the rest of the Watson family joined Mother for the second service of church. When I asked Mother why she attended both services, she joked, "I need that much of God's grace and more." Seeing how concerned I was for whatever she was guilty of, Mother quickly added, "Oh, Shirley, you know it is so I can spend time with you."

On our arrival back at the Watson house, everyone helped with the meal and sat down to a heavy Sunday supper. Afterward, I would go for a long drive in Uncle Harris's Ford traveling car with Aunt Madge and Grand Mother. Sleepy and lazy from the drive, the four of us would have a light dinner and then gather around the radio to listen to the news and children's stories.

My favorite story was Snow White. Uncle Harris declared he could compare each of the seven dwarfs to people he knew in real life. Aunt Madge and Grand Mother shook their heads in disbelief. One stormy evening when we had no electricity, Uncle Harris lit candles and directed us all to sit in the living room. In great detail, he described the very people whom he knew were Dopey, Grumpy, Sneezy, Doc, Bashful, Happy, and Sleepy. Grand Mother was so tickled tears were running down her face. Aunt Madge was speechless with laughter.

After school, I would run into the kitchen for kisses to both Aunt Madge and Grand Mother. They would tell me to run off and play until dinner. Whenever they baked cookies or brownies for dessert, I was given a small plate to take to Tootsie's house to share. If they baked a pie, they made a separate small pie for the two of us.

While Aunt Madge and Grand Mother were washing the dinner dishes, Uncle Harris pulled me up on one knee to read the paper with him and to laugh at the funnies. He had a nervous habit of running his fingers through his thinning brown hair. I took on the habit too, and he chuckled when I admitted, "I want to grow up to be just like you."

He loved Aunt Madge. They held hands and kissed each other on the cheek. Aunt Madge was plain and neat, always dressed in a white blouse and dark skirt. Grand Mother combed Madge's long brown hair every morning and then twisted it neatly at the top of her head, pinning in all the loose ends, for a perfect bun.

Mother continued to work at the telephone company. Uncle Harris worked downtown too, as a CPA for an insurance company. Aunt Madge and Grand Mother cleaned and cooked most of the day. On Saturdays, Aunt Madge and Uncle Harris would sweep all the floors and shake out or beat on the clothesline all the rugs in the house. They seemed very pleased that Frank had Mother's company, and they were content with me. I was certainly carefree and happy at the Watsons'.

Frequently, the Watsons would welcome Big Lee, Uncle Harris's brother, and his wife, Sarah, to stay at their house. Big Lee, as he was known not just to family, was indeed a large man. His huge pants were attached to black suspenders that were as long as I was tall. Without those suspenders, I doubt he would have been able to keep himself decent. Big Lee was a sought-after auctioneer who traveled the country holding auctions for wealthy clients.

In my second year at the Watsons', I became acquainted with Uncle Harris's nephew, Little Lee. His occasional visits were filled with stories of big cities throughout the United States that I had read about in the school library: Chicago, New York, Cleveland, Philadelphia. Little Lee had supposedly been given his nickname to avoid confusion as to whom you were speaking, but the fact was he was a slight man and somewhat odd. Little Lee spoke with a female voice and wore bracelets. It was hard to imagine anyone confusing him with Big Lee.

I enjoyed listening to Little Lee describe the theater, plays in which he had a cameo appearance or small speaking part, and cities he had visited while performing on tour. I was not aware of his exact talent, only that he had the most graphic way of describing a person. You could visualize them just at his telling.

Little Lee came to the house one Saturday morning, just as Mother and I were returning from a walk. He was accompanied by a man he introduced as Tyrone Power. Little Lee announced that he was driving with Tyrone through Cincinnati on their way to California, to put Tyrone in the movies. When they departed, Mother looked at Aunt Madge and exclaimed, "He's gorgeous!"

I turned to Aunt Madge to ask what that meant. When Aunt Madge saw my face, she laughed and enlightened me. "Why, that is a very pretty man!"

As a special treat, Aunt Madge and Uncle Harris took me to the movies once a month. The movies that were the most popular were those starring Shirley Temple. She was a very talented little girl with blonde ringlets who could sing and tap dance. I remember going to see *Now and Forever, Little Miss Marker,* and my favorite of all, *Bright Eyes.* We all clapped when we heard on the radio that Shirley Temple, a little girl just like me, had won an Academy Award!

By the third year with the Watsons, I had a bank account of twenty-eight dollars, toys, and a two-story white dollhouse Uncle Harris made me for Christmas. Grand Mother made all my clothes, with matching outfits for my dolls. My favorite outfit was a dark brown knit jacket and skirt, with a brown velvet hat that tied with a brown satin ribbon on the side, and a matching brown velvet coat. It was called a Shirley Temple outfit. There was a brown plaid skirt too.

After an unusually quiet dinner one night, I was upstairs in the bathroom brushing my teeth when Mother walked in and shut the door. She demanded, "What did Aunt Madge say?" (I had to call her Aunt Madge, using the "proper" pronunciation—not *ant* but *aunt,* because Madge told me an ant is what crawls on the ground.) I told her what I had overheard earlier in the kitchen when I came home from school.

Mother asked suspiciously, "Are you lying?"

I was shocked. "No, I'm not lying, Mother." Mother went shock white and started pacing the bathroom. She was despondent. "I thought we were all family. How could this fall into such ruin? I don't understand. Aunt Madge was talking about adoption? How could she even speak of such a thing?"

Well, I must say she was not the only one who did not understand. Though I hinted at not grasping exactly what had happened or how what I had repeated had led to such disappointment, Mother never did come right out and tell me what I could do to fix the problem.

The next day was Saturday. Mother and Frank announced at breakfast they were separating, immediately. Their news was met with silence. I did not know what to say. Then Frank began arguing with Mother in front of us all about Aunt Madge and Uncle Harris wanting to adopt me. "I thought that was what you wanted, a family for Shirley. How could Mother and Harris adopting Shirley be such a horrible request? We could have a life of our own in Florida, and Shirley would be more than well taken care of here."

Mother declared, "No, no, no, and that is final! I will not, not ever, have my daughter taken from me. She is mine. Do you hear me? She is mine, and I am hers." She took me by the hand and we walked out the front door.

Without realizing what had been arranged between them, I came to understand that we were headed toward Frank's and Mother's apartment. Frank stayed behind to temporarily reside with his mother and Harris and Grand Mother. The specifics of what had transpired with the Watsons or between Frank and Mother never were revealed to me. I had thought we all got along famously.

One week later, Mother and I moved from the apartment she and Frank had shared. It was a cold and rainy Saturday morning, and my spirit was as low and miserable as the gray weather. Frank had borrowed a truck to help transfer Mother's clothes and personal items to a new address. I can't remember the exact location of our new place, only that it was the third floor of a white clapboard house. Actually it was an attic that had been renovated to be an apartment.

The largest space at the top of the stairs was a pale green kitchen with a table and two chairs positioned in the center of the room. To the left, there was one bedroom painted yellow and a small bathroom in the same color. To the right was a larger bedroom painted pink with a closet along one entire wall. Because the roof was sloped, the attic gave Mother some fits when she tried to stand upright in the bathroom or the closet. Every room was just the right size for me.

Frank took it upon himself to pack and move what little furniture Mother had brought into their relationship, including the green couch. He also packed and moved her clothes and shoes as well as the jewelry he had given her as gifts. There was no such consideration for me. All my clothes, toys, even the dollhouse Uncle Harris had made for me, were left behind at the Watson house.

No words were spoken between them during the move. When everything had been safely deposited in our attic apartment, Frank reached for Mother's hand. My heart was pounding, and I was hopeful they would kiss and make up. Frank merely said, "I'm sorry," and kissed her on the cheek. He took from his pocket a small red satin box tied with a white velvet ribbon. He knelt at her feet and said, "No matter what you decide, please accept this." He pressed the gift in Mother's hands and disappeared down the stairs.

Mother did not shed a tear. She seemed defiant, almost angry. Mother busied herself with arranging her things and then unpacking a box of foodstuffs into the kitchen cupboards. When she discovered Frank had purchased us a set of dishes, pots and pans, and dish towels she called to me to help with the unwrapping. I didn't care a lick about new stuff. I was heartbroken. And she didn't even ask me how I felt.

Purely sensual love is never true or lasting,
for which reason first love is, as a rule, but
a passing infatuation, a fleeting passion.

—Richard Von Krafft-Ebing

Sam

Sam considered himself to be a young man, a viable
bachelor. On several occasions, pals presented him
to women who were friends of their wives. No courtship
developed. Despite conversations on interesting topics
of the day, Sam did not enjoy the company of anyone to
whom he was introduced. Friends and neighbors gave up
their matchmaking efforts. They decided Sam would have
to fend for himself in life or find a woman on his own.

He contacted an agency to search for a suitable housekeeper. Grace was tired of managing the household
chores and raising Janet in addition to her full-time job.
Sam interviewed several ladies of advanced age. One
Friday evening, a much younger woman from the agency appeared as scheduled to speak with Sam. When he
opened the door, Sam was surprised by her youthful appearance. He immediately looked for her birth date in
the agency records she presented and noted that she was
fifteen years his junior. Sam was impressed by her enthusiasm for housework as well as her excellent references.

That evening at dinner, Sam told Grace and Janet that
he had made a decision about a housekeeper. Elizabeth
Krall came to the house on Sunday evening carrying a
small cotton satchel of her personal items. Sam felt rather
strange welcoming a woman who was not a family member to live in his home. He had become accustomed to being in personal proximity with only his mother and sister.
Grace and Janet were horrified that a stranger had been
instructed not just to cook and clean but to actually come
and live in the Disser home.

Sam distanced himself from Elizabeth as much as he
did from Grace and Janet, not knowing what to say. If he
had something to relate, Sam would state it in a matter-
of-fact way and finish with the topic without need for casual conversation. When Elizabeth asked him about the
household accounts and his daily routine, Sam was truth-
ful and brief in his answers.

He was quickly and happily lulled into a sense of security. Elizabeth had been proficient in acknowledging the needs of the family from the first day and was supportive of his schedule. Wondering if he would ever find a partner with whom he could imagine spending the rest of his life, Sam recognized how convenient it was instead to have Elizabeth manage the household.

She also addressed the basic needs of Grace and Janet. His interaction with both of them diminished considerably, and he was relieved. Sam no longer had an expectation or desire for marriage. It was a burden lifted off his shoulders to have the matters of the home attended to by Elizabeth and to have Grace's complaining come to an abrupt end. Sam was satisfied to be left to himself.

Over time, Elizabeth's cordial updates on the household accounts turned from mundane facts to detailed discussions with Sam on what should be done with the house and the thrift of a vegetable garden in the side yard and herbs grown on the kitchen windowsill. She had a coy and flattering way of engaging Sam, pulling from him opinions and preferences, beginning with the day-to-day requirements of the household and extending to maintenance items requiring his financial approval.

A transforming occasion was when Elizabeth and Sam were alone one Saturday evening for dinner. Aunt Grace had taken Janet downtown to a Cincinnati Ballet performance of *Romeo and Juliet* at Music Hall as a special treat.

Elizabeth cooked all of Sam's favorite dishes, served the meal in courses, and sat down in a chair beside him to eat.

No longer was Sam a confirmed bachelor but a normal man, with feelings and desires and needs. He recognized he did not wish to daydream how a woman's lips, her kisses, and the warmth of her body would feel. He wanted to know the touch of Elizabeth's skin against his skin.

**The average man is a conformist,
accepting miseries and disasters with the
stoicism of a cow standing in the rain.**

—Colin Wilson

Janet

The flood of 1937 caught everyone in the city by surprise, especially Father. He was not as prepared as
were most of his competitors to take advantage of one of
the worst catastrophes in the nation's history. Water levels
of the Ohio River reached eighty feet, the highest since
the city had started keeping such records. Rushing water
swept away riverfront businesses and homes and swamped
downtown hotels and restaurants with filthy river muck.

More than fifty thousand residents were left homeless. The Red Cross and other agencies of assistance were inundated. Citizens on higher ground in close proximity to the city center were called upon to volunteer their homes as temporary shelters.

Hearing the news of the flood, Father pulled Grandfather's car from the garage on Saturday morning to drive Aunt Grace and me downtown to witness the melee. The Carew Tower, opened in 1931, was the tallest building in the city. Inside the Tower were two department stores, the H. & S. Pogue Company and Mabley and Carew, a hotel and commercial offices. On the top floor was an observation deck from which visitors could see all three of the neighboring states: Ohio, Indiana, and Kentucky.

I don't know how he did it, but Father was able to arrange for just the three of us to ride the elevator to the observation deck. What was meant to be a pleasant vantage point for travelers to the city was instead a panorama of water roiling with broken furniture, tree branches, and remnants of homes. Homeless families, crying babies, and the moaning of the hungry could be heard over the incessant sweeping of the streets below. Father was mesmerized. Aunt Grace and I were overcome with despair.

My nightmares diminished over time but grew in vivid detail the first few nights after witnessing the gloom of the flood. In my dreams, I was caught in the water, barely holding onto a large tree branch, yelling for Grandfather to save me. I was panicked at my inability to swim.

Flood walls were not completed by the Army Corps of Engineers until 1942. Construction companies that had stockpiled materials and maintained a healthy cash flow began reaping the benefits of the contracts with city leaders almost immediately. Father never maintained inventory of any materials. Repair and replacement contracts went to his competitors. Though he maintained the commute between the office and the house, at all other times Father was in the study with the door closed.

I was adamant that I wanted no trips to the city center. The next time I ventured downtown was with Aunt Grace to see a movie. She had to promise me the only sound in the city streets would be the din of new commerce.

To exist is to change, to change is to mature, to mature is to go on creating oneself endlessly.

—Henri Bergson

Shirley

I had only the clothes I was wearing when we left the Watson house. Mother had taken me to a secondhand shop close to Frank's and her apartment the first week we were on our own to buy a dress, an undershirt and underpants, and a spare pair of shoes. At night, I stood at the bathroom sink in my slip to wash the dress I had worn so it would be dry for me to wear the next day. Alternating two dresses was easy at first. Then the other children at school started to make fun of me.

In the new attic apartment, I walked twelve blocks so I could continue going to Avondale School. There was no other school near where Mother and I now lived. My salvation was that it was the end of May and there were only two weeks of school until summer vacation. Mother had told me going to Avondale School would guarantee comfort and stability in knowing my classmates and my teacher. I decided not to disagree.

The landlady lived on the first two floors of the house. Mother made arrangements with her to watch me from the time I came home from school until Mother came home from work. On my first day of summer vacation, I promised Mother, "I can take care of myself all day. I won't be a bother to anyone." As she turned to leave for work, a little rug placed at the top of the stairs caught one of Mother's high heels. She slipped on it and went down the two flights of steps, flipping this way and that, with me standing at the top of the stairs screaming.

The landlady took us in her car to the emergency room at Christ Hospital. She waited with me until the doctor came out to tell us what had happened. Mother had cracked several ribs, scraped both arms, and snapped off her tailbone. A surgeon had put silver cement at the end of her spine. Mother was to remain in bed for six weeks.

All that summer, the landlady was kind and generous. She brought us breakfast, lunch, and dinner every day. I was Mother's nurse and caretaker. One afternoon, without announcing he was coming to visit, Frank strolled up the front walk.

I was standing at the kitchen sink washing our lunch dishes when I looked out the window and noticed it was Frank getting out of a car at the curb. The landlady remembered him from the move and welcomed him into the house. He climbed the stairs to our attic. Walking past me without a word he went straight into Mother's bedroom. I followed him.

Mother was pleased to see him. She held her hand out to welcome him, and he knelt beside her bed. With a raised eyebrow directed at me, Mother gave the distinct impression that I was to leave the room. I did walk outside her bedroom, but I lingered in the hallway to be close enough to hear what they were saying.

Frank was leaning in so close to Mother that I couldn't catch even one word. Before he left, Frank went to the car and brought Mother a large book and a radio. After that, she never heard from him. Mother told me Frank was moving to Florida. He had accepted a promotion as partner in an architectural firm in Miami and the oceanfront home he had designed was completed. Frank had informed his family and Mother that they would never see him again.

There we were, Mother and me, alone and together. It was wonderful. Of course Mother was off work. Whether

Frank paid the hospital bill or our rent and board or paid it all, I don't know.

The book he had brought for Mother to read during her convalescence was Margaret Mitchell's *Gone with the Wind*. She read a new part of the book to me every night. I know she skipped certain parts of the story because she would hesitate and turn the page quickly. Those parts of the book must have been excerpts she considered too graphic a description of the Civil War battles.

When Mother started to feel better, we began adding morning and then afternoon walks to our daily routine. Our schedule included lunch in front of the radio to listen to the *Fibber McGee and Molly* program. Initial excursions were short walks to the end of the block and back. We gradually progressed to walks all around the neighborhood. During our walks, Mother found us another apartment. This one was in a newer building and was much larger, with a living room, dining room, bedroom, and bathroom. I thought we were rich.

With the help of two neighbors and our landlady, we moved into our new apartment. Mother made arrangements with the two little old ladies in the apartment across the hall from us to watch me every day when I came home from school. At the start of the school year, I had a ten block walk, but in the opposite direction of the walk from the attic apartment.

This was the best time of my life. When I came home, I changed clothes and listened to *Your Hit Parade* on the radio to learn the latest songs. On my ninth birthday, Mother bought me my first store-bought card and a bakery cake with tiny glass candles. We danced to music on the radio and laughed until it was time for me to go to bed.

It is not a lack of love, but a lack of friendship that makes unhappy marriages.

—Friedrich Nietzsche

Claire

In the 1930s, divorce was talked about openly, but it was not as common as discussions on the subject. Legal reforms had taken place that gave a wife property and a stipend for any children. A woman had no choice but to work to make ends meet. The children had to be old enough to go to school and responsible enough to wait at home until the mother returned from work.

Male politicians were certainly eager enough for the female vote, but men were not eager to offer women the best jobs or high-paying jobs for fear of competition. The ladies Claire knew and worked with were in the same predicament. Working women held low-paying jobs at wages set by men anxious to keep women at a minimal level of income. Claire was barely able to afford an acceptable standard of living for herself and for Shirley, with no money left over to save or pay for emergencies.

Claire was more than grateful that Frank Wilson had paid not only all of her hospital and doctor bills but also three month's rent and board at the attic apartment. The real godsend was the bank account he established in her name with one hundred dollars on deposit. She was actually more appreciative of the telephone company and her supervisor Miss Katherine, who agreed to give her the same switchboard work at the same pay when her back healed.

Even though it was made clear there was no opportunity for advancement, Claire gave telephone operation her best effort every day. She had been an exemplary employee and continued to be dedicated to the telephone company. Every review Claire received showed excellent marks for customer service, attendance, attitude, punctuality, and appearance.

She took pride in her appearance. Each evening, she polished her black leather heels and ironed a dress or a blouse and skirt to look professional. Claire wanted to be not only a mother but also a good example for Shirley, for girls Shirley's age and older, that women could make it on their own.

Cosmetics were Claire's weakness. Seasonal changes in makeup fashions and colors tempted Claire as she ambled past department store counters during her lunch break. Irresistible transformations were possible for eyes, face, and lips. Advertisements showing instant popularity with the opposite sex filled the pages of ladies' magazines. Even the local newspapers regularly featured ads and articles on the seemingly endless quest for beauty and self-confidence with the mere purchase of the latest in cosmetics.

Regardless of her income, Claire had been adept at stretching her money and her cosmetics to last and to have the best effect for her. The salesladies at the department store cosmetic counters were so enamored with her beauty and glamorous presence that they convinced her to be their "model" at lunchtime. Claire was engaging and enlisted customers for all the cosmetics brands. For compensation the salesladies treated her to bags upon bags of samples of the latest in perfumes, eye makeup, foundation, lipstick, and moisturizing creams.

Claire reveled in the attention, the compliments, and the free cosmetics. She offered recommendations to the salesladies and their customers on what products were beneficial and which were the longest-lasting. She longed for female friendships with the salesladies or their customers but found that her beauty did not inspire close relationships. A coworker confided, "You are too beautiful to compete with."

**Marriage is the triumph of imagination
over intelligence.**

—Oscar Wilde

Sam

Despite the radical changes in the law and viewpoints on divorce when Sam's father was alive, he had insisted a separation was more economical and socially acceptable. In the United States, the proportion of divorced men and women among those couples who married in the 1920s was twice that among marriages before the war. In the years since the war, Ohio had eased divorce requirements, stating marital happiness was more important than economic security. The judge who granted the separation of Sam and Claire was a friend of Sam's father.

He had agreed to whatever Samuel Sr. requested to avoid the two Disser children having to be wards of the State of Ohio.

During the late nineteenth and the early twentieth century in America, the courts automatically granted custody of any children to the father, in either a separation or a divorce. Women were not financially independent, nor were they capable of showing economic support unless it was from family members. Certainly that had been Claire's predicament. It was Mr. Disser who was in control and who dictated the terms of the separation. Sam earned his entire income from his father. Mr. Disser would be the only one to determine the fate of the children.

"The crucial difference between divorce and separation," Sam remembered his father explaining to him, "is that a divorce ends the marriage. This is not acceptable for a Disser. Divorce would scar Janet and mark the Disser name with the stigma of an improper heritage." Separation was deemed appropriate at the time to allow for Claire and Sam to live apart from one another, to lead separate lives. In this way, the Disser name would not be tainted with the term *divorce*, and Sam, once the separation was declared final, would have no legal requirement to support Claire or baby Shirley.

Separation had been agreeable to Sam at the time and had been mostly forgotten up to this point. As Sam was discovering, his physical needs and self-esteem were being tempted every now and again by the woman in his employ. After thoughtful consideration, he made the decision to test his interest in the opposite sex. Free from his father's concern for the disgrace of divorce on the Disser name, Sam dispatched an attorney to file the required divorce papers to permanently rid him of Claire.

**All change is not growth; as all movement
is not forward.**

—Ellen Glasgow

Janet

To my way of thinking, Father was quick to grieve the loss of his parents. Just three weeks after we buried Grandfather, he hired a housekeeper, Elizabeth Krall. He claimed she had been recommended by a friend of the family. Father insisted she take over the spare room on the second floor and live with us.

At seven o'clock the next evening, Elizabeth Krall appeared on our doorstep. Aunt Grace was appalled by her unannounced arrival, without deference for our schedules. Aunt Grace introduced herself and said, "Your bedroom is at the top of the stairs, all the way at the end of the hall. It's lavender." She stormed back to the kitchen to portion dessert on three plates and brought them into the dining room.

"Was that our new housekeeper at the door?" Sam inquired.

"Why didn't you tell us she was coming, Sam? We've had no opportunity to meet her prior to this evening, and suddenly she is moving into our home?" Aunt Grace was fuming.

Sam responded, "Why, this is the help you've been asking for, Grace. Your difficulties are now properly addressed and you can quit your complaining." Sam was pleased with his decision.

I did not know what to think of their disagreement. Soundlessly, Elizabeth appeared in the doorway of the dining room. Aunt Grace flushed when she saw Elizabeth, uncertain how long she had been standing there. I stared at her. She was plain and as tall as Aunt Grace, five foot seven or so. A square pale face set upon a short square neck must have forced her to buy the blouse she wore that had no collar. Her long brown hair was braided and pulled to one side to spill over her right shoulder like a schoolgirl's.

Elizabeth acted timid and withdrawn. However, her influence over Father was immediately apparent. Without counsel with us, Sam waved his hand in her direction and stated, "Elizabeth, welcome. As you and I discussed, you have full responsibility for this household." Eager, too eager, to establish her position, Elizabeth nodded first to Aunt Grace and then to me, "Well, I will rest now and tomorrow I will begin to organize this home in as efficient and inexpensive a manner as possible. Good night."

Because Father had never wanted to be in the cement business, he had struggled to keep the business as vibrant as it had been under Grandfather's ownership. As if the 1937 flood and his lack of an inventory of construction materials was a sign from God, Father announced, "I am actively pursuing the sale of the family company." On my fourteenth birthday, he happily declared he had found a buyer. Weeks after his announcement, Father signed over The Disser Company customer list and became a plumber once again.

Now Father was able to spend more time at home. With a regular job, rather than arriving from work after I was in bed, he was able to roll up the drive while it was still light outside. He engaged in conversation with me and was pleasant. My schoolwork was suddenly of interest to him, and he asked to be made aware of activities involving parents. Aunt Grace was mildly annoyed. She had attended my school functions, knew my teachers and the curriculum, and helped me every night with homework.

It was around this same time that Father instructed Elizabeth to bring all the serving dishes to the table and join us for the evening meal. He talked to her as if she was part of the family. Aunt Grace and I were admonished if we interrupted Elizabeth. Father laughed at her jokes and smiled directly at her when she spoke to any of us. I was disgusted and tried to enlist the support of Aunt Grace. She politely refused to join in my mounting loathing of the woman.

Winter arrived early that year. Jumping in piles of leaves in the backyard was out of the question. The colorful autumn lasted less than two weeks. Leaves lost all color and fell to the ground in clumps of brown discards. I retreated to the attic as soon as I arrived home from school to avoid Elizabeth's constant chatter and incessant whistling. Boxes full of old toys, broken parts of this and that, and clothing and hats that had belonged to Grandmother and Grandfather were stacked in no particular order.

In the far corner, a tall, black, shiny box with matching lid caught my eye. It was closed with a black satin cord that came from two punched holes on either side of the box and tied in a bow on top of the lid. The bow came free easily, and I slid back the lid. Inside was a white felt top hat. I took it to my room to present to Father after supper.

Before Father appeared in the dining room, and while Aunt Grace was in the kitchen helping Elizabeth scoop food into serving bowls and onto platters, I hid the top hat under the table. The meal was too slow for me. I was so excited to share my discovery! When Elizabeth disappeared into the kitchen to portion the dessert, I could wait no longer.

I pulled the top hat from beneath my chair and handed it to Father. He was delighted. It was precisely the reaction I had hoped for. "Were you an entertainer?" I asked.

"Yes, as a matter of fact I was, and darn good at it too. Elizabeth? Come in here. I want to show you what a debonair Fred Astaire is seated at this table!"

"Ooh, you look positively dashing in that hat, sir," Elizabeth gushed and curtsied. "Would you be so kind as to entertain us?" Whatever Father sang or danced for Elizabeth, I do not remember.

In my mind's eye, I am looking across the table at Aunt Grace to see her shaking her head slowly from side to side in sympathy and caution against my anger. She recognized my hope for his performance to be directed at me, at us. Instead, his attention was fixed solely and intently on Elizabeth. He sought her approval and pleasure, and she gave it, willingly and constantly.

Life is just a chance to grow a soul.

—A. Powell Davies

Shirley

Our next move was to the Walnut Hills area. This meant I had to go to a different school—Hoffman Elementary. I was used to moving now. We had an apartment there, but Mother didn't care for it. Three months later, we moved again, this time to People's Corner, into one half of a two-family house. This time my enrollment was in Windsor School.

Over the summer, I had to remain with Aunt Clara and Uncle Fred, Randall and David. Mother was rightfully concerned there was no one to watch me in this neighborhood during the day while she was at work.

So, as I had before, I faced David's harassment. I guess he really hated sharing his family with me, especially sharing his mother. Well, I didn't much care for being his victim or listening to his mother defend him and irritate me with her secrets about Mother's life.

Finally the day came in September, as I was starting a new school year in the fourth grade, when Mother proclaimed, "Okay, Shirley, you are now old enough to live with me all the time, including next summer."

"Live with you *all* the time?" I shouted. No more staying at Aunt Clara's house and being tormented by David? I hooted and hollered and hugged Mother until I thought I would squeeze all the air from her belly.

Mother and I spent all day Saturday and Sunday together. During the week, we had breakfast at the same time and then Mother caught the bus to work and I walked to school. I was glad when school began serving lunch so I did not have to figure out what to prepare and pack each morning.

I did have to check in with the lady next door when I got home, but I unlocked and then locked our door and stayed in our half of the house until Mother came home. Every night Mother and I fixed dinner together. We would go to the store on Saturday morning. After we unloaded our groceries, we would walk to the park or take a bus to the zoo.

The zoo was a fascinating place. Its proper name was the Cincinnati Zoo and Botanical Gardens, the second oldest zoo in the United States. In our history lessons at school, we were taught that the zoo had opened in September 1875 with three deer, eight monkeys, two buffalo, a tiger, a hyena, a talking crow, an alligator, an old circus elephant, a pair of grizzly bears, a pair of elk, six raccoons, and four hundred birds. By the time Mother and I were making our regular visits, there were also lions, bears, zebras, and seals. I never grew tired of watching the animals play.

Once in a while, we would take the *Island Queen II* steamboat to Coney Island. The *Island Queen II* was a 280-by-80-foot side-wheeler capable of carrying four thousand passengers, one of the largest steamboats of its day. I would run all over the *IQ II* while Mother sat and read old fashion magazines.

We could walk up from the boat landing right into Coney Island. Mother was daring enough to go on most of the rides with me, especially the merry-go-round, but not the Wildcat roller coaster. She loved the merry-go-round, and we both repeated the water ride the Mystic Chute as often as the operator would allow us to get back in line. We would spend the day there and then take the steamboat back into town.

One Saturday, after spending the entire day at Coney Island, our feet hurt so much that we took our shoes off. I walked in my bare feet and Mother in her stocking feet to find a seat once we were safely on the boat. By the time the steamboat reached the public landing downtown, our feet were so swollen they would not go back in our shoes. So we both walked without our shoes across the cobblestones of the public landing to the streetcar station. We laughed the whole way.

People on the sidewalks laughed at us laughing. We took the streetcar back to the two-family house and, still carrying our shoes, ran up the stairs to soak our feet in the bathtub sitting on the tub's edge, side by side.

> **The future has a way of arriving unannounced.**
>
> —George Will

Janet

When I was twelve years old, my father told me I had to go and live with his cousin Zelda, known to family and friends as Mother Z. When I asked, "Why do I have to live with Mother Z? Have I done something wrong?" Father recounted the story of her daughter's drowning while swimming in a lake at the beginning of summer vacation. Seeing my concern, Father added, "Your stay is to give her stability, a normal routine." Aunt Grace confided that my real purpose in living with Mother Z was to try to

246

reduce her depression. It frightened me to think Mother Z might expect me to take her daughter's place.

Father could not tell me how long I would be living away from my home and from Aunt Grace. He merely answered, "As long as it takes." One July morning, Father put my red suitcase in the trunk of his Cadillac and drove me to Mother Z's house in Westwood. It was a small brown brick house, not far from the sidewalk. The best feature was a large wooden porch that had a dark shingle roof and two white porch swings, one at either end.

Mother Z was a somewhat familiar figure. I had met her several times before when she had come to our house during Aunt Hannah's visits. She was short and slight, with very large feet encased in big black tie shoes. Her short brown hair was curly and mussed as if she did not own a comb or brush. Mother Z dressed every day in a shirt and pants that alternated between light brown and dark brown.

She took my hand as if I were a small child and led me to the back of her house to the guest room. Between two windows was a polished single brass bed covered in a pink and green patchwork quilt. A whitewashed dresser leaned on three short feet against the far wall. Mother Z had placed fresh pink roses from her garden in a slender green vase on the bedside table. This would be my room for the next two years.

Each week, I organized my clothes, packed, and re-peated my good-bye to Aunt Grace. Father picked me up at Mother Z's house every Friday night after work. On Sunday nights, he dropped me off again. This way I was able to keep up my friendship with my two best girl-friends, Anna and Patricia, and spend time with Aunt Grace as well.

For my best friends Anna (christened Anna Marie) and Patricia (christened Patricia Marie), we chose the nicknames AM and PM. We thought we were very clever. To make our threesome complete, we chose Noon as my nickname. The code word for our little threesome was Time. If someone asked what we were up to, we would simply shout, "Time!" and giggle at our secret. Weekends with AM and PM went by all too quickly.

The attention Mother Z paid to me during the week when I wasn't in school was sweet. She fixed breakfast for me every morning. We washed dishes together and played board games. She taught me the simple, fun card games Crazy Eights and Go Fish. We worked in the garden tend-ing to her rose bushes and planting begonias and gerani-ums in the backyard.

Mother Z always made sandwiches for lunch and then chose a book from the shelves on either side of the fire-place to read to me. By midafternoon we were both asleep on the couch. At four o'clock every afternoon, Mother Z would awaken from her nap with a start and kiss me on the cheek. I helped her prepare dinner.

School interrupted our routine, but only to steal away the time for card games and gardening. Mother of Mercy's bus came to pick me up at her house. When I came home, I read and took a nap at the same time as Mother Z, and then I lent a hand with the evening meal. Mother Z and I developed an easy friendship. She taught me to cook and bake, tend a garden, and know the names of all the trees and birds and insects in her backyard.

My memory is not clear as to the reason why I returned to Father's house on a permanent basis. It was June, and Aunt Hannah was visiting. She had convinced Mother Z to spend a few nights at Father's house. No one explained if she would stay or go back to her own home. When she left, Father stated simply, "Your time with Mother Z has ended. There is no further need for your company." I felt empty and sad.

Life was expected to resume as if I had been in the house the entire time I lived with Mother Z. My summer was boring. Even my best friends AM and PM were boring. We had nothing to do. During the school year, my afternoons were the same. I never did any homework. I was not that good of a student. Aunt Grace was a confidante and study partner from September to May. Aunt Hannah's return the following June was the high point of my summer.

Aunt Hannah was Aunt Hannah to everyone who came in contact with her when she was in residence at the Disser home. One of her most endearing qualities was her undivided attention when you spoke to her.

A physical distraction for me (I couldn't help but to stare at her feet) were her bunions. All her shoes were stretched out of shape and slapped against her feet when she walked. Apparently the bunions were very painful. It was not proper to slip off your shoes in the presence of others, so the only relief she had was when she was sleeping.

After seeing Mother Z's large feet and then the trouble Aunt Hannah had with her big feet, I intently watched my feet as I grew in height. What a relief it was to me that my feet did not grow at the same pace.

Grandmother and Aunt Hannah had not only been sisters; they had been best friends. Aunt Hannah had called Grandmother "my buddy." They complemented one another. At family weddings, Aunt Hannah had designed and created the table favors and flower arrangements and the bridesmaid and bridal bouquets. Grandmother May had sung and played the guitar, playing hymns or popular songs—whatever the bride chose.

To Grandmother's dismay, Aunt Hannah had married an alcoholic. He was an excellent carpenter who built their house and helped raise their five children. When the last child married, Aunt Hannah's husband drank more than ever before. They lost their house to unpaid bills. Aunt Hannah left her husband and stayed with each of her children, moving from one child's home to the next, spending most of her time with her daughter Ida in Akron. Spring and summer, she gave Ida and her husband time to themselves, staying with her other children and relations until she could sense she had worn out her welcome.

When Aunt Hannah went to visit Major, her eldest son, she would have the most interesting adventures. His legitimate first name is a mystery to me. He joined the service during the war and decided to make a career in the army. After many promotions, he was made a major, and that is what everyone called him.

One summer during Aunt Hannah's stay with him, Major got permission to take Aunt Hannah for a ride in a tank. Another time, he took her for a ride in a fighter. She loved the flight more than anything in her life, "Oh, Janet, the weightless sensation, looking down on everything, being among the clouds. I was temporarily an angel, lifted to heaven." I never tired of listening to her stories.

Her favorite stay was with us, even after Grandmother had died, because she claimed Elizabeth offered the best meals. She taught me to play pick-up-sticks, solitaire, and gin rummy.

One summer morning, she invented a midmorning "snack lesson." She told me to pretend we were "two hungry hobos, an old lady and a little girl, resting (if you please) on a back porch swing." After Elizabeth brought out to each of us a plate of homemade biscuits topped with honey, Aunt Hannah proceeded to tell me about ants. "Drop some crumbs on the walk to the garage. Call out to our friends, the ants, 'Welcome friendly ants, welcome!'" Well, we waited and we waited. I thought the ants would never appear. Then, sure enough, some ants came by and carried off the crumbs. "You see, Janet, this is not only a lesson in the science of ants, but also a lesson in patience. Those ants took their good natured time stopping by to see us, didn't they?"

I cherished the lessons and the gifts from Aunt Hannah. On the first day of her summer visits, she would present me with a book or two. They were not typical children's books. I am not certain of her source for the books she chose. They were filled with graphic illustrations, paintings, and artists' renderings. Her explanations of color, technique, style, and content were riveting.

When Father was agreeable to a shopping trip during her stay, Aunt Hannah would purchase and apply numerous artists' materials to canvas. I wish I had kept even one of her watercolors. They and she are still vivid, wonderful, charming memories. I hope the bit of artistic talent I possess came from her.

**Poverty don't cause no shame when you
don't know nothing else.**

—Anonymous

Shirley

Mother and I tried to go to church, but by Sunday morning she was usually too tired to do much. Most Sundays I would wake up and crawl into bed with her, and we would sleep the majority of the day away.

We lived with lots of other poor people in People's Corner. Mother didn't care. On rainy weekends, we rode around the city on the streetcar and bus line. Mother would point out the landmarks and neighborhoods around the city and declare we could choose anywhere we wanted to live.

The Main Street Incline and the Mount Auburn Cable reduced bus time by half, forcing metal on metal in a steady ascent up the hills of Cincinnati. I was thrilled to be living together. It was just me and Mother, and I never wanted it to end.

To be sure I was the best daughter I could be. I was well-behaved at the Windsor School. The principal was Mrs. Knucklebaum. She was a large woman who swished when she paced the corridors. Mrs. Knucklebaum spoke with a sweet voice and had a good humor. She welcomed me to school every morning.

Most of the students had been going to school together since kindergarten. Fortunately, I had Mrs. Neiman for my teacher. She made me feel a part of her classroom from the first day. She was pretty—a redhead if I remember right—with the longest legs I had ever seen. Her class was fun. I worked on extra projects to bring home my A-plus papers to Mother.

One of my girlfriends was named Anna Cordone. She lived in an apartment building down the street from Mother and me. Her mother was divorced, and Anna didn't know her father either. Anna and I got along very well because we had a lot in common. We played in the playground after school and then walked home together.

Henry, a boy who lived in a red brick house at the end of the street, was also in our class. He teased me about my curly hair, "Curly Shirley, little curly Shirley Temple." I told him to quit it or I was going to hit him. He just snickered and kept on tormenting me.

One day, I hid behind the door of the coatroom at school. As he came around the corner, I smacked him up the side of the head and warned, "Leave me alone." He did.

My other girlfriend was Consetta Sicardi. She confided that her mother wanted me to come to her house for dinner because she was sorry I did not have a father. From the moment I walked into their house, I loved the smell of Mrs. Sicardi's cooking. At supper, she kept giving me more and more food to eat because she thought I was too skinny. I had never seen so much food served at a single meal. And, though I never offered the thought out loud, I was afraid of eating too much or I might expand and grow up to look like Mrs. Sicardi.

After I finished my schoolwork, I would sit on Mother's bed and look out the window to wait for her to come home. When I told her how much I liked Italian food, we started walking down Vine Street one night a week to eat at Scotti's restaurant. The Scotti family featured buffet dinner three nights a week and only charged for adults to eat. The owners adored Mother and they loved me. They would say "Oh, here comes our Disser-i family!" We would eat until our waistbands could expand no further. Mrs. Scotti would kiss Mother on each cheek, whispering in her ear that the food was no charge. Then we walked home.

All I did as a kid was walk. On cold and snowy days, Mother and I would only walk to the corner of the block and back for her to go to work and me to catch a city bus to school. One Saturday, even though it was cold, I remember Mother and I walked to the end of the street after we had eaten dinner at home.

That was the first time I met Cecil. He proceeded to walk with us from the corner, around the block, and back to our door. I kept looking at him and looking at Mother. Mother was busy listening to Cecil the entire time we were walking. The more he talked to Mother, the less I liked him.

"Mother, what do you see in that man?" I inquired when we had returned to the privacy of our apartment.

"Why, Shirley, that's a rather bold statement from someone as young as you," Mother was shocked.

"What do you see in him?" I repeated.

"Well, to be honest with you, he is stable and sincere. That is something I have missed and longed for since Frank and I separated."

"And love? Mother, what about the love we read about in books?" I was worried she had not mentioned love.

"Oh, Shirley, love exists only in books, and between you and me," Mother sighed and pulled me close.

A man can't make a place for himself in the sun if he keeps taking refuge under the family tree.

—Helen Keller

Janet

E ven in the worst of the Depression years, Grandfather had insisted I enjoy every moment of my childhood. He had taken great delight in making me smile. I never knew the extent of the hardship on most people. I came home to play with the girls down the street, and day-to-day life seemed pleasant enough. Grandfather had always talked about the "good times" and the "better times to come." He had told me I would witness changes that would give me a life of freedom and happiness.

Grandmother had been fun when family was together, especially when Aunt Hannah came to visit in the summer. We had played the board games Monopoly and Scrabble. Aunt Grace had claimed Grandfather cheated at Scrabble, using words that did not exist.

Aunt Grace and Grandmother—and when she was with us, Aunt Hannah—had played pinochle, canasta, and bridge. I had tried to understand the cards and the rules by watching them play, but it was too boring for me.

Father never participated in any of the games our family had played. Now that Elizabeth was in the house, Father changed his mind about games. He joined in Scrabble as long as Elizabeth was able to play too. Father came home one evening with a phonograph and several big band records. He thought it would be fun for us all to learn how to dance.

When Aunt Grace and I realized the music was meant for Father and Elizabeth to enjoy, without interference from us, Aunt Grace purchased a puzzle. She dumped all the pieces out on the parlor table and propped the cover with the picture on it against the lamp. We could be in the same room as Father and Elizabeth while politely ignoring their laughter and spinning around.

It took almost two weeks to assemble the puzzle. When we were finished, we enjoyed the completed project for a day or two, then threw the puzzle pieces up in the air, and stored them away in the original box. Aunt Grace brought home yet another puzzle, and then another, until we had almost ten puzzles in our collection.

Elizabeth told Father it was not fun to dance without our joining in or complimenting them on their progress. Aunt Grace and I were pleased, without showing it of course, that we had achieved what we had hoped would be the end of record playing and foolishness for just the two of them. What I did not realize was that it was an obvious, not-so-coy request for Father to take her out dancing; which is exactly what he did.

PART THREE

Divorce and Marriage

> **If you do not tell the truth about yourself, you cannot tell it about other people.**
>
> **—Virginia Woolf**

Claire

Despite the declarations of newfound female independence, a woman who did not have a husband was expected to work for wages her entire life. While wives prided themselves on their cleaning, cooking, and parenting skills, single mothers were expected to be the housekeeper, protector of their children, as well as the eternal breadwinner.

Claire was blessed that Shirley was such a good child. On Saturdays, when they would board the *Island Queen II* for Coney Island, Claire would marvel at the way Shirley adapted herself to every situation and easily made new friends. The river was fairly calm in the summers when barges and pleasure boats competed to disturb the glassy surface. It gave Claire a chance to reflect on her life and what lay ahead for her and for Shirley. The trip downriver to Coney Island was comforting, a chance to breathe the fresh air and observe Shirley's energy.

In the Cincinnati winters, the overcast skies and rain or gray melt of snow increased the river level to brown swells. Claire dreaded the cold weather and the chill of being alone. One particularly dismal winter day, Claire received the ultimate gift in the mail: a decree of divorce from Sam. She was free to pursue a marriage, consolation in another man's arms. What more could she ask?

Cecil was the answer. He had been a bachelor all his life. His bank account was substantial. For almost twenty years, he had been the right-hand man to the owner of a very successful company. Most important of all, Cecil was desperate to have Claire as his wife. She was fifteen years his junior, and he was thrilled she had taken an interest in him. Yes, Cecil was a man upon whom she could depend for the rest of her life. He would be the eternal breadwinner.

> **No person is your friend who demands
> your silence, or denies your right to grow.**
>
> —Alice Walker

Shirley

Mother had met Cecil face-to-face two months before our walk and thought he was sincere, a snappy dresser, and well-mannered. She had spoken with him many times over the previous year, connecting his business calls. Cecil had become interested in Mother by engaging her in phone conversations. When he made an excuse to visit her at the telephone company, Cecil became enamored with Mother.

When a sales position in the company he worked for became available, Cecil offered her a starting position. The offer was for ten dollars more each week as the local sales representative for women's stockings at the Real Silk Hosiery Company. Mother put in her two-week notice at the Bell Telephone Company and went to work for Cecil.

Real Silk Hosiery made socks and hosiery for men and women. For Mother, this was the career she had longed for, with an increase in salary that allowed us to shop in the department stores. Within six months, Mother had signed on so many new clients that she was promoted to Regional Sales Representative. With her success came a company car. I loved taking drives with her in that car on Saturdays to Ault Park and on Sundays after church in the country.

Cecil started coming to the apartment on a regular basis to join us on our evening walks after dinner. There was Cecil then Mother and then me. Cecil did not speak to me. He talked the entire time we walked. He liked to hear himself talk, and Mother listened. It was obvious to me that Mother wanted me to become acquainted with Cecil. It was just as obvious that Cecil wanted nothing to do with me.

Three months after Mother started her new job, Cecil gave her instructions to go to Bloomington, Indiana. It was June, the week of my tenth birthday, and I was out of school. Mother was able to take me on the trip with her. I was thrilled. She told me to give her the directions as she was driving. We had the best time. Our stay was in a lovely rooming house in the center of town.

The shoe factory in Bloomington was one of her largest customers. Mother was supposed to present to the owner of the company a one-year contract for socks and hosiery. The lady who managed the rooming house understood that I was to remain inside during the day. She loaned me books and games to keep me occupied. In the evenings, she recommended where we should eat and go for walks. Every night when Mother returned to the room, we explored the little town square.

By the third day, Mother had become very quiet. Cecil was supposed to have sent a letter with the details of the contract, but there had been no mail for her at the rooming house or at the factory. Thursday morning after breakfast, Mother drove us home. When she went to the office on Friday, Cecil admitted that he had sent the instructions to a shoe factory in Bloomfield, Indiana, instead of Bloomington. What an idiot he was.

Cecil was now coming to the apartment for both dinner and our walks. I really didn't care for him. He was a large man with thinning brown hair and brown eyes—not handsome or well-bred. He was not at all the type of man I believed Mother deserved. Cecil boasted about the people he knew and the important sales deals he closed each day. He never gave Mother or me a chance to speak. Cecil didn't care what we had to say, what we were interested in, what filled our days, or what made us happy or sad. Cecil was selfish. I hoped Mother would see him for the man he was and make him go away.

On August 15, 1937, Mother came home from work and announced, "Cecil and I are married." I thought the sky had fallen on top of me and the world had gone dark. My heart sank, and I felt as if I was suffocating. I was crushed. I objected, cried, wailed, and stamped my feet in objection. I would not believe it was true. Mother shouted, "Stop! It's done. Cecil is your new father." I was furious. I went for a walk, a very, very long walk. The next day he moved in with us.

Ignorance is preferable to error, and he is less remote from the truth who believes nothing than he who believes what is wrong.

—Thomas Jefferson

Sam

Elizabeth was more than a decade younger than Sam, yet she took pleasure in what he liked, waltzes and musical theatre, rare steak, and chocolate cream pie. Elizabeth cooked his favorite foods without regard for Grace's or Janet's preferences. She took note of how he made his bed and tucked his clean sheets around the mattress in the same way. Elizabeth folded and nested his clothes in each dresser drawer in the precise order he had practiced for years.

Sam led a simple life. Elizabeth took pleasure in meeting his basic needs to ensure his comfort. Was it possible that a woman who observed him in all the unguarded moments of his personal life could find him desirable?

She looked lovingly at Sam whenever they were alone in the same room. She brushed his arm with her arm if he passed her in the hall. Elizabeth asked for Sam's help carrying the groceries from the car to the house. With a gentle hand on his back, she leaned around to face him with a smile and a "Thank you." Her gaze lingered when she caught Sam's attention.

Surely a marriage with Elizabeth would secure her devotion and dedication to him forever. What could he possibly have to offer her? She would be the mistress of the Disser home and she would have his eternal gratitude. Was that enough?

Long gone and forever forgotten was life before Elizabeth. Sam was a different man. Having spent his early years wishing to be left to his own decisions, he was now at a loss without direction. Elizabeth could be his helpmate and partner.

The day the divorce decree came in the mail, Sam felt the courage he needed to ask Elizabeth to marry him. While Grace and Janet were setting the dinner table, Sam fell to one knee beside Elizabeth in the kitchen. With the decree clutched in his left hand he reached out to touch the hem of her dress. As she turned to look down at his face, he was overcome with love.

"Will you be my wife? Will you please be my wife, dear Elizabeth?" Sam looked up at her face for a hint of the answer. Elizabeth fell to her knees and threw her arms around his neck. "Yes! Yes, oh yes! I want nothing more than to be yours!" Elizabeth cried tears of happiness.

Sam felt a sense of freedom. He sighed a deep breath of relief and knew his life was finally going to be everything it should be. He helped Elizabeth from the floor and they walked from the kitchen into the dining room, arm in arm, to share their wonderful news with Grace and Janet.

People change and forget to tell each other.

—Lillian Hellman

Janet

I begged and pleaded with him not to marry her, "She is our *housekeeper!* And I hate her!"

He would hear none of it. "You have no say in the matter. You are fourteen years old. Why, in a few years you will be out on your own. This is my happiness, for once, my happiness that matters."

Aunt Grace stood silent and stoic. I was angry with her for not saying anything. I stormed up the stairs to my room. As soon as I heard Aunt Grace pad up the stairs and shut the door to her room, I stormed down the hall and entered without knocking. "Why don't you stand up to him? This is your home too!"

She replied slowly through clenched teeth, "All Disser property belongs to Sam. I am merely family, just like you."

Her truth stung, sucked the air out of my lungs, and left me speechless. When she realized my reaction to her words, she ran to me and fell to her knees asking for forgiveness. "We are all we have, you and me. Let's accept that and be the pals we have always been, shall we?"

No, not any more. I decided on the spot that I was not going to trust anyone, not a single adult, certainly not Father and now not even Aunt Grace.

Father married Elizabeth in a brief ceremony at the courthouse downtown on July 16, 1938. A reception, wedding cake and all, was held at the house that afternoon. Oh, I was pleasant enough to all the guests, saying hello and how wonderful the occasion. Then I excused myself for the remainder of the day and settled in the attic.

My retreat in the attic became permanent. If I was not at school, I was in the attic, searching through Grandmother's clothes or Grandfather's hats and jackets for treasures that might have been left in their pockets. AM and PM called and called for me, but I refused to come outside or go to their houses to listen to records and talk about boys.

Lingering in the attic, I read my grandparents' letters to each other over and over again. I sat inside their old mahogany wardrobe trying to conjure memories of them. I became depressed. Their voices and conversations were slowly fading from my memory, and I was left with little reality of them, of Grandfather. There were times I surely dozed or daydreamed that his voice was whispering in my ear or his hand was reaching near to hold my hand. Awakening destroyed the echo, his touch. Eventually, I emerged from the attic without solace or relief.

The personal life deeply lived always
expands into truths beyond itself.

—Anais Nin

Shirley

His cruelty began the first evening he lived in our apartment, at dinner. Cecil scolded me, "Sit up straight!" I looked at Mother. He warned, "Don't look to your Mother. I am the man in this house now. Do as I say!" Again I looked at Mother. She was looking away.

Cecil pushed his chair away from the table and went to what was now their bedroom for a pillow. He shoved it down my chair against my back. "When I tell you to do something, you do it. Understand?" I ate that night and every night thereafter in silence.

Then he demanded we rent a different apartment. So Mother and I packed to move again. The Naomi Apartments were located next to the French Bauer ice cream factory. When I was able to sell the scrap I found in the apartment lot or adjacent lots, I took my pennies to the French Bauer factory customer window for a cone of freshly churned chocolate ice cream.

This apartment had only two rooms. Two rooms, can you imagine? Only a living room and a bedroom—for three people. Of course, there was the green couch for me to sleep on at night and for use as a couch to sit on by day. Cecil declared that we had to live frugally and save as much money as possible. It was the way he had always lived.

Adjacent to the living room was a short hallway to the front door. In the hallway sat a squat white stove and a white box refrigerator. Off the hall from the living room to the bedroom was a closet that housed a sink and a toilet. Mother and I had to wash dishes in the bathroom sink. The place was so very small…the smallest apartment of all.

The only good part was that I had never experienced an outside container for milk. Every morning the milk man would deposit two fresh bottles of milk in the metal container beside the entry door. I would hear the milk being slipped into the metal box at 7:00 a.m. sharp. That was the exact time I needed to get up and get ready for school. I poured cereal in a bowl and added milk, sat on the couch/my bed to eat my breakfast, and took a stand-up bath over the sink. That was how I started every day.

As I had so many times before, I got acquainted with the kids in the apartment building. There was a patch of ground at the back of the building beyond the parking lot and a car lot the other side of it that was empty at night. Those were our playground and meeting places. We played the simple games hide-and-go-seek and drop the rag. Not one of our families had money to give to us to do anything else.

I went to the same school, but it was the fifth grade, which meant a new set of teachers. It was a thrill for me when the school year started and there was the school principal, Mrs. Knucklebaum, to welcome me back. I had a different class teacher but I liked her. Her name escapes me now. She was older, with gray hair and stiff-collared shirts that were held together at the neck with a different pin every day.

My class from the previous year was together again. When Mother registered me at the front office, she gave the school her new name, Claire Phelps. The secretary congratulated her on her marriage and asked if my last name was also changed. "No," Mother advised, "Shirley's last name remains the same. Her name is Shirley Disser."

Those were interesting times. We were cramped in that tiny apartment and Cecil barely spoke to me. The loving relationship between Mother and me continued when Cecil was not present. She must have had her own, separate relationship with him.

During supper on Christmas Eve, Cecil grabbed my arm and stated matter-of-factly, "Even though your mother has my last name, you will not have my last name. I have family of my own." He released my arm and went back to eating his dinner. Mother was quiet. I tried to be still, but I could not contain my curiosity.

"Do you have children?" I asked.

"No," he replied, "I have cousins."

That evening as he was taking out the trash, I heard him holler at the apartment manager, who lived in a building across the parking lot from us, "I told that brat she is not mine and never will be. And I don't want to hear another word about it from you."

The apartment manager yelled out in return, "What do I care? All I asked for was the names of the members of your family."

Cecil fumed, "Listen here, old man, that brat came with the package, the ugly duckling. All I care about is the swan. You don't need the name of the brat, understand?"

A relationship with step-siblings is absurd.

—Janet

Janet

Father and Elizabeth were ecstatically happy. I was furious. It wasn't even a year after they were married that Elizabeth announced she was pregnant. "Won't it be wonderful?" she gushed at me. "A little brother or sister for you to play with." In the first place, I didn't think anything about Elizabeth and Father was wonderful. In the second place, I didn't play anymore. I was not a child. I was a young woman. What was she thinking?

The baby was born, and it was a boy. I have never seen Father so thrilled. He ran around the house exclaiming, "I have a son, a son!" What was the big deal? Anybody could make a baby. All our neighbors had children. David—they named him David, for cryin' out loud. Elizabeth was convinced that naming her firstborn after the great hero in the Bible would ensure strength and long life. Besides, she wanted a *D* name to go with Disser. Oh, for heaven's sake.

No more than two years later, Elizabeth was pregnant again. This time it was a girl, and wasn't I pleased? No. I didn't care. They named her Donna. How awful. Who would think to choose the first letter of their kids' first names to match the first letter of our last name? It was stupid.

You would have thought my father did not already have a daughter, me. Donna and David received all his attention. It was, "Oh, and yes, of course, there's Janet." Yes, the afterthought, thank you very much.

Elizabeth had problems with the third pregnancy. She passed blood one evening after dinner, the details of which I didn't wish to hear. Father was distraught and discussed Elizabeth's condition with Aunt Grace and me at great length the next evening. Doc Simmons had confined Elizabeth to bed rest. She was Father's sole focus and concern. He was worried this child might be small or have ill health. The baby lived only three weeks. All births ceased with the death of their second son, Dennis.

After many months of mourning, Elizabeth began to return to her normal habits. The household schedule and all attention revolved around David and Donna. David and Donna Disser were the beautiful and gifted children. They were given subject tutors and music lessons, taken on trips, and introduced to all of Father's friends as his children. I spent more time in my room or with my best friends AM and PM, out of sight and out of mind.

**Father or Stepfather—those are just titles
to me. They don't mean anything.**

—Oliver Hudson

Shirley

About a year after she and Cecil were married, I heard Mother crying and gagging on the floor beside the toilet. Cecil's girth kept me from seeing all but a glimpse of her kneeling on the tile. He finally backed out into the living room and called an ambulance.

I knelt beside her and tried to think of something comforting to say. I did not know what was wrong. "Are you sick? What can I do?" my voice shook with fear. "Did Cecil hurt you? What did he do to you?"

Two men in dark blue uniforms held my Mother between them as they carried her out of the apartment and placed her inside the ambulance. I grabbed the jacket of one of the men as he was walking out, crying and begging, "What is wrong with my mother? Tell me! Where are you taking her? Please, please!"

Cecil walked out of the apartment and got into his car as the ambulance doors were closed. I screamed at him, "What is wrong? Where are you going?" He gave me no reply. I ran back into the apartment to look in the bathroom. The toilet was filled with blood.

I waited and waited and waited for Mother to come back home. I cried and cried and prayed. I was so afraid I would never see my mother again. Cecil came in the door in the middle of the night and announced, "Your mother is very ill. She will be in the hospital for a while."

"Please take me there. I have to see her." My begging seemed to please him. He was delighted to repeat the hospital rule, "They do not allow children."

It was true. Hospitals did not allow a child to be a visitor. I begged him for more details. "Will Mother be okay? What is wrong with her?"

He grunted, "Go to sleep. I'm tired."

For two days, I appealed to Cecil to tell me what was wrong with my mother. He never gave me an answer. His stares and silence were agonizing. On the third day of her absence, Cecil conceded, "Well, your mother had a tumor on one of her ovaries, and it burst." In the first place, I didn't know what an ovary was, and in the second place, I didn't know what a tumor was. "She is going to be in the hospital for a while longer. We will have to manage without her." What was he saying? I took care of myself. There was no "we" that included him and me.

Sometime during the ten days Mother was in the hospital, the Real Silk Hosiery Company went out of business and closed their doors without notice to the employees. Mother and Cecil were out of work. Evidently he had seen or known that the business was failing. That was the reason for our move to such a small apartment, to save as much of his money as possible, not knowing how long it would take him to find another job.

Cecil left the apartment every day to look for work. I busied myself getting ready for school, going to school, coming home to do homework, cleaning the apartment, and then going out to play. Cecil came home at dinner time and made us supper. We sat in silence and ate. Then he would leave to go to the hospital. I did the dishes, got ready for bed, and fell asleep on the couch. I never knew when he came back to the apartment after his visits with Mother. He never woke me to tell me of her progress. He just left me to sleep.

On Saturday, Cecil insisted, "It's time for us to do the laundry." Mother had always done the wash. We went down to the basement. "Now," he directed, "you have to learn how to wash and iron." I was incredulous. He showed me how to sort the dirty clothes and how much detergent to put in the washing machine. Then he got the ironing board down from a peg on the wall and the iron off a shelf. He ironed most of his things but showed me with each piece how to iron. "Don't do it any differently from the way I am showing you. Understand?" Now I was doing wash, folding laundry, ironing, doing the dishes, cleaning the apartment, and taking care of myself.

As it turns out, Mother had been pregnant and had miscarried. The doctors were forced to make two incisions on her stomach, one starting at her belly button and running down to her female parts, and one across her stomach from hip to hip. The baby was a boy, and she was four months along. Cecil and Mother had planned to name him Paul, after Cecil's brother.

I did not know the implications for Mother until she came home. The doctors had told her she would have to rest and remain calm. Cecil decreed she would never work again. We heard about that decision for years and were expected at each telling to compliment him on his generosity.

Cecil had complained to me the day before she returned, "You know the doctor asked your mother why she wasn't getting any better. And your mother confessed, 'My daughter is home alone, and I'm worried about her.'" I didn't care that Cecil was unhappy because Mother missed me. I missed her. I was thrilled she was coming home. It was the middle of June, and I spent the whole summer taking care of her. When she would take a nap I would go outside to play, running in and out of the apartment from time to time to check and see if she needed me.

When I had the chance, I asked Mother, "What would have been baby Paul's last name?"

She seemed surprised by my question but answered easily, "Why, it would have been Paul Phelps."

I asked, "If you two are having children, then why can't my name be Shirley Phelps?"

Mother dropped her head back against the pillows and stared at the ceiling. Before she answered, she motioned for me to lie with her on the bed, folded in her arms. She whispered in my ear, "I don't expect you to understand this, but Cecil would have to adopt you to give you his last name. He does not have any intention of claiming you as his daughter." While she held me, I cried. I was not sure why I was upset, but I cried until my head ached. I finally stopped crying and went to the bathroom sink to splash cool water on my face. Then I went for a very long walk.

In the blocks I walked away from Mother, I tried to understand why she would want a man who did not want me. Had I been such a disappointment to her that she would accept Cecil and allow him to reject me? Then I knew that I was and always would be a Disser. That was my heritage, my unique place in Mother's life. No one could change our history or our devotion. If Cecil did not want me, that was fine. I did not want him.

I fixed breakfast and lunch for Mother and me. Cecil would go to the grocery on Saturdays and fix our supper each night. One hot and humid August night, Cecil did not come home until very late. When he walked through the door, he announced, "I've signed a contract to sell Franklin College materials. Actually, Franklin College is not a college at all but a series of correspondence courses. I'll be selling packages of materials and tests to prepare men and women interested in getting specific jobs with the US government."

Mother was proud of him, "That's wonderful, Cecil. You will be good at that."

He had committed to travel every week, Monday through Friday, signing potential students. That suited me just fine. I gave no thought to Cecil being on the road. Every night, I ate dinner with Mother, we chatted like old times, and then I went to sleep on the couch. His whereabouts were not my concern. Life was good. I was happy again to be the sole beneficiary of Mother's time and attention.

One week that winter, it snowed and it snowed and it snowed for several days and nights. A whimpering noise woke me up in the middle of the night. I called for Mother. She didn't answer. I walked down the narrow hallway to their bedroom. Mother was sitting up in bed and crying. "It's still snowing and I don't know if Cecil is safe or even alive."

"Oh, Mother. He's fine." I got in bed with her and curled up behind her back so she could fall asleep.

Of course Cecil never called, or thought to call, to let Mother know he was okay. He just showed up late Friday night and acted as if she should not have been worried. Well, I wasn't worried. Why was she?

The day before Thanksgiving that year, Cecil came home with a twenty-two-pound turkey, a free gift from the Franklin College. We had nothing big enough to cook it in. Cecil insisted, "I'll find something." Finally, he took the icebox insert and, tearing off long sheets of aluminum foil, he completely covered the bottom and sides. "There" he said, "that was easy." Mother and I couldn't suppress a fit of laughter. The bird still did not fit. So Cecil chopped off its legs and cooked them separately in a boiling pot. The turkey and legs cooked all day long. We didn't sit down to eat until nine thirty at night. I was starving. Mother never did forget that story. She repeated it every Thanksgiving.

We moved again, to Park Avenue in People's Corner. There were three apartment buildings in a row. Mother chose the center building because the apartments were more spacious. The one she picked had a bedroom for me, a bedroom for them, a living room, and a kitchen. Now that was living! I had a bedroom of my own. Of course the green couch came with us. This time it was used solely as a couch. I was able to continue to go to Windsor School, and I played as much as I wanted to in nearby Eden Park.

A year after we moved in, the landlord decided to transition the apartments to living quarters for University of Cincinnati students. We moved to Evanston, renting the upstairs of a house. I had to change schools and go to the sixth grade at Evanston School. This was a large neighborhood, friendly and filled with kids. I made lots of new friends.

Cecil was still traveling Monday through Friday. It was wonderful to have him outside of our normal routine during the week. One day he came home and told Mother he needed to go to Portsmouth, Ohio, for the entire week and wanted her to go with him. He said that, at ten years old, I was certainly able to stay by myself. Mother made arrangements for Mrs. Lyons, who lived below us, to feed me. She did—every meal I had eggs. Eggs were cheap.

While Mother was gone, I was so lonely. Mrs. Lyons brought up a plate of eggs in the morning and again in the evening. A neighbor lady across the street, Marilyn, had made friends with Mother. She stopped me as I got off the school bus Tuesday afternoon and asked how I was doing. When I told her I was going to have eggs every meal she invited me over for dinner every night. I ate my eggs then went to her house. Marilyn had two little girls, Betty and Ruth. We played jacks until it was time for them to go to bed. Friday afternoon she offered to take her daughters and me to the movies. I had a few pennies and a nickel to share. It was so thrilling to be going to the movies with them that I bought candy for Betty and Ruth.

Marilyn remarked, "You are so funny. Any time anyone does anything for you get so tickled." Well, why not? I was not used to having people do things for me. While we were at the movies, Mother and Cecil arrived home and could not find me. Thursday night's and Friday morning's dirty dishes with remnants of egg left on them were stacked in the sink. Mother was upset with me, and Cecil was prepared to give me a lecture and a spanking.

When I saw Cecil's car parked across the street, I ran back to the apartment and clung to Mother. Crying and hugging her around the waist, I told her I had been given eggs for every meal. Mother was furious with Mrs. Lyons but more upset with herself for leaving me. She stomped her foot and told Cecil she would never leave me alone again. I stopped crying and smiled, my face still buried in her coat.

The next move was to Dayton, and I was enrolled in a private school. The apartment we lived in was barely big enough to fit the green couch through the door. It was close to the downtown area and one block away from a movie theater. On Saturday mornings, Cecil would give me money to go to the show for the afternoon. One Saturday I put a dress I had made from a rag and safety pins on my doll and took her to the movies with me. The woman who sold the movie tickets asked, "Are you taking your doll to the movie?" When I explained my doll was my only friend, she let me into the theater for free. I kept that movie money for myself and never told Cecil that I didn't spend it.

We stayed in Dayton six months. I remember I didn't like our stay there. The school had high stone walls up both sides of the walk to the front door. It was creepy. I had two classes in an attic and one class in a cellar room next to the school boiler.

This was the first time I was required to get up in front of class and speak. We were assigned a book to read and a day and time to give a book report. I got up in front of the class and my knees started to shake. At the end of my report the teacher commented, "Why, that was very good." She asked the class for any comments.

One classmate pouted and said, "Well, she just looked straight ahead and not at any of us." They were lucky I didn't pass out. Thank God we left that school before I had to give another book report.

If there was a choice between compromise or a show of strength, men would always choose War.

—Anonymous

Janet

What took everyone's attention off the new children was the start of World War II. Father began reminiscing about his service in the First World War. Every night at dinner, he proclaimed what would be the outcome of the international conflict. Father was certain the United States would enter the war and was disappointed President Roosevelt did not make a commitment to the Allied Powers right away.

Stories of political and economic instability in Germany were the feature of every radio program and newspaper. Father claimed Germany was still bitter over their defeat in World War I, which he had helped single-handedly to win, of course.

Accounts of the Nazi Party and its leader Adolf Hitler began to fill the news. Hitler had signed alliances with Italy and Japan to oppose the Soviet Union. In a bold move, he had sent his troops to occupy Austria in 1938 and then to annex Czechoslovakia in 1939. Two days after signing the German-Soviet Nonaggression Pact, Hitler invaded Poland. Two days after the invasion of Poland, on September 3, 1939, France and Britain declared war on Germany.

"Now," Father predicted, "now Roosevelt will show the world that the US will come to the aid of our friends." But the president continued to observe, as did the rest of America, while Hitler satisfied his newfound thirst for communist dominance. Early in 1940, the Soviet Union divided Poland with Germany, occupied the Baltic States, and overwhelmed Finland.

In April 1940, Hitler went on to conquer Denmark and begin a strike on Norway. In May, his forces swept through all of The Netherlands as well as Belgium as part of an eventual, planned invasion of France. France surrendered to German forces in June. Then Hitler launched massive bombing raids on Britain in preparation to occupy England. To his regret, after losing a significant battle (the Battle of Britain), he postponed the invasion.

Who was this "new father"? Never was there a man as lacking in love and affection for children as Cecil.

—Shirley

Shirley

We moved from Dayton back to Cincinnati at the midpoint of the school year. I was placed in the same year of school, the sixth grade, back at Windsor School. I have no memory of our apartment. We were only there a few months and moved again, to Norwood, which was close to Cecil's office. The rooms were so tiny even the green couch was too big and had to be put in storage. Cecil purchased a used child's trundle bed that he put in the living room for me to sleep in. How embarrassing. I had to pull it out from under the dinner table to get in and out of bed. When I slept in it, I had to be on my side with my knees bent up toward my chest. It was torture, pure torture.

We were not in Norwood long when Mother became quiet and serious. I asked what was wrong, and she admitted, "Oh, sweet Shirley, I have to go to the hospital again. My first surgery only took care of part of the problem. I have to have another surgery to be better."

When she lost the baby, the surgeon had removed one ovary. A return to the hospital was required to have the other ovary removed. A complete hysterectomy was performed. Mother was home after little more than a week in the hospital, and she rested in our apartment for ten weeks.

This was the same year Mother intimated that she needed to describe for me how women and men are built. She put two potatoes in our round boiling pot as an example of a woman's ovaries. At a loss as to how to describe a man, she opted for a banana and two pears.

I asked Mother why she was explaining a man's anatomy to me. Mother confessed that she wanted me to understand not only the details of her surgery but also the "workings" of a man's privates. When she raised the banana and placed it in the pot between the potatoes, I was appalled.

Many years later, I would relate this bizarre demonstration to a girlfriend of mine when we were riding the streetcar to work. She and I laughed the entire ride to our offices downtown.

Mother timed her surgery so she would be home from the hospital just as my summer break began. It was a grand plan. After she recovered, we moved back to Hyde Park. Mother was so pleased. The apartment was big—two bedrooms and a living room, a dining room and long kitchen with deep cupboards for storage. Since Cecil had opted to move to one side of the street instead of the other, I could not go to Hyde Park School and had to register for seventh grade at Horace Mann School.

This year at Horace Mann School was the first time I attended class with mostly colored people. I had had no problems getting along with either the whites or the coloreds in any of my other schools or neighborhoods. Then the colored girl who sat behind me, Mariah, stole one of my pencils. At the start of the school year, Mother had surprised me with a box of pencils with my name stamped in gold. It was the only one I had used, and it was missing. When everyone else went to recess, I opened the top of Mariah's desk and saw a new pencil in the tray. It had my name on it. I put it back in my desk, in my pencil tray.

I went out to the playground and saw Mariah pointing and laughing at me. I threatened, "Don't laugh at me. I know what you did."

"What do you mean you know what I did?" Mariah mimicked me in front of all her friends.

"You took my pencil."

"How do you know I took your pencil?"

"I found it in your desk."

"How dare you look in my desk!" she said. And with that she grabbed my hair and started pulling on it. I thought my hair was going to come out at the roots. It hurt. I punched her in the stomach. The playground teacher only witnessed me punch Mariah in the stomach and came over to put a stop to our fight.

The principal and my teachers thought I was an excellent student. They did not think so much of Mariah. She had poor grades and a nasty mouth. The teacher asked me first what the fight was about, and I told her Mariah had stolen my pencil. The teacher said, "That is no reason to fight."

I protested, "I didn't pick a fight with her. She pulled my hair and it hurt. I wanted her to stop."

"No matter," the teacher answered, "you never punch a girl in the stomach."

I didn't care. I knew she wouldn't give me my pencil back unless I stood up for myself. From then on, Mariah and her friends didn't want anything to do with me. Wouldn't you know, in high school we ended up playing basketball on the same intramural team? She was guard, running and scrambling with me all over the court. She tried every move and maneuver to get me to take a fall or have an injury.

Finally, I went to the girl's coach and declared, "I will not play basketball. Mariah and I do not like each other."

She warned, "You have to play. You signed up to play and you will play."

I refused. "I am not going to play with her." The coach told me she would talk to Mariah. She went over and told her to stop harassing me.

Mariah made up an excuse. "Well, I guard her closer than anyone because she is one of the best players."

The coach warned, "I'll take you out of the game and tell your gym teacher to fail you in class unless you behave." She stopped tormenting me.

Cecil, however, continued to torment me. I didn't wear my clothes correctly. My shoes weren't polished. I combed my hair the wrong way. I was too fat. Every time he saw me it was pick, pick, pick. I avoided the very sight of him. Whenever Cecil was in the apartment, I chose to leave.

A pretty teenage girl named Celia lived in the apartment building next to ours. She went to Horace Mann

School too but was two years ahead of me, in the ninth grade. We rode the bus home together every day. Celia had coal-black hair and black eyes and wore bright red lipstick. I looked to her for advice on my clothes and my hair.

Celia and I had a lot in common. Her mom was absent most nights gambling at Castle Farm, where her dad was a bartender. Castle Farm was a popular nightclub, restaurant, and casino on the west side of town. Celia was left to cook and care for herself and her little brother Frank. Most nights, I could be found in her family's apartment. I did my homework while Celia read magazines and Frank played with his toys on the living room floor.

Celia's older brother Jimmy, age eighteen, was in and out of their apartment trying to hold down two jobs and spend time with his girlfriend. Jimmy adored my mother. She called him Gingy. Mother teased Gingy all the time about his girlfriend, Rose. Rose was a delicate blond with pale creamy skin, just like a much younger model of Mother. Rose was quite a contrast to Jimmy. He had black wavy hair, big muscles everywhere, and was very good-looking. Jimmy told Mother that he hoped Rose would grow up to look just like her.

Jimmy got away with everything with my mother. He brought a dessert to her every night from the downtown restaurant where he was a cook. She made over him and gave him change and small bills from her purse every Friday night. One day he came home with a gun that belonged to a friend. He told Celia he would just point it up and aim it like a cop. Unfortunately, his finger squeezed the trigger and a bullet shot the light fixture right out of their dining room ceiling. His mother was furious. We could hear her yelling at him clear over in our apartment.

At least one night a week, Celia and I would walk down to Bole's Drugstore (it would later become Pack's Drugstore) to buy the latest song sheets. Mother and Celia and I would sit around and sing. Our captive audience was Celia's little brother. When we got tired of singing, Mother would watch little Frank so Celia and I could play kickball in the dead-end street. We didn't come in until the street lights came on. Mother always said I was the first one out in the morning and the last one in at night.

There was a gravel driveway at the end of the street that was graded up a hill and then flattened at the top. That winter, Mother gave me a pair of her old riding boots to go out in the snow. Celia and I took big pieces of cardboard we found stacked beside Bole's Dumpster to sled down that driveway. Trees that lined either side made it a bit of a challenge.

One afternoon it had snowed and then rained and then snowed again. I came home from sledding at the driveway and couldn't feel my toes. Mother took the boots off me and I winced. She asked what was wrong. I told her I thought my toes were frozen. She assured me, "I can fix that." Mother ran water in the tub.

When she put my feet in the tub I shrieked, "That's crazy cold!"

Mother explained, "All you can do with frozen toes is to start with cold water and gradually warm it up." She was right. The water was finally hot, and I thought I would melt. Mother wrapped my feet in several towels and then went to the kitchen to make hot chocolate with marshmallows for both of us. My toes were fine. The hot chocolate was perfect.

A "down-home" couple, as Cecil described them, had moved into the apartment directly below us. Fred and Ruby were honest and simple people. Mother and Ruby became the best of friends. Ruby had a face filled with freckles and strawberry-blond hair that she wore in a single long braid down her back.

Fred worked for Turner Construction and was a brute of a guy with bright red hair and a smile that spanned from ear to ear. Mother and I came to learn that Fred was a very picky eater. He insisted all vegetables and meat be chosen and purchased fresh from the market every day. While Mother and Ruby agreed fresh was best, Ruby did not always want to spend her day riding the bus to and from the Findlay Market downtown and then washing the food and preparing the evening meal.

Ruby and Mother had a secret that they eventually shared with me. Ruby bought canned vegetables and packaged meats from the local A&P grocery and put them in our kitchen. She would come upstairs in the afternoons for ingredients to put in her casseroles, soups, and stews. Fred never knew the difference. At least we never heard he knew the difference. During the day, Ruby and Mother walked and talked and shopped when they wanted to.

The next spring, Fred was offered a long-term contract in Detroit. He and Ruby moved. Celia's brother Jimmy was drafted to fight in the war. Mother was devastated by the loss of her two and only friends.

How strange to think of yourself as an only child for so long, and then to have your life include siblings.

—Janet

Janet

It was early 1941, and Hungary, Romania, and Bulgaria had been added to Hitler's new empire. German troops quickly overran Yugoslavia and Greece. In the summer of 1941, Hitler abandoned his pact with the Soviet Union and launched a surprise invasion of Russia. Just outside the city of Moscow, his troops met with strong resistance. The Soviet troops, who were used to the brutal winter weather, stopped Hitler's advance. In the meantime, Japan expanded its war with China and seized all colonial holdings. On December 7, 1941, Japan attacked the US military bases at Pearl Harbor. On December 11, Germany declared war on the United States.

Finally, President Roosevelt committed the United States to the war. Father was so angry and frustrated that he spoke against the president whenever he had the opportunity. He disagreed with Roosevelt's policies and decisions regarding WWII. Father had particular contempt for the president's federal tax policy to pay for the war. Prior to US involvement, about 10 percent of all workers had paid federal tax. Roosevelt pushed to impose a blanket tax and, by 1944, every employed person was paying federal income tax.

As if the tax issue was not enough, Father was even angrier about the controls placed on the US economy and trades. The most important were price controls, imposed on a majority of products and labor. In addition, the military published priorities that directed industrial production. Plumbing jobs were halted mid-project and necessary materials were redirected to the war effort. Work for Father became erratic, and his moods followed the same pattern.

Blackouts were practiced in every city, including Cincinnati, reaching down Harrison Pike to the Disser home. All lighting had to be extinguished to avoid helping the enemy target major metropolitan areas at night.

Actually, the real purpose was to remind people that there was a war on and to provide activities that would engage those not otherwise involved in the war effort.

In spite of all his grumbling and at Elizabeth's urging not to scare the children (their children), Father did create a bomb shelter in the basement.

Father stored blankets, canned goods, and an old radio on empty shelves. All the while, he complained to Aunt Grace and me, "Roosevelt must be out of what is left of his mind if he thought there could ever be a bomb attack from enemy aircraft over southwestern Ohio. The enemy doesn't even know or care where Cincinnati is, much less where Ohio is, even if they had a map. He is such a fool."

When I was sixteen and a half, I wanted to apply for a job certificate so I could do my part in the war effort. I went downtown to the courthouse to get the required copy of my birth record. There was no record of my birth. The clerk found a birth document filed by a midwife that was for a Jennette Grace Disser, with no birth date or month, just the birth year: 1924. I brought a copy home and showed it to Aunt Grace.

It was then that Aunt Grace chose to tell me about my mother and my sister. "Jennette was your grandfather's name for you. Your mother named you Janet the day you were born, but he was not going to let that be the last word. Your grandfather insisted on his preference for you,

Jennette, which he believed to be a more appropriate family name. Jennette had been the name of their first child, who died at age sixteen. So, at his instruction, the midwife recorded Jennette on the birth document she filed. Everything else is correct. The month and day we have always celebrated as your birthday is September twenty-eighth. The year of your birth was 1924."

Realizing that this might be the only time to tell me about my birth, Aunt Grace elaborated. "As a matter of fact, you were born in this very house in the lavender room. Your mother was young, beautiful, and very much in love with your father. Despite their love for one another, however, your grandfather did not approve of their marriage. There was a vast difference between your father's and your mother's ages and a significant concern about her upbringing. Sam and your mother married without your grandfather's blessing or knowledge."

Taking a deep breath, Aunt Grace continued the story of Janet's mother and father, fearing she would never again find the time or the courage. "Your mother became pregnant again when you were three years old. When your little sister was born, your father and your mother were separated. It was your grandfather who dictated that you would stay in this house to live with your father."

I had barely opened my mouth to ask one of the many questions tumbling from my head when Aunt Grace put a finger to my lips, "No questions, Janet. I do not have the answers. All I know is what I have told you."

"Is my sister still alive? Where does she live?" I had to know.

"As I say, all I know is what I have told you." Aunt Grace walked away and never tolerated discussion on the subject of my family history again. The topic was closed.

I returned to the courthouse the next day. Paying a small fee, I added my birth month and day as September 28 to the recorded year of 1924. I legally changed my name to Janet Lee Disser, not quite the same spelling as the famous movie star Janet Leigh, but close enough to make me feel special and defiant.

The closest to perfection a person
ever comes is when he fills out
a job application form.

—Stanley J. Randall

Shirley

The day I turned fourteen, I applied for a job certificate, because Cecil would not give me any spending
money or an allowance for my chores. Mother stretched
the house allowance he gave her each week as much as
she could to keep us fed and clothed.

I went downtown to the courthouse to get a copy of my
birth certificate. The clerk found a birth document for a
Shirley Mae that was filed by a midwife for June 10, 1927.

Mother's name had been misspelled as Claire Dissere. I brought a copy home and showed it to Mother. She disagreed with the spelling of the last name and agreed with me that it should be changed.

That evening, she showed it to Cecil and declared she was going downtown with me to correct it the next morning. He took the birth document from her hands. "No, you don't want to do that. Leave it the way it is. It will cost money to make changes." My birth document had to be correct. At the clerk's office the next day, I confirmed June 10, 1927, as the date of my birth and requested the spelling of my last name to be Disser. The cost was two dollars.

Upon receipt of my work permit, I applied for and interviewed at Shillito's department store to be a retail clerk. I was hired on a Monday and started work the same week, on Thursday. I boarded the three o'clock streetcar from school to the city. I worked from three thirty to nine o'clock, with half an hour for dinner. Dinner was provided free of charge in the cafeteria. Saturdays I worked from eight in the morning to five at night, with no free lunch. The lunch break was forty-five minutes, so I packed my lunch and ate on Fountain Square in good weather and in the Carew Tower arcade in bad weather. I worked evenings through the school year and every day the following summer.

For the first time, I was able to purchase clothes and cosmetics with my own money. I had all the assistance I wanted at Shillito's cosmetics counters. During lunch breaks on Saturdays, I would go to the clerks who looked the prettiest to ask for their recommendations. It was refreshing to buy personal items for myself. I took pride in my appearance and tried to stay current with the latest styles.

Whenever I could, I purchased beautiful scarves and undergarments for Mother. She giggled with delight as I handed her packages, for no occasion whatsoever, the contents of which I had carefully wrapped in scented tissue paper.

Cecil could not have been more disgusted with the young woman I was becoming. He ridiculed my "pittance" of a salary, told me I applied my lipstick incorrectly (never from one corner of your mouth to the other, Shirley, only apply it in the middle), my hair made me look like a little girl, and I used too much shampoo and toothpaste. I could never do anything right.

You're no good unless you are a good assistant; and if you are, you're too good to be an assistant.

—Martin H. Fischer

Janet

Worth War II had brought prosperity to Cincinnati companies that were engaged in metalworking and food processing. I had my choice of two positions as secretary to the purchasing manager at Smith & Hill Shapers or at the Kroger Company. I chose the job at Smith & Hill, enticed by an hourly rate that was five cents higher.

Even though I worked in the Roselawn area of town, I was not far from the city by bus. On the weekends,

Fountain Square was my favorite meeting place in downtown Cincinnati. The square was a public gift from Henry Probasco in memory of Tyler Davidson, his brother-in-law and business partner. A glorious fountain of the Genius of Water, named the Tyler Davidson Fountain, graced the square. I used to tell people, "Meet me beside the fountain. You can't miss her. She is nine feet high, raised on a six-foot pedestal, and cast in a flowing gown with outstretched arms that stream water."

The Genius of Water stood witness to hundreds of people waiting for friends, engaged in conversation, and taking a breath of fresh air. She may not have warranted so much as a glance from those who rushed through the square as a shortcut to the streetcar and bus stations. I would always look at her as an ironic testimony to the Flood of '37 that nearly lapped at her feet.

Weekend meetings with friends became increasingly more important after I met Dave Fredwest. Friends and Dave and I met at the square every Friday night. He worked as an assistant buyer at the exclusive department store Gidding Jenny on Fourth Street. Dave and my boss Charlie were friends. Charlie had introduced us.

Dave was ten years older than me. Dave had been drafted before he graduated and was now home from his service in the war. He had been assigned to an aircraft carrier but ended up serving as a submarine spotter on the east coast. Because of a hernia he suffered while folding a wing below deck, the aircraft carrier had departed without him. He rarely talked about his days as a service-man because he regretted not being able to carry out his assigned duties overseas in the heat of battle.

Thanks to a strong work ethic that was ingrained at an early age by his parents, Dave had started work in a neighborhood notions store at the age of twelve. He never questioned his family's need for his income or their insistence on his excellent marks in school regardless of the hours he worked.

At the notions store, Dave had developed an eye for high-quality fabrics and became an excellent negotiator with the store's suppliers. I had excelled in my history, math and English classes and had a knack for gab. I was confident we complemented one another.

I was pleased to be part of the workforce and spent less and less time on my schoolwork the last year of high school. President Roosevelt had insisted civilian support was critical to winning the war. I was doing my part.

You're braver than you believe, and
stronger than you seem, and smarter than
you think."

—Christopher Robin to Pooh

Shirley

For all four years of high school, I was able to stay at one school, Withrow High School. It was exciting to rally with school friends at sports events. There were football games every Friday night in the fall, basketball games on Saturday nights in winter, and baseball games and track meets most weekends in the spring. Mother gave me permission to stay out late on the weekends. My curfew was ten o'clock.

Since my grades placed me in the top 5 percent of my college preparatory classes, Mother encouraged me to participate in after-school activities. I was a soprano in the choir, secretary of the Girls' Glee Club, and treasurer of the Spanish Club. Choir was the most fun; Mr. Graeter was an entertaining choral director. The week before Christmas, he took choir members out of their regular classes for a half-day of caroling through the school hallways.

Classes were much more interesting and the teachers less strict in high school. My history class was one of my favorites. I loved the teacher, Mrs. Rosen. She would ask a question, and I would be the only one to raise my hand. She finally told me to put my hand down and insisted others answer her questions. She had a snappy new car with a rumble seat. She did not offer a ride in her car to any students except me, but I did not accept a ride from her for fear my classmates would see me.

The one course I did not get an A in was algebra. It took me forever to understand algebra and even longer to catch on to geometry. Mr. Mathias, who was also the assistant principal, taught both math classes. I think he felt sorry for me because I worked so hard on his homework assignments. The entire football team and two other girls were in my math courses first thing in the morning.

Everyone in class had to get up and work a math problem at the blackboard and then explain their work to the rest of the class. At home one night, I was complaining about having to work the math problems in front of the other students. Cecil grabbed the pencil out of my hand and said, "It's not that difficult. Here, I'll show you how it's done."

It didn't take long to see that Cecil didn't know the first thing about geometry. He couldn't figure out a single problem in my homework. I interrupted him, "That's not how Mr. Mathias showed us how to solve the math problems."

Cecil replied, "Well then, the hell with you. Do your homework yourself and stop complaining."

It was a godsend to have a best friend who was a math genius. Joyce Ewall was my best friend through all of high school. Joyce loved my mother. Her mother was sweet but really old. My mother always wore the latest styles, fixed her hair in an elaborate French twist, and shared beauty secrets with us. One day Joyce and I laughed at Mother because she was all dressed up to go shopping downtown but walked out the door of our apartment in her slippers. She had to come back in to put on her high heels.

Cecil's income had increased with expansion of his territory to include Indiana and Kentucky. I contributed half of every paycheck to Mother. She was shopping again and constantly cheerful.

In an attempt to stay current in fashion with Mother, Cecil purchased tailored suits with matching short-brimmed hats and overcoats. Mother's dresses were pale colors; her favorite was lavender, with skirts cut on the bias for a smooth draping that grazed her knees. Underneath her clothes, she was particular about her choice of lace slip, girdle, and stockings. Mother and Cecil made quite the pair when they stepped out to the theater or to go to church on Sunday morning.

In the heat of the summer, Joyce and I would dress up too and venture downtown on Sunday afternoon to the Albee Theater to sit in the air conditioning for the feature matinee. After the movie was over, we would stop at the Fanny Farmer candy shop for a chocolate treat to eat on the bus back home. Joyce and I would each select a chocolate to take home to Mother as well.

Throughout high school, I looked forward to going to college. Everyone in class talked about what university they were planning to attend. I even did a book report for my English teacher Dr. Fredericks about going to Miami University. Mother came to parents' night my junior year of high school and introduced herself to him. She said afterward that it was like shaking hands with a cold, dead fish. However, she glowed with pride as she told me, "Dr. Fredericks could not stop saying great things about you." He told Mother I was very smart.

> We must let go of the life we
> have planned, so as to accept the
> one that is waiting for us.

> —Joseph Campbell

Janet

Dave and I listened and danced with friends to Big Band music at the Western Hills dance center. My favorite band was Glenn Miller. Dave insisted the music of the Tommy Dorsey band was better. Late one evening, Dave pulled his car over to the curb on the way back to my house. He asked me to marry him. Without hesitating a second, I yelled, "Yes!"

"Wait, do I need to ask for your father's permission first?" Dave was a little bit panicked.

Again without hesitation I yelled, "No!" We laughed and hugged and kissed and made plans for our big day.

As my wedding day approached, I resisted both Elizabeth's and Aunt Grace's help selecting a dress. I found myself wondering about my mother. My heart ached for knowledge of her, as it never had before.

As a couple, Dave and I had discussed my taking on the traditional role of wife, homemaker, and eventually mother. And yet I had become enamored with the work I was doing. It was a traditional female job, but I had gained the respect of my peers, and management had asked for my assistance on several important purchasing projects. The confidence in my abilities was intoxicating.

Most jobs in which a woman worked with all men immediately or eventually revealed she possessed the fewest skills. On the contrary, Smith & Hill Shapers found that women brought a new set of skills that included more attention to detail and a willingness to work longer hours. Most days I outperformed the male clerks regardless of their age and abilities and for much less pay.

Did I want to be a wife, homemaker, and mother? Was my mother now a wife, homemaker, and even a mother to more children than the sister I had never known? For me, being a wife and working woman would be a dream come true.

The reason people find it so hard to be happy is that they always see the past better than it was, the present worse than it is, and the future less resolved than it will be.

—Marcel Pagnol

Shirley

In anticipation of college entrance requirements, I took a biology class the summer before my sophomore year. It required the dissection of animals. Mr. Caldry was my teacher, and he was an odd little man. His wire-rimmed glasses were broken on one side. To fix the earpiece, he threaded wire though the attaching post hole, wound it around the side stem, and then wrapped it around his ear covered in medical cotton affixed with masking tape.

There were two students at every lab table. I had a nervous partner at my lab table, Regina. She did not want to touch an animal, much less dissect anything. We made a pact. "If you will record all our findings, I will do the dissecting," I offered. She agreed. We started with worms, then butterflies, and finally a frog. Thank God it was summer school and our semester ran out before Mr. Caldry made us dissect a cat.

Regina and I became friends and stayed after biology class. Summer school was held at Hughes High School, across from the University of Cincinnati. Regina and I felt so grown up as we went out for a sandwich after class at the same deli that the college students frequented. After lunch, I caught the bus downtown to work at Shillito's.

Summer school before my junior year, I took college preparatory English. I went to class and then on to work at Shillito's. My extra efforts pleased Mother and gained more of her attention. She was proud that I was earning my own money and especially pleased with my marks in school.

My junior year in high school, I had Mrs. Atkins for English. She told Mother I was her prize pupil. I think Mrs. Atkins was the smartest teacher I ever had. She had traveled all over the world during summer breaks. I loved to hear her stories. The guy who sat behind me whispered, "Get her to talk about one of her trips so we don't have to take the test." Mrs. Atkins caught me telling him no. He regularly got the students around him into trouble.

One of our English requirements was to write a short story during the class period. I don't know what ever happened to the short story I turned in. Mrs. Atkins asked if I had ever thought of writing as a career. She smiled and said, "Your short story was so good. Do you mind if I keep it and show it to my colleagues?" I didn't think it was that great. It was the story of my relationship with Mother.

Toward the end of my junior year, Betty Ann Markison (she lived across the street) asked if I would be interested in working the summer before my senior year in the front office of the A&P grocery store where her father Ed was manager. He needed someone to fill in every time one of the clerks went on vacation. Cecil came home that night and said, "I got you a job at the A&P." Like hell he did. Betty had asked me at school, and I had already agreed. The A&P where Betty Ann's father was store manager was at Brighton Corner, not too far from where my ancestor William Crockett had had his first grocery store.

Every day that summer, I took the streetcar to People's Corner, then the streetcar to Vine Street, and at the top of Vine Street I caught a third streetcar down to Brighton Corner. My work was behind several different desks in the grocery office. Since I had already taken clerical courses in school—typing, shorthand, general business, and Dictaphone—I had no problem completing the daily tally sheets of sales and purchases. I rotated from one desk to another as the ladies took vacation throughout the summer months.

When the final sales tally was audited, I walked the day's paperwork to the main office, which was housed in an A&P warehouse. The men working in the warehouse wanted to know who the new girl was. It was flattering to catch their attention every day. Walking every day through the store and to the warehouse, getting admiring looks and whistles, that was great.

One night, I could not find a specific figure in the accounting ledger. It was getting later and later, and I was getting more and more upset. Betty Ann's father finally came to my desk and asked me, "Are you having a problem? I've never seen you here this late." I told him I couldn't find a certain dollar amount in the daily ledger. He found it right away, as a footnote in the margin, at the binding. The amount was $1.57.

Ed was very pleased with my work at the A&P store. Each desk was new and a challenge, but I was a quick learner. I was thrilled to be setting aside half my paycheck. Having my own money for college expenses was going to be a dream come true. The A&P job paid twenty-two dollars a week. At Shillito's, the most I could make in a week was eighteen dollars.

My senior year in high school, I elected to take advanced English. I was assigned to a seat between the two smartest and most popular guys in my graduating class. I was surprised they were nice to me. We had so much fun. The teacher, Miss Dover, was right out of college. She had long brown hair and a cheerleader personality.

I don't know if she realized what she was doing or not, but she used to sit on top of her desk in front of the class with her legs crossed. Miss Dover always wore a short skirt, and she had a nervous habit of pumping her one leg up and down. Of course all the boys were much more interested in watching her skirt move than in listening to what she had to say.

At the end of first semester, she gave us a midterm exam. The three of us who were seated together received the highest scores. The boy on my right got an eighty-five out of one hundred points. That was the best grade in the class. The boy on my left received an eighty-two, and my score was eighty. The rest of the class, about thirty in all, failed the test. When we all compared our grades, we were in shock. The three of us who were the smartest in class were accustomed to scoring between ninety-five and one hundred on tests.

Miss Dover came to class the next day and apologized. Apparently the exam she had given us was the equivalent of a college test. Mr. Peoples, the principal of Withrow, came in to talk to the class. He explained, "Your teacher tried very hard to prepare you for this midterm exam. I looked over the questions, and I have to admit this test was extremely difficult. So I have regraded the exam on a curve." The three of us ended up with As, with scores of one hundred, ninety-seven, and ninety-five (me). The rest of the class received Cs. Now that was fair.

The total of my course credits and grades were more than enough for acceptance into college. In January, I appealed to Mother, "Can I please go to Miami University in the fall? That is where all the smart kids are planning to go next year. Even though applications aren't due until the end of March, I know it may take some time for you to convince Cecil to give me the money for tuition."

The first of March, Mother told me Cecil would not give me the money. I took another long walk. He was making seven thousand dollars a year and could afford to pay my tuition. I had balanced his work accounts several times and knew his income and his expenses. And he knew I knew.

I argued with Cecil about tuition for college. He sneered at me and said, "What would you do with a college degree? The only things you are going to be good for will be to snatch a man if one will have you, get married, and have babies. That is the day I look forward to—when you are out of this house and out from under my feet."

There is no substitute for victory.

—General Douglas MacArthur

Janet

I t had been obvious to everyone that the media supported what the US government deemed appropriate to publish about the war. This was most apparent in
posters and even in movie scripts, which had to be preap-
proved to ensure promotion of national support for the
war. Some portrayals of the enemy were benign and others were extreme. Disney cartoon characters made fun of
the Germans, while some of the posters resorted to evil
creatures to depict the Nazis and the Japanese. Smith &
Hill had war posters in every manufacturing area and
hanging in the front office too.

Recycling was a requirement for all civilians and for Smith & Hill employees. Neighborhood drives were a weekend event at the old house on Harrison Pike. Dave and I became experts at gathering rubber, tin, waste fats from cooking, paper, lumber, and steel.

Materials needed for the war efforts were sometimes a scarce resource in the neighborhoods. What was most important was rallying around the call to give to the war without spending personal income—a way for people to show their support. Rationing of food supplies began in 1943, so the entire city of Cincinnati was one of thousands of cities to initiate neighborhood "victory gardens" to grow and share fruits and vegetables.

In the fall of 1943, my precocious step-brother David and his young friends decided to focus a few spare evenings gathering apples out of the orchard down the road. The property was owned by an older couple, the Tackers. Tradition held that old Mrs. Tacker took the entire fall season to bake every apple from their orchard into apple pies, apple dumplings, and apple tarts. She sold them at the church festival two weeks before Thanksgiving. She donated half of the money she received to her church and the other half she kept as her "pin" money.

I suppose honesty got the better of him, because David confided in me, "Janet, a few friends of mine picked those Tacker apples." I had to admit to myself that what he and his friends had done was an admirable stunt to pull off. However, I advised, "David, I think your friends need to either confess to their parents that they stole the Tackers' apples or they need to use their little red wagons to gather the apples from their current hiding place and present them to the Tackers. What do you think?"

He thought for a moment. "I'm not sure I can do that." I leaned into his face and interrogated: "A few friends but not you?" As his head fell to look at the floor, I suggested, "Why don't you tell Mrs. Tacker you gathered the apples for her this year? If you hang onto the apples, what are you going to do with them all anyway?"

Logic or honesty prevailed. David and his friends rounded up the apples and returned them to the Tackers. David related to me that he declared to Mrs. Tacker, "Me and my friends here organized your apples." She actually believed that innocent face and even gave him five dollars. What a stinker.

If you tell the truth you don't have to remember anything.

—Mark Twain

Shirley

I was consumed by trying to decide what to do for a life on my own. I gave considerable thought to my real father. Was he still alive? Did he have the money to send my sister to college? What if I were to apply to Miami University and tell them to send the bill to him? Didn't he owe me something? What story would I tell? Wouldn't that first story have to lead to other stories? No, after all these years I did not matter to him so he need not matter to me.

Mother never would tell me what had happened to separate her from my father. Every time I asked, she would reply, "That was a long time ago." The one statement she did share, and repeated, was that she had requested a divorce from my father because of desertion; that he had never so much as come to see me. Perhaps that was her way of deterring me from looking to the past to determine my future.

In April of my senior year, Cecil came home to announce a new opportunity for me. *Oh, really?*

"Listen to me, Shirley," Cecil demanded, "the air force is sponsoring a select work group requiring clerical skills at the Salmon P. Chase College downtown on Ninth Street. The work schedule has been assigned two college credits. Surely you should be able to fill out simple government forms and documents?"

Was he kidding me? The clerical skills they were requiring were the same skills I had already taken in classes and excelled at in high school. I called the college and the receptionist confirmed the pay was twenty-five dollars a week. The class schedule was 8:00 a.m. to 5:00 p.m. every day, with half an hour for lunch. Lunches would be available down the street at the YWCA. I thought to myself, *Why not?* What else was I going to do?

The Monday after graduation, I reported to the all-day air-force work group, repeating the exact skills I had already mastered. Within the first week, a young woman came in from the front office to talk to my supervisor. She was a nice-looking, professional gal. Her name was Miss Irma Gabe. She walked back to where I was seated and said, "I spoke with your supervisor to confirm you have the highest output and accuracy in the group. Would you like to work for us here at Salmon P. Chase College?"

As it turned out, the air force was planning to terminate the work group. It was obvious to the world that the end of World War II was very near. Veterans would be returning to the United States, and the college needed to prepare to enroll large numbers of these men in regular college courses once again.

The Servicemen's Readjustment Act, better known as the GI Bill of Rights, was intended to allow returning servicemen the opportunity to get a college education. College was to become available to everyone returning from the war. This would offer a college education to many more than the privileged few who had previously paid their own college tuition.

Miss Irma Gabe promised, "I will personally train you. You are to be my assistant and will have the office next to me." At the age of eighteen, I was going to be given the title of assistant and my own office? In the next several weeks, Irma would teach me all the skills I needed to be the college registrar.

Most women had to give up their jobs for the men who came back home and needed to work. I was going to enjoy my own pay, the potential for a career, and the power of money in the bank. Little did I know that had the war continued, those of us with the top skills in the work group were to be offered jobs with the War Department in Washington, DC. How excited I would have been to have had a career in our nation's capital!

Returning veterans were given government opportunities to come to the college. I enrolled male and female students in the college to prepare for peacetime jobs. My salary was increased to $28.50 for five days a week plus one Saturday each month. My bonus was free attendance at the College Law School, in the evenings of course.

I came home and was in the middle of telling Mother how excited I was about my new position when Cecil demanded, "You can give your mother fifteen dollars a week for room and board."

I was incredulous, "Out of twenty-eight dollars fifty?"

He yelled at me, "Yes! I know you already have money in the bank from working before this job." He stormed out of the room. Mother just sat there and didn't say anything. I had to admit Mother did do all my washing and ironing, cooked my breakfast and dinner. I relented without argument and gave Mother fifteen dollars a week.

**The truth is always exciting...
Life is dull without it.**

—Pearl S. Buck

Janet

How unfortunate that President Roosevelt passed away in April 1945. On May 8, 1945, the president at the time, Harry Truman, was able to declare V-E Day. Japan had surrendered after two atomic bombs were dropped on Hiroshima and Nagasaki. Dave and I married six weeks later, on June 23, 1945.

I finally relented and asked for help with the selection of my wedding dress. Without much shopping, Aunt Grace and I found the perfect gown. It was crisp white linen with cap sleeves trimmed in lace that repeated on the high Victorian collar. Aunt Grace worked with the florist to fill the cathedral with the perfume of white gardenias. My bouquet was one spray of gardenia nestled in white stephanotis and bursting with pink roses. The fragrance was glorious as I walked down the aisle to the strains of the Trumpet Voluntary.

After a noon ceremony and high mass at Our Lady of Lourdes, the midday heat in the closed cathedral mixed with the floral scents became sickening sweet and suffocating. As I walked to the statue of the Virgin Mary for the devotion, I felt my knees weaken and my sight blur. I prayed I could stand upright to walk back to Dave. He noticed I was failing and strolled calmly to my rescue and escorted me back to the altar. At long last, we were pronounced husband and wife.

Aunt Grace had helped me dress in my wedding gown that morning in a small lady's room at Our Lady of Lourdes. She returned to the same room with me when the receiving line witnessed the last guest to offer congratulations. Undressing was much more laborious than dressing. I was glad to be relieved of the weight of the wedding gown and the remaining fragrance of gardenia.

Elizabeth had insisted my traveling suit be pink. I was delighted to have found a plain, pale pink linen suit to change into. Dave had changed too. He was standing at the open doors of the cathedral dressed in a navy blue double breasted suit and white shirt. He shyly held out a corsage of baby pink roses for Aunt Grace to pin on my suit jacket.

Father insisted he pay for a wedding brunch at Vitor's Restaurant. The owners, Vincie and Joseph, had children who went to school with and had remained friends with Aunt Grace. The Vitors stationed high wooden planters down the center of the main dining room to cordon off the front area of the restaurant for our guests. A wide bank of windows looked out over a grove of protected fig trees and potted plants. It was a lush green background for ten tables set for six, covered in starched white cotton tablecloths with pink cotton napkins. Tiny silver bud vases holding delicate pink rosebuds crowned each place setting of pink luminescent china.

When the last guest left the wedding brunch, Dave and I gave hugs and quick good-byes to Father and to Elizabeth. Aunt Grace stood behind Father and Elizabeth, choosing to remain in the doorway of Vitor's to wave to us from a distance. Even though she believed she was hidden from my view, I could see tears on her cheeks glistening in the sun. Dave and I quickly settled into his car and set off on the drive toward our new life together.

Within one week after our wedding, we were settled in an apartment in Ventnor, New Jersey. Dave had agreed to return to New Jersey where he had served in the navy for three years. Dave had been selected to be a Navy Reconciliation Officer, helping returning servicemen find full-time jobs and gain college placement.

I was anxious to put my skills to work and applied for a clerical position at the Ventnor Boat Works. Ventnor Boat Works had been founded by Adolph E. Apel in 1902 in Ventnor, New Jersey, on the water. Mr. Apel implemented gasoline engines in his boat designs and was fascinated by changes in hull shape and size that resulted in improved ratios of speed to horsepower.

He labored on his theories and devoted the company's engineering capabilities and increasing facilities to the invention of boat designs that would guarantee top performance. Adolph's son, Arno A. Apel, accepted the presidency of Ventnor in the 1930s to continue his father's legacy. His passion was modifications in marine designs for increased speed. He became known as "The Speed Merchant."

When the United States entered World War II, Ventnor Boat Works was commissioned by the War Department to build military vessels. Military specifications required plywood. Ventnor boats were constructed of mahogany planks. The change in raw materials, new designs, and large orders had necessitated the hiring of additional staff.

Talk about being in the right place at the right time. My application was appropriate for two reasons. First, the purchasing agent was at his wits' end with his current secretary. He was demanding a replacement that was proficient in shorthand and typing. Second, the revision in materials required by the War Department had consumed all the purchasing agent's time and efforts. He was demanding secretarial support with purchasing experience.

In my interview with the purchasing agent, he dictated two letters and asked me to complete a standard purchase order from a government requisition. I took the shorthand in pen, typed the two letters without errors, and completed the purchase order with every required detail. He was very impressed and hired me on the spot.

The company had grown from less than two hundred employees in 1942 to a staff of more than six hundred in 1945. Ventnor manufactured, tested, and delivered marine launches, patrol and air-sea rescue boats, and sub chasers for both the army and the navy. In 1946, the company earned the Army-Navy "E" award for excellence. Even though it was the end of the war, Ventnor continued to fill military orders at the same time they were returning to the design and building of recreational and racing boats.

When the war ended in Europe, the United States encouraged individual drive and determination to help revive America's economy. World War II had promoted a patriotic workforce, ready to realize the economic potential of fighting men who had come home to take jobs, marry, and start their own families.

The first few months after the end of WWII were filled with excitement. Working women and men home from service transformed war support to a culture of growth and seemingly limitless opportunity. In the months immediately following the end of the war, streets and restaurants were overflowing with newfound prosperity and goodwill. An onslaught of weddings, new housing in the suburbs, and increasing employment resulted in demand for personal goods, appliances, and automobiles.

Television, too, had a powerful impact on daily life. By Christmastime 1945, the average family watched television four to five hours a day. Popular shows for adults were the situation comedies like *I Love Lucy* and *Father Knows Best*. Americans of all ages were glued to their sets at regular times each day.

We were thrilled to purchase one of the first televisions in our neighborhood. TVs were readily available to Mr. Apel. He was generous in his offer to staff to be added to the list of people desiring a television. Our console was enormous. It took up one entire wall of the living room in our apartment. Dave and I had a selection of thirteen stations, most of which featured news, a few soap operas during the day, and live plays in the evenings. We became quite popular with our neighbors who wanted to witness TV and enjoy this new form of entertainment instead of sitting around a radio.

My favorite evening pastime continued to be writing letters home to Aunt Grace. She reciprocated with letters several times a week, filled with family updates and local news. In the midst of my excitement over the end of the war and my new life with Dave, Aunt Grace included a newspaper clipping in a letter of news from home. The newspaper headline read, "Launching of a New College Comes at Opportune Time." Beneath that was a photograph of Miss Irma Gabe and Miss Shirley Disser, executive secretary to the director and registrar for Salmon P. Chase College of Commerce of the YMCA. There, in my hands, was a photograph of my sister. She was beautiful.

From error to error one discovers the
entire truth.

—Sigmund Freud

Shirley

Even though I was busy working, making my own mark
on the world, I still held my relationship with Mother
near and dear to my heart. I asked for her counsel on
what to buy and how to budget my money. She was insistent on my investing in well-made clothing, "solid" pieces
she called them, whenever I could afford it. Mother also
suggested I set aside a specific dollar amount each week
in a savings account.

Mother had become obsessed with the fashion of celebrities, especially the stars of Hollywood and radio who came to life in television. During the war, the most famous stars had been called on to donate their time to be civilian defense marshals to inspire regular citizens to do the same. These famous stars never appeared in the same outfit twice. Mother took note not only of the cut of the clothes but the colors and the stars' hair and makeup.

Bond drives had requested Hollywood stars to make personal appearances to help finance the war effort. At work we were urged to buy war bonds with as much as 10 percent of every paycheck. You paid three-quarters the face value of the bond and received the full value after a set number of years. Compliance with the "ten pledge" was expected.

Cecil was never interested in celebrities or in, as he called it, "throwing good money after bad to see those puffed up egos" on the big screen. Mother and I made quite a production of dressing up to go downtown for lunch and a movie on Saturdays. My favorite films were *Casablanca* and *Yankee Doodle Dandy*. Mother preferred *The Best Years of Our Lives* and *Going My Way*.

She had been truly concerned when the Hollywood studios allowed Clark Gable and Jimmy Stewart to enlist. Newsreels shown before the movies provided updates on the progress of the war and reminders to ration and support scrap drives. They also encouraged audiences to purchase war bonds and create neighborhood victory gardens.

These times with Mother were precious to me. She always dressed and looked like a movie star herself. Men would turn to watch her walk down the street. Women commented on her beauty. She dressed in the latest fashions with matching hat, gloves, and high heels. All the sales clerks at Pogue's department store knew her by name, and she knew their names. At each counter, Mother would ask the salesperson about his or her family and health. They, in turn, would focus all attention on her.

I was invisible to Mother's admirers, but I did not mind. What a joy it was to watch her, so envied and admired. Mother was taking the money I gave her each week and the pittance of an allowance Cecil gave her to buy happiness.

Mother's favorite winter outfit was a dark purple velvet suit, a jacket, and a skirt that came with a white silk blouse with ruffles at the V-neck and on the cuffs. For the holidays, she looked striking in a black velvet dress with fitted waist, full skirt, heart-shaped neckline, and sheer black chiffon sleeves embroidered with tiny red holly and green leaves. Then came springtime, and she glowed in a vibrant yellow linen dress with matching cropped jacket, a lavender Easter dress with matching long overcoat, an orange sundress with spaghetti straps, and a white-and-orange striped sweater.

In the fall of 1945, I surprised her with a gold lame A-line raincoat with matching umbrella. At the apartment, she lounged in cropped silk pants split on the sides and lightweight chenille over sweaters or long blousy cotton shirts belted at the waist. We had matching floor-length black silk bathrobes for summer and red quilted ones for the colder weather.

Mother declared, "I am finished with pink, forever. My new favorite color is yellow." We purchased deep yellow-gold draperies for the apartment and a yellow-and-white brocade chair for her living room. I placed it beside the infamous green brocade couch in the hopes she would, after all these years, donate it or put it out to the curb. The green couch remained.

To understand a mother's love, bear your own children.

—Chinese Proverb

Janet

On Valentine's Day 1946, I gave Dave the best gift of our love. I was pregnant with our first child. My doctor gave me strict instructions to gain no more than fifteen pounds. That was not difficult. It was easy to treat myself to a few heavenly bits of chocolate each week and no other sugar. Besides that one temptation, I had no unusual cravings or appetite for certain foods.

From the time we had begun talking about raising children—more than one, perhaps three or four?—I feared I may not experience a mother's bond with my babies. Isn't motherhood a learned, sacred lesson passed on through the generations? And yet my mother did not protect or cherish or even pursue me. How would I know what to feel?

I needn't have worried. A strong maternal instinct triggered inside of me with the first sensation of my baby stirring. After that sensation, I had few fears or worries about what kind of mother I would be. My excitement and anticipation grew with every month that passed.

On September 11, Dave and I had a little girl and named her Sherron. A big, bouncing, good natured baby girl, Sherron was born with blond hair and green eyes. "Where on earth did the blond hair and green eyes come from?" I asked Father on the telephone when we called him with the good news. He claimed all babies had blond hair and green eyes. I had heard that was only an old wives' tale.

The look on Father's face the first time he held Sherron was undeniable. She had my mother's features, hair, and eyes. I knew it. As she grew up, Sherron remained blond and green-eyed. Father kept his distance from her as if the obvious reminder of my mother was too much for him to bear.

I don't wish to be everything to everyone, but I would like to be something to someone.

—Javan

Shirley

In the evenings, I went home after work to eat dinner with Mother and Cecil. His disgust with everything about me continued. I could not chew my food properly. I left my arm on the table while I was eating. I cut my meat incorrectly. I could not wait for him to leave the table and retire to their bedroom to read so Mother and I could wash the dishes together and then listen to the radio in peace.

Saturday nights, I went with the girls from work to hear live bands play the most popular tunes and local singers take on the latest hits in a dance club on Hyde Park Square. It was at the club that I met Cliff Park. All the returning servicemen gathered at clubs throughout the city where there were crowds of single girls.

Weddings of girls and returning GIs had become a frequent event. Churches were booked for marriage ceremonies every weekend and some weekdays. The justice of the peace was a very busy man for those who could not or would not wait for an opening in their church's schedule. Not long after the weddings came the baby showers. Every soldier was anxious to start a family and buy a house—the American dream.

Cliff and I were dating for several weeks when we introduced each other to our parents. Mother thought he was "adorable" and hoped he was the one for me. Mr. and Mrs. Park were pleasant enough when we met. They were an affluent family from Hyde Park, and I had the feeling I did not live up to their expectations for Cliff. He repeated to me his mother's remarks that I seemed "pleasant and reliable." Her comments sounded more descriptive of a cat or dog than a girlfriend.

I was still working for the Salmon P. Chase College. Cliff was working as an administrator for the AMVETS (American Veterans) during the day and attending general education classes at night. It was a requirement of his government employment that he obtain his high school diploma within one year.

He had been drafted into the war mid-May 1944. That had been a difficult time for his mother. The oldest son, Joe, was twenty-eight and fighting in the war in France. The middle son, Bill, age twenty-three, was fighting in the war in Italy. Cliff did not want to "miss" the war and joined the army when he was called for service. Fortunately for Mr. and Mrs. Park, all three sons returned from the war, even though all three were wounded in battle. Each of their sons was a medaled hero.

I have to admit I was eager to leave my current home situation, and so was Cliff. We were both living with parents, desperate to be out on our own. Cliff confessed he loved me and asked me to marry him. I agreed. We had met in August and were married in November. The ceremony was held over the Thanksgiving holiday weekend, on Saturday, November 26, 1948, at Knox Presbyterian Church in Hyde Park.

My Uncle Paul Knost played his violin for the prelude, processional, recessional, and postlude. His music selections were soft, light, and joyous. Our ceremony was led by Reverend Edward W. Stimson. Mother wanted to wear a black dress and satin heels, but I insisted on a more appropriate deep green dress with matching gloves, hat, and heels. All other details of the service escape me.

Both sets of parents, relatives, and close friends greeted us afterward at the Hyde Park Country Club for a dinner reception. The open bar and five-course meal was paid for by Cliff's father, Mr. Benjamin Park, a well-liked and generous man who owned several automobile dealerships around town. In the wedding day photographs, Cliff and I look like kids, and just like kids, we look scared to death. There was no honeymoon trip. We went to church at Knox Presbyterian on Sunday morning with Mother. Both of us returned to work Monday morning.

Before marrying Cliff, I had certainly heard about and seen photographs of the horrors of the war. The stories of cruelty and torture had been just that, stories. As soon as I heard an accounting of the war camps or saw pictures of the war dead or dying in the newsreels, I quickly turned my head and dismissed them for my own peace of mind. That part of the war was removed, distant, and had nothing to do with me. During the next weeks and months, I was to discover how horrors seen and known were to remain with the men who experienced them first-hand.

Local draft boards, led by community leaders, were given quotas that dictated how and who to draft into the war. There had been very little resistance to the draft. If a man was called, he answered the call as his patriotic duty.

At the beginning of 1944, there was a severe manpower shortage. Cliff was drafted just days after his eighteenth birthday. As soon as his division of teenagers landed in France they were pressed into active duty in the field. He confessed he was terrified by the abrupt initiation into combat against the German forces.

The most difficult part of his tour of duty would come after he was released from an army hospital in France, having had surgery to remove a bullet lodged in his left knee. He was reassigned to the 104th Infantry, Timberwolf Division, under the command of General Terry Allen. The division's first action came in October 1944, during the taking of Achtmaal and Zundert in Holland. They then participated in the Battle of the Bulge, advancing through the Siegfried line into Cologne.

Breaking out of the Remagen Bridgehead on March 25, 1945, the Timberwolf Division was teamed with the Third Armored Division to advance more than three hundred miles deep into the heart of central Germany. Hitler's forces were collapsing, but attacks by pockets of resistance continued. In a persistent push eastward, the Timberwolf Division eventually arrived in the town of Nordhausen. It was the morning of April 11 and, at first sight, Nordhausen appeared to be like every other town the 104th had liberated.

Nordhausen, they discovered, was different. It was the home of the Mittelbau-Dora Concentration Camp. The sights and sounds and smells were indelibly etched on the minds, eyes, and the recesses of the souls of each American soldier. The division found five thousand corpses and six thousand inmates in various stages of human decay. Malnutrition was the prevalent means of torture. Corpses were human skeletons covered in tissue-thin flesh. Those who were still alive were found lying in disease and filth, being eaten away by diarrhea and starvation.

Several men were found alive at the bottom of a pile of corpses. They had been struggling for days to get out, but the weight of the bodies piled on top of them had sapped their strength. In one corner of the camp were piles of severed arms and legs. All division medical personnel were dispatched to the camp to undertake the grueling task of discerning who could and could not be helped.

Those who could stand feebly staggered toward their rescuers, attempting to salute or reach out to shake their hands. Tears trickled down their cheeks and those of their American liberators. Swollen, bulging feet were bare, and striped camp uniforms hung loosely on emaciated frames. Most men in the camp who were still alive had not only been starved but also beaten, the lash marks engraved on their bodies in raised scars.

Angry beyond words, General Allen demanded of his men, "Search every house in the village and round up every able-bodied male citizen. Bring them to this camp." When they were assembled before him, the men of the village swore to General Allen they had had no knowledge of the camp. He did not believe them. The stench of human death and decay was overpowering.

General Allen was horrified by the conditions at the camp. Division personnel were instructed to supervise the men of the village as they transported the barely living to medical tents and dug mass graves on a knoll just outside of town, overlooking the town square. When a sufficient number of graves were excavated, General Allen directed every resident of Nordhausen to carry the corpses from the camp, through the town, and up to the knoll for proper burial.

In disbelief, the division found another concentration camp just two miles northwest of Nordhausen. It was an intricate underground V-bomb factory consisting of two long tunnels, each one several miles in length plus forty-eight smaller feeder tunnels. The V-bomb was Hitler's secret weapon, a pilotless radio-controlled aircraft capable of carrying a high explosive bomb.

The factory was run by the Nazi SS, an abbreviation for Schutzstaffel, meaning an elite squadron. From 1943 to 1945, they had forced sixty thousand prisoners to produce the V-1 and V-2 bombs. Twenty thousand prisoners had died from starvation and execution. Those prisoners who were too weak to work were left to die of starvation in the forty-eight feeder tunnels or were burned to death. The camp incinerator had extinguished the lives of an estimated one hundred prisoners each day over the two years.

When he entered the service, Cliff was a boy of eighteen who knew only the best of what his Hyde Park lifestyle could offer. When he came home, he was a man who had observed the darkest face of human character. Much as he tried to forget the sights and sounds of what he had been called to do, he could not erase his own actions or the actions of his enemies.

He attempted to numb the pain with alcohol. Even though the alcohol lulled him to sleep, the nightmares continued, driving Cliff between the mattress and box spring to avoid incoming bombs and deafen the screams of dying men. During his waking hours, bursts of temper and shocking fits of anger were frequently the result of his inability to control the images of the war and the concentration camps.

Happy is the son whose faith in his Mother remains unchallenged.

—Louisa May Alcott

Janet

Three years after the birth of Sherron, we had our first son, Steve, on November 8th, 1949. He had little hands and little feet, a small round mouth, and big brown eyes. Dave and I agreed it was time to move back home to Cincinnati as we started raising our growing family.

We purchased our first home in a neighborhood in Colerain. The house was a picturesque white cape cod with black shutters and a black front door. Dave returned to Gidding Jenny department store downtown. He was

promoted to Lead Buyer. I went to work as the office secretary at LaSalle High School. Aunt Grace came to live
with us. She had retired from her career as a secretary at
the Internal Revenue Service.

Rather than spend her days in the Disser home, she
presented her support to us for as long as we would accept it. Dave and I were grateful for the offer. We knew we
could not continue to work as we needed to and support a
family without her constant presence.

She was everyone's favorite aunt. No one questioned
why she had never married, or if she had ever thought
about marrying. To be honest, I have no idea if she ever
had a boyfriend or a lover or if I just was not aware of one.

Her companionship was invaluable to the entire family. She would simply appear at our side exactly when one
of us had the need of her company and care.

Grey-haired, old-fashioned, and conservative, she became known as Aunt Grace to neighbors, friends, and
church members. She doted on everyone and was a friend
to people I did not even recognize. Shopping at the grocery or taking leisurely walks with the kids around the
neighborhood, Aunt Grace would strike up a conversation with people I do not remember having met. She was
our own ambassador to the community.

**There is no such cozy combination as man
and wife.**

—Menander

Shirley

Mother and Cecil moved one last time, to an apartment in O'Bryonville on Paul Street. The apartment had a galley kitchen with a window overlooking Paul Street, a large dining room and living room, a small solarium with a bank of windows facing Madison Road, a nice-sized bath, and a walk-in closet. Their bed was hidden in the wall adjacent to the closet, pulling down into the center of the living room when needed for sleep.

I knew Mother was despondent. She was desperate
for a house. A vacant home was for sale at the end of the
same street. Cecil would not hear of a mortgage, a commitment that would last longer than he could foresee the
economy supporting the need for his correspondence
courses. Mother showed me that house two, three, maybe
four times, hoping she could convince me how serious she
was about buying it. I agreed with her. Cecil never did.
A long-term mortgage commitment instead of a monthly
rent payment made no sense to him.

My first place with Cliff was in Pleasant Ridge, a one-
bedroom apartment in a four-family red brick unit with
white trim. It was owned by Cliff's father, and we paid no
rent. Cliff was responsible for managing our building and
the apartment buildings on either side of us.

Just four months after our wedding, I knew I was
pregnant. The obstetrician referred me to Dr. Benjamin
Spock's book *Common Sense Book of Baby and Child Care.*
Mother read the first two chapters and decided she did
not agree with Spock's advice. Since she did not offer any
alternative advice I had few other options for information.

Cliff and I had been married two weeks shy of one year
when our first little girl was born on November 8th, 1949.
Sandra had a full head of brown hair, brown eyes, and
a very pleasant disposition. Cliff would have been happy
with one child. Having grown up as an only child, I was
insistent on more, at least one more.

Four years later, I was finally pregnant again. We moved to a two-bedroom apartment in Mount Washington. In April 1953 our second little girl, Beverly, was born. She was bald and fat, and she came out screaming. She didn't stop screaming, thanks to a bout with colic, for six months. The only person she was silent for was Mother. Mother was ecstatic. "I have two girls! I have my very own two girls."

Our two-bedroom apartment was becoming smaller as the girls were growing bigger. When our youngest entered kindergarten, we purchased a brand new home in Mount Washington. It was a standard three-bedroom tan brick ranch with two bathrooms, living room, dining room, kitchen, single car garage, and a full basement. It was within walking distance of Mount Washington Elementary School. The sprawling basement housed a laundry room, a playroom, and a den for Cliff. Our private yard and covered front porch were the gathering places for neighbors and friends.

The radio was happily relegated to the basement in favor of a television set. I was delighted to see my long-treasured radio shows on TV. *Red Skelton* was my favorite. The girls loved the Abbott and Costello and Bob Hope movies. Cliff's favorite was *The Jack Benny Show.*

Mother bought a new car from Cliff's father, a yellow '56 Chevy she nicknamed Tweety Bird. Every weekend, Mother drove out from O'Bryonville to Mount

Washington to play with the girls. She doted on them, spoiled them, and cherished them. As each of the girls turned five, Mother alternated taking one of them each Friday night through Saturday at Cecil's and her apartment to lavish them with love and attention.

Holidays were spent with both sets of parents. Cliff's parents typically chose lunch celebrations while Mother and Cecil preferred dinner gatherings. Of course, Mother still couldn't cook, so Cecil and Cliff handled the meal preparation, allowing the girls and me to smother Mother with our love.

Cousin John had continued to write to Mother and send photographs. The pictures of him and Henny and their children gave the girls an opportunity to learn about the Doppler family history from Mother. Mother reminisced, "In my youth, Cousin John was the center of my universe."

You don't choose your family. They are
God's gift to you, as you are to them.

—Desmond Tutu

Janet

Dave and I and our two children, Sherron and Steve, spent holidays at the Disser home, celebrating with Father and Elizabeth, David and Donna, and Aunt Grace. Father took great delight in regaling us with stories of his youth. His appetite grew with his imagination. He developed a rather large girth, in obvious agreement with Elizabeth's good cooking. There was salad, meat, potatoes, vegetables, and always a homemade dessert. Without fail, at the end of the meal, Father would declare, "That was delicious, now what's for supper?"

Of particular interest to the children were Father's stories of World War I. His participation in the war became quite a narrative of fiction. His telling of being in the European Theater ended one evening when Aunt Grace could stand the untruths no more. In the midst of one of his creative tales, Aunt Grace interrupted with, "You were just a cook in New Jersey. You never even left the United States." The room fell into a deafening silence.

Within a few seconds, Father replied, "Why, everyone knows an army lives on its stomach!" And off he went on a story about his work as a plumber.

Father was pleased with his life. There was more work for plumbers than ever before, and the pay was increasing all the time. Americans were buying appliances that had not been available before WWII, which created installation and repair opportunities for men in the plumbing business. The growth of American industry was beneficial to men in the trades, and he was glad to be away from the toil and sweat of the construction business. He often commented, "I never planned to work as hard as my father. The hours were too long. I never could stand the smell of cement."

David was approaching his teen years. Father's greatest concern was that the United States would engage in another war that would entice or draft his son. When President Harry Truman approved production of the hydrogen bomb and sent armed forces to Korea, Father was furious. For the 1952 presidential race, Father campaigned vehemently for Dwight Eisenhower. "Now there is a man who has experienced the ravages of war." True to Father's promises to the entire family, Eisenhower was elected and US troops were withdrawn from Korea in 1953.

In April of the same year, Dave and I were blessed with another son, Mark. He was a handsome boy, sprouting light brown shoots of hair and quietly gurgling when we held him.

Steve and Sherron were becoming a handful. Steve was enamored with science fiction. He tried his best to convince family and friends that there was life in outer space. Sherron constantly had her nose in *Life* magazine to see the latest fashions and to imitate the biggest Hollywood stars. She knew the names of blond actresses she wanted to copy, especially Marilyn Monroe, and the clothing she planned to someday purchase for herself, designed by Dior, Chanel, and Givenchy.

I was thrilled to see my children growing up in the "new conservative" world, as Father called it. At school, Steve was asked to recite the Pledge of Allegiance with the addition of the phrase *under God*. We went to St. Mary's Catholic Church on Sunday. The other families who attended became our friends. We socialized and sponsored dinners and outings at the church and in one another's homes.

Sherron tried desperately to teach her brother Steve about girls. She even attempted dance lessons with him to rock 'n' roll music. Her forty-five records, by artists like Bill Haley, Elvis Presley, and Jerry Lee Lewis, were repeated over and over again on her portable record player. "Mother," Sherron complained to me, exasperated, "Steve is such a poor pupil." She gave up on him and practiced with neighborhood boys and girls in our basement. Dave and I could empathize. We preferred dancing to the new songs of the day sung by Perry Como and Rosemary Clooney.

Dave delighted in taking Steve to the Cincinnati Reds baseball games at Crosley Field to watch Jackie Robinson and Hank Aaron play ball. I was at a loss as to what to share with Sherron. She was not at a loss without my companionship. Her girlfriends and classmates kept her busy with dancing and parties at their houses and ours.

PART FOUR

Discovery

> **From time to time I have seen someone who looks as she must look, but the similarity is gone by the time I have convinced myself to look away.**
>
> **—Janet**

Janet

Department store sales, lunches on Fountain Square, concerts in the city parks—when were you there? Were you there, right next to me? How could I miss seeing you, a part of me? I wasn't looking.

Shirley

How many times did we cross paths? Did we both work in the city? Mother and I shopped downtown and went to the movies on Fountain Square. Did I sit beside you on a streetcar or a bus? I don't remember thinking of you very much.

> Families are a mystery. Despite having all
> the clues there may never be an end to the
> questions.
>
> —Anonymous

Shirley

The summer of 1957, a marvelous new discovery came into Mother's life: her older sister, Laura. Actually, Laura found Mother. She was at the courthouse in downtown Cincinnati to confirm a deed to property when she inquired if there were any records for Clarissa Doppler. The clerk found two records. One record was for Aunt Clara, Cousin John's sister. The other record was for Clarissa Doppler, who was now Claire Phelps. Laura hurried home on the next bus and looked for Claire Phelps in the telephone book. She phoned her sister. Mother and Laura talked for hours that day and every day thereafter.

Cliff and I took the two girls out to Laura's home the next Saturday, promising to meet Mother and Cecil there and bringing as much food as we could fit in the trunk of the car. Mother had told me Laura was married and had six children, four boys and two girls. Laura's children were not really children. They were also married and had children of their own.

We turned off Clough Pike and crept up Newtown Road looking for a dirt drive. The first dirt drive we came to had Laura's address hand-painted on a board that was nailed to a tree. The lane was level, but the right side of the drive fell off gradually on the right into a valley and stream. About a mile and a half down the lane, we saw a gray clapboard house straining to remain secure on a stone foundation, hanging off the right side of the drive. We tumbled from the car, fumbled for the food in the trunk, and made our way to the front door.

It was wide open, revealing a giant bed in the front room. Behind the bed was a kitchen, noisy with the sounds of several adults and many children. The kitchen door was open as well, offering a direct view from the front door to the opposing hillside. We made our way around the bed and were greeted with shouts of joy at our coming. Introductions followed and were quickly forgotten. Throughout the day, there were reminders as to who was who and belonged to whom.

The property belonged to Mother's sister, Laura, and her husband, Edwin, whom everyone called Irv. Irv explained that he had built the house himself. We were very complimentary. Laura took us on a tour, which led us through a total of four large square rooms, including the kitchen. My youngest daughter looked perplexed and asked, "Where is the bathroom?"

To which Irv replied, "Why there is a privy out there by the garden." I knew the next question from my curious youngster would be "What's a privy?" so I cautioned her against more questions with a raised eyebrow and a soft pat on the fanny to scoot her back outside.

Settled in a dip in the hill beside the house on lawn chairs and stretched out on blankets, we each had time to observe Laura and Mother together for the first time. Where Mother was blond and fair, Laura was a brunette and fair with the addition of freckles across her nose and scattered on arms and legs. Mother's build was strong but shapely, and Laura had full sloping bosoms and wide hips, perhaps more the physical evidence of six children than her natural profile. Laura's and Mother's eyes were the same shape, but Laura's were hazel and Mother's eyes were green. Laura's nose was sharp at the tip, where Mother's was rounded and flared.

We found ourselves thinking they could not possibly be sisters—then we heard them laugh. Yes, they were most definitely sisters! We could not help but laugh and cry with joy in celebration of their discovery of one another.

**It was easier for me not to
wonder about you.**

—Claire

And I felt the same wonder.

—Laura

Laura

Laura had been born to William Crockett and Margaret Ann Fein. She had vague recollections of the Crockett family life—poor but happy. That was until their mother passed away when giving birth to Laura's little sister Clarissa. Father told Laura her brother Willy was being sent off to a farm. She and her baby sister would be very

372

well cared for by her mother's sister, Aunt Louisa, in the big city of Cincinnati.

Aunt Louisa was a large and rather frightening woman, giving Laura instructions on how to care for her baby sister. It seemed she was to be her sister's caretaker, and Aunt Louisa wanted no part of the responsibility of a baby. By the tender age of four, it was obvious that Laura was not adept at caring for or minding a baby sister. And Aunt Louisa was discovering she could not manage both girls. While the baby had been silent and passive, Laura was energetic and boisterous. Aunt Louisa's frustration mounted, and her intolerance erupted in fits of screaming and hissing at Laura.

One evening, a family discussion was convened by Aunt Louisa with Fred and Elizabeth Fein. Fred Fein was Louisa's and Margaret Ann's younger brother. Aunt Louisa pressed the issue of the Feins lack of a pregnancy and their continued desire for a child. She demanded the Feins take Laura to their home to live with them and avoid contact or future communication with either Aunt Louisa or Clarissa.

Fred and Elizabeth Fein were soundless and reverent. It was not until Fred drove into the ghetto of downtown Cincinnati that Laura's fears escalated and she began to panic. He stopped and pulled her out of the backseat to witness the orphan children lying on the sidewalk in filthy clothes and crying out to no one in the night for their mother, for food, for help.

Upon their arrival at the Fein home, Laura was admonished to speak to no one and to stay indoors to be sheltered, fed, and educated. Fred and Elizabeth held church councils and prayer meetings at their home several evenings each week. Laura was instructed to go to her room and remain there to play and then sleep.

As the weeks and months passed Laura would tiptoe from her room to the top of the stairs to listen to the conversations and Bible study when the house was filled with congregation from the Oakdale Methodist church. One particular evening, the Bible study focused on children and the teaching of children about family. Laura took this as a sign from God.

Though Fred was quiet, he could be pleasant and helpful. Elizabeth, on the other hand, was blunt and principled. Laura had prepared her question in advance of breakfast the next morning. "If you please, could you tell me, where does my father live?" Being a rather tall man, Fred pushed his chair back from the table and came around to the side of the table where Laura was seated. He nodded at his wife knowingly and then bent down to look at Laura. "He is with the Lord. And we are with you." He patted her lightly on the top of her head and walked away.

She never asked again, as she neither understood what he had said nor did she believe it. In her eavesdropping, Laura had come to realize that Fred and Elizabeth—Mr. and Mrs. Fein to her—repeated lofty phrases and

Bible verses when in the company of members of the congregation but had very different things to say in the privacy of their home.

Laura's childhood and education was controlled by Fred and Elizabeth. Mrs. Fein schooled her in the basics of education and instructed her in Methodist teachings. The school room was the kitchen table, Monday through Saturday mornings from 7:15 a.m. sharp until 12:00 p.m. sharp, with one break for what Mrs. Fein referred to as "the relief of fluids." Laura was not allowed to go outside other than to play by herself in the fenced backyard one half hour from 12:00 p.m. to 12:30 p.m. for time with "God's air and nature." After lunch, Mrs. Fein directed Laura in cleaning, dusting, washing, and ironing.

The truth was that Fred and Elizabeth were getting older and had had a decreasing interest in having children of their own. However, when presented with the desperate plea to take on Fred's niece, the church congregation prayed with them to follow the one truly Christian response. They agreed to take her into their home, and the church praised them for their selflessness and generosity.

It was at this same time that the Feins had been searching for a housekeeper. Laura was of a mind and demeanor ripe to train to dust and mop. Elizabeth was pleased to be seen as an educator and cultivator of Laura's young mind. She approached each new day with lessons that allowed her to impart her wisdom as well as maintain a strict cleaning schedule. Given the fact that Laura was family and confined to the house, Elizabeth was assured that all her earthly assets and personal effects would remain exactly as she had purchased and arranged them.

The Fein home was not impressive. Fred and Elizabeth maintained a standard gray stone house in the little burg of Oakwood on the north side of the city. There were three bedrooms, two bathrooms, a parlor, dining room, study, and kitchen. A small square foyer allowed visitors a brief reprieve from inclement weather. The basement and attic were void of any belongings or treasures from time gone by. When Laura was able to manage the steps and the weather permitted, she was directed to sweep and air out the attic and basement as part of her afternoon cleaning routine.

Every room was painted white with the exception of the kitchen and the bathrooms, which were painted yellow. Fred was not pleased with the yellow paint exception as he methodically walked around the house on weekends with a bucket of white paint touching up any walls or woodwork that had chips or scratches. Dark crown molding and a large dark entry door made the white walls appear frosted.

Fireplaces in every room had black-and-white tile hearths and dark mantels. Mirrors of all shapes and sizes were hung on almost every wall. Elizabeth took advantage of a glance at her image at every opportunity.

Dark floors were meant to show as little dirt as possible. Oriental area rugs in purples, reds, greens, and oranges kept dust collected and provided a kaleidoscope of colors that were echoed in furniture and pillows. Elizabeth had chosen complimentary ceramics of birds and flowers that she placed on tables and bookshelves. Elizabeth was particular that each ceramic be replaced precisely as she had positioned it. "Dear, you must place my birds and flowers exactly as I selected their placement. Is that understood, dear?" she reminded Laura day after day, every day.

Laura curtsied and kept her eyes fixed on the floor. "Yes, Mrs. Fein. I will always do what you tell me to do." The answer had been instructed and was repeated instinctively.

Fred was absent from the house six days a week, appearing only in time for supper Monday through Saturday. He was the station master for the railroad. Fred was a thin man in and out of his station uniform, with dark hair, long sideburns, and a beard. Elizabeth was pale and also thin, with sharp features, long straight brown hair, and a constant concern for the effect of her clothing on her appearance.

Laura's room was the smallest bedroom at the back of the house—up the staircase, at the end of the hall. She slept in a small wooden bed with white sheets and white blankets. She wore all white clothes to signify her purity and innocence. The church ladies complimented Elizabeth on her work with Laura, commenting, "Your effort to contain her knowledge to only what is necessary is extraordinary."

It was not until Laura was approaching a maturity of sixteen that the members of the congregation increased their polite but persistent questions about Elizabeth's restriction of Laura to the Fein home. On Christmas Eve of 1918, Elizabeth provided Laura with a virginal white wool suit that had become too small for her. Dressed in the white suit and a white wool coat, Laura accompanied Fred and Elizabeth to the Oakdale Methodist Church for evening service.

That evening, she met Edwin Hirschauer. He was entering the church for the Christmas Eve service with his parents and siblings. Edwin also worked at the railroad and greeted Mr. Fein with holiday wishes as he stepped into the church's nave. When he noticed Laura, he tipped his hat to her and requested a proper introduction. For Edwin, it was love at first sight. As he walked down the center aisle with his family trailing behind him, he insisted everyone sit in the pew directly across from Fred and Elizabeth and Laura.

Edwin was five years older than Laura and had been searching for a wife who would be acceptable to his parents. There she was. Laura was a treasure dressed in white to match her ivory skin. His two sisters snickered and giggled at Edwin's stares in Laura's direction. Placing an arm around Edwin's shoulders, his mother whispered in his ear, "Now that would be a perfect match for my son."

Under the watchful eyes and constant chaperoning of members of the church, the two were able to meet, talk, hope, and plan for the future. Four months after their Christmas Eve meeting, Edwin and Laura confirmed their love and were joined in holy matrimony. Their marriage was celebrated with repeated and sincere blessings of a pleased and proud congregation. Fred and Elizabeth were publicly proud and privately disappointed. Who could be trusted to clean and wash and cook for them now?

Regret for the things we did can be
tempered by time; it is regret for the things
we did not do that is inconsolable.

—Sydney Smith

Claire

Claire made many visits to see Laura. Once they
found one another, they swore they would never
be separated again. Laura was overjoyed to have Claire's
friendship for herself and her two grown daughters, Janet
and Dottie. Both Janet and Dottie were close to Shirley's
age. Janet was three years older than Shirley, and Dottie
had been born in the same year as Shirley.

Laura was thrilled that her sister Claire wanted to come out to see her. Laura shared the abundance of her flower gardens with Claire. Claire treasured the blooms in cut glass vases she refreshed throughout her apartment to remind her of a generous and loving sister.

When Shirley's two daughters accompanied Claire on her trips to see Laura, Irv insisted everyone go swimming in the lake below the house. The cool and clear waters were the final culmination of the Turpin Farms valley streams. With no hint of charity, Claire regularly took food, cash, and clothes to Laura. The only way Shirley knew what Claire was doing was when she noticed canned goods stocked on the pantry shelves, new cookware in the kitchen, and some of Claire's dresses on Laura and her daughters. Cecil and Cliff had no interest in returning to Laura's farm, so they were not aware of the offerings Claire and eventually Shirley took to their extended family.

Perhaps it was the recounting to Laura of her life (compared to what it should have been) that was so draining for Claire. The coincidence of letting go of her own daughter—also named Janet—had created a hole in Claire's heart that was reopened. The role of provider for herself and Shirley combined with the loss of Janet revisited her every dream. "If I had not looked after myself and Shirley," she defended, "what would have become of us? When Cecil came along, even though his infatuation was limited to me, I was so weary of working and worrying." Had it been the right step to take, to marry Cecil? Should she have made more attempts to have a place in Janet's life? Laura patted her hand and sighed, "Life is heaven on earth today. Yesterday has vanished."

Was it the guilt of a life lived less than it should have been for herself? For Janet? For Shirley? God had graced her with one loving daughter who had brought to life two beautiful little girls. Was it marrying a man she did not love and who cared nothing for Shirley? Tedious apartment life, fading love from a now-bitter husband and rare friendships closed in on Claire.

Despite finding Laura and hearing how similar their childhoods had been, a sudden onset of migraine headaches began without warning and then increased in frequency, intensity, and duration. The remedy for Claire's migraines was a teaspoon after another of several crushed aspirin dissolved under her tongue, and two days or more in bed without sound or light, until the migraines would dissipate.

It may have been so much aspirin that resulted in the stomach cramps, or all the black coffee and heavenly bits of chocolate she craved during the days of good health. Vomiting and diarrhea weakened Claire and then evolved into severe constipation. She took weekly trips to Dr. Dornheggen and made regular visits to consult with her friend Forest, the owner of Pack Pharmacy in

O'Bryonville. Dr. Dornheggen prescribed Kaopectate, more aspirin, and codeine. Nothing relieved the migraines or the stomach cramps. Years passed, and there were no remedies and no relief.

Our home is merely visited with the cares of the past. I like this home the best. It is now filled with hope for the future.

—Sam

Sam

In the end, it was Grace who had been a nagging reminder to Sam of his past. She was the one who was intimately familiar with all the skeletons in his closet. Sam was glad when Grace left the house to reside with Janet and her family. What a relief it was to have her permanently away from the Disser home...his home. Let Grace observe and mentally record someone else's life for a change.

Elizabeth had given Sam the much sought-after Disser son, a young man to carry on the Disser name. Then she brought to life a talented daughter. Their children took on Sam's common sense and Elizabeth's solid appearance.

David was rugged and born to play sports. What a blessing it was for Sam to finally have a son. Neighbors and parents of David's school chums remarked about David's aptitude for his studies and his natural athletic skills for football and baseball. Donna played the piano and the flute and had a voice like her mother. She was given solos at the school concerts and was a source of pride as well. It was sweet to have a mirror image of Elizabeth in the house.

Elizabeth and Sam selfishly rejoiced in sole ownership and control of the Disser house—their house—and their children. They shared their existence with no one. David filled the house with friends, and Donna continued to please them with her musical ability and awards.

> Who is it that loves me and will love me
> forever with an affection which no chance,
> no misery, no crime of mine can do
> away?—It is you, my Mother.

> —Thomas Carlyle

Shirley

After more than a week without a bowel movement, Mother could barely function. Rather than risk driving to his office when she was feeling so weak, she chose instead to ride the bus to see Dr. Dornheggen. When she arrived at his office, she fainted in the waiting room and woke up in Christ Hospital. A nurse at the hospital called Cecil. He rushed to her side and conferred with Dr. Dornheggen. Specialists performed surgery immediately only to discover a stomach that was beyond repair.

An entire day passed before Cecil called to let me know Mother was in the hospital. I rushed to her side and was appalled to find her in such ill health. Two days later, Mother was dead. I was in shock. No one could console me.

As she had lay dying, Mother had insisted the girls not be allowed to be in attendance at her funeral. The day of her funeral, I left Sandra and Beverly with a neighbor and my best friend, Noni Benigni. Noni told me later they cried the entire time I was gone.

I was dismayed at the lack of people who came to the funeral service. Mother had no close friends. She had many acquaintances at her church, in the neighborhood, and at the department stores, but her life had revolved around me and the girls.

At her death, I knew of only two people to call: Aunt Laura and Cousin John. Cousin John and Henny boarded a plane in Orlando and flew to Cincinnati for the funeral. Henny had to help John into the funeral home and past Mother's casket. He was severely crippled with arthritis and was overcome with grief.

Aunt Laura and her entire family came at the start of the service and stayed until the funeral director informed us of an evening service for which his staff had to prepare the same grieving room. It was time for us to leave.

Mother's burial at Spring Grove Cemetery the next morning was a blur. I couldn't bear the thought of putting her in the ground. My tears kept coming. I did nothing to stop the flow. Cliff led me back to the car.

At home, I melted into a chair and stared into space. I had no mother. I was no longer anyone's child. I was a ghost, an apparition of one woman's spirit. I had never imagined there would not be many more years to celebrate life together. Even while she was taking her last breaths, Mother had tried to tell me not to think of her as leaving me. I was devastated by her absence.

We were partners in life—the best of life and the most difficult. Our love transcended what other people could only hope to possess. No one understood the intensity of our feelings for one another. There would never be a single day when I would not think of her and miss her.

Cecil was disconsolate. During the night, he packed all of Mother's clothes, hats, shoes, and gloves into shopping bags. The next morning, he attended Sunday church service. At the end of the service, he gathered the women of the church together and offered them every piece of Mother's belongings, including her intimates. He left the women to take what they wanted and drove to Aunt Clara's home in Mt. Lookout. He presented Aunt Clara with Mother's jewelry box filled with her treasures and gifts from holidays and birthdays now past. When he returned to the apartment, he threw all of Mother's photographs, all of my photographs, and all our keepsakes in the trash bin beside the apartment garage.

He distributed all physical evidence of Mother anywhere else but to me. Everything that held the scent and the glamour that was my mother was donated to people who held no regard for her. Her most prized possessions were given to a woman who had spoken ill of her at every opportunity. All tangible memories of our wonderful life together were thrown into the garbage as worthless pieces of paper. He despised her love for me. I despised him with a hate and a loathing I could not forgive.

It doesn't matter who my Father was; it matters who I remember he was.

—Anne Sexton

Janet

Dave and our children absorbed all my attention and energy. Holidays and birthdays were the only times I saw my father. I neither neglected him nor contacted him. It was Elizabeth who called to make arrangements for us to come to the Disser home for celebrations.

Besides, I was pregnant again. With Mark tucked safely in my arms, I arrived at Father's house to collect Sherron and Steve after a day of baking Christmas cookies with Elizabeth. That was just about the time my sweet stepbrother David was turning sixteen. He was enamored with the new Buick Skylark convertible and insisted Father purchase one for him for his birthday. I left before the discussion reached a successful conclusion for David.

Our son Greg was born in the summer of 1956. It was with this beautiful blond, green-eyed bundle of joy that we decided not to have any more children. Four was enough to feed, clothe, and educate. Aunt Grace's presence was truly a blessing to us all, but even her patience was beginning to wear thin.

I watched my children grow and mature with a new respect for how blessed life can be. I had become a good mother, strict and steady. I respected Dave as a father. He was a strong role model who never hesitated in his affection or gentle discipline. Dave was fair and honest, treating each child with the same temperament.

Was my sister a mother too? From time to time I would daydream about her. Did my father ever think of her? I doubted he did. I had thoughts of her, imaginings. I would picture my sister in the way dreams are spun from wishes, and then I would gladly continue my life with the thoughts of her I had invented.

All that we are is the result of what we have thought. If a man speaks or acts with an evil thought, pain follows him. If a man speaks or acts with a pure thought, happiness follows him, like a shadow that never leaves him."

—Buddha

Shirley

The girls were growing up so quickly. They were involved in school plays and activities with friends. I found myself having more time on my hands. Cecil telephoned repeatedly to insist we continue a relationship. He was aging and had no one in his life, no friends and no family. His beloved cousins lived in California and had not seen him in more than twenty years. I didn't care that he had no one. I hated him. He had taken away all material evidence of my mother, of my childhood.

After a great deal of prayer and soul-searching, I visited Cecil one time. He was pleased. My visits became more frequent while the children were at school and Cliff was at work. My time at the apartment increased when his business was failing, and I saw the need to balance his accounts and process the mass mailings that were his only source of income. On holidays, Cecil came to the house for dinners and was present at celebrations of the girls' birthdays. He never showed affection toward me or the girls but was appreciative of our invitations.

I searched for solace in the Bible and popular authors of the day such as Norman Vincent Peale with *The Power of Positive Thinking* and Bishop Fulton J. Sheen's *Life Is Worth Living*. The comfort and guidance was temporary. Nothing filled the void I felt every morning I woke up and knew Mother was gone.

The girls' favorite books *Cinderella, Frog Went A-Courtin'*, and *Chanticleer and the Fox* gave me brief escapes. I focused on making as normal a family life as possible for the girls. The youngest liked Barbie dolls and the oldest preferred climbing trees. Both of them could slap around in the inflatable pool in the backyard or play with silly putty and slinkys for hours.

In the evenings, the girls and I chose our favorite television shows, and when a specific program was over, the girls had to go to bed. *Lassie, Father Knows Best,* and *I Love Lucy* were the most popular shows. On Sunday night, we scheduled dinner to end before *The Wonderful World of Disney* and *The Ed Sullivan Show.*

Cliff grew tired of watching television sitcoms. He purchased a small television to put in the basement for his solitary enjoyment. He left us upstairs as soon as dinner was finished and retreated to the basement to watch football, basketball, boxing, track and field, and the news programs.

Alone and searching for closure, I wrote to Cousin John to thank him for making the arduous trip to Mother's funeral. In my letter, I remembered, "You were always on her heart and the person she spoke of fondly with every memory of her childhood." Whether it was to relieve some of the anger I felt for Cecil or part of my outpouring of grief, I relayed what Cecil had done with Mother's possessions, her treasures, and our photographs.

Cousin John replied more than a month later. Enclosed with his letter of condolence was a journal, dictated to and written by Henny, filled with memories of Mother. Tucked in between the back page of the journal and the back cover were two photographs. One was a picture of Mother as a child of two or three in the arms of John Disser Sr. The other photo was a Disser family photograph with Mother at age seven (noted on the back) perched on Cousin John's knee.

I read and reread Cousin John's words. Mother's life before me and after my birth gave me a new appreciation for her strength and her independence. Rather than being consoled with the knowledge of her early life, however, I was devastated. If only I had known all that she had sacrificed for me, I would have been more grateful for the woman I adored and cherished.

**The gift of believing means heaven is never
too far away to call out to our loved ones.**

—Anonymous

Janet

On Valentine's Day 1962, my rambunctious stepbrother David was driving his pristine Buick Skylark to his girlfriend's house to propose marriage. Whether his concentration was focused only on what he was going to say or if he was impatient to get to her house and had failed to completely close the driver side door, no one knows. The police who arrived at Father's house were only able to relay the news of David's death as he leaned out to grab the open door and it slammed back with such force against his head that he died at its impact. His car had been found sitting in the middle of a farm field. The engine was still running.

Elizabeth and Father removed themselves from each other and chose to grieve the loss of their son David in individual and private ways. Donna was isolated from their common shields of sorrow. Left to fend for herself, Donna focused on finishing high school and planning for her own future.

Aunt Grace passed away on January 15, 1972. Born Grace Dewey Disser on May 21, 1899, she had lived a long and full life of work and family. Despite her glorious seventy-three years on earth, I had foolishly let myself believe she would be a constant in my life and the lives of my children for many years to come. It was difficult to let her go. She had not been sick a single day in her life, had never missed a day of work, and had enjoyed good health despite caring for the various illnesses each of us had experienced.

One of the children, I can't remember who, had come down with severe bronchitis. Within a few days, Aunt Grace could not stop coughing. One week later, I felt her hand slip away from my grasp in the chill of pneumonia. She was resting, cool and calm in her bed. My throat closed and I gasped for what to say. The tears came in a flood until I was too weak to stand. The family let me sit in her room, alone with the tranquility of her final, still moments.

I knew that if she could see me weeping, she would have scolded me for crying and insisted I be strong for the children. Her absence in my life gave me a shiver. Who would care for me as only she did? Who would show me how to survive the coming years?

Father died of stomach cancer on January 27, 1980. His death did not inspire the same feelings I had when Aunt Grace passed away. I did not really know my father at any time in my life. He was an enigma to me.

On the precipice of his leaving this world, I held thoughts of longing for the father he believed he was to me. He never delighted in his own father the way I did. He never knew what made me smile or laugh. He never knew Aunt Grace whispered "You are loved" to me each night just before I fell asleep. Did he ever love me? I never blamed him for the life he chose to lead, without my mother. But he had so easily dismissed me, first to be cared for by his parents and then to be cared for by Aunt Grace. My father neglected me. I never understood why. All I could whisper at his deathbed was "Good-bye."

When you are sorrowful look again in your
heart, and you shall see that in truth you
are weeping for that which has been your
delight.

—Kahlil Gibran

Shirley

Cecil passed away in January 1972. I don't remember the exact day. The surgeons had scheduled a procedure to remove prostate cancer, but Cecil did not survive the anesthetic. Cliff and my youngest daughter and I had visited him in his room at Christ Hospital the night before his surgery. We had promised to visit him the next day to celebrate his recovery.

His passing was a burden lifted from my shoulders. It was a release. I no longer felt an obligation. What I was not prepared for were the arrangements he had made for himself at the same funeral home as Mother or the burial plot by her side at Spring Grove Cemetery. The sight of Aunt Laura and her entire family at Vielhauer's Funeral Home in East Walnut Hills, so far from their own homes, was a blessing and a sharing of memories of Mother that came flooding back for us all.

I made arrangements with Mr. Vielhauer to bury Cecil at a time convenient for the funeral home. There was no need for anyone's attendance or for a service at the cemetery. Without thought for any of Mother's possessions remaining in the apartment, I set about cleaning and deciding what of Cecil's possessions to keep and what to donate.

The very first thing I did was to offer the green couch, that horrible green couch, free of charge to any neighbor who would come and get it out of my life. A moving company came to pack and transport the remaining furniture to my house. I would cherish the pieces Mother had selected and placed in their small apartment, especially her treasured yellow chair.

To my surprise and delight, Mother had hidden keepsakes, handwritten notes, and jewelry in the apartment. Silk and ceramic flowers pulled from china vases Mother had placed high atop the mahogany wardrobe, the glass front china cabinet, and the walnut secretary revealed

Pogue's and Mabley & Carew receipts for clothes and shoes, hats, and gloves. Beneath the handfuls of receipts in each vase were blessings from heaven. A gold circle pin embedded with emeralds, a single cultured pearl on a gold filigree chain, and an unopened red satin box containing a diamond engagement ring wrapped in a handwritten love note from Frank Watson were initial elements of surprise.

The true fortune was found in the maple breakfront in the dining room, behind the shelving that held Mother's lily-of-the-valley-china. A thick packet of scented letters had been secreted away, tied in lavender ribbon. Mother had written the letters to Laura expressing regret for the years they were separated. Laura had returned the letters to Mother, writing on the reverse side heartfelt reminders of the love they now shared and the glory of God for bringing them back together.

In Cecil's death, I found fragments of Mother's life. I cherished what I could now hold in my hand, jewelry to wear and letters to read. Remembrances and celebrations of Mother's love came flooding around me in a warm cloak of peace.

I thought about who I might have become had I stayed with Mother to be a friend and constant companion and had not married. I had been so desperate to be out of our home situation that included Cecil. Cliff loved me, and I loved him. Our love gave Mother her two precious granddaughters.

Oh, Mother, after your death so much changed in my life. Cliff began to lose jobs, one after the other, and his alcohol intake increased. Much as I didn't want to, as my Mother had to, I went back to work. The girls were home alone after school and during the summertime. They were alone from the time I left the house to catch the bus until I was able to return in the evening.

We had to make ends meet, to pay the bills. It was the only way. I hated it. I began to hate Cliff too. More jobs came and went for Cliff, and with each change escalating arguments about how to make ends meet. I developed medical problems, and that, too, became a source of conflict. The girls went away to college and my fights with Cliff escalated. My illnesses worsened. I experienced aches and pains that were both imagined and real.

After forty-seven years of marriage, my husband purposely had me served with divorce papers on my seventieth birthday. My youngest daughter came to pick me up to take me out to lunch. I was sitting in a lawn chair in the driveway, shaking. She was angry at her father when I told her the sheriff had just left after handing me the court documents. I still had the declaration in my hands.

The middle of November 1999, exactly one week before what would have been Cliff's and my fiftieth wedding anniversary, our divorce was finalized. Our daughters moved me into a lovely two-bedroom apartment, close to the same neighborhood I had come to know and love. Friends and the girls were supportive and caring. I reached in and pulled up a strength and independence I had not exercised in a long time.

To have a loving relationship with a
sister is not simply to have a buddy or a
confidant—it is to have a soul mate for life.

—Victoria Secunda

Janet

Christmas of 1999, my youngest son purchased an ancestry.com subscription for his wife. She had developed a keen interest in investigating her family history. Many months passed before she began receiving feedback to her genealogy inquiries. Caught up in her excitement over the ease of online research, I thought it would not hurt to ask her, when she thought of it, to inquire as to the Disser lineage. To be honest, once the appeal passed my lips, I did not consider it again.

She posted a request on ancestry.com the same day of my request, June 27, 2000. It was a simple appeal for information. The subject line read: "Missing Disser—Claire, Shirley." The message: "Would anyone have information on Claire, who married Samuel Disser in the early '20s? They had two daughters, Jennette and Shirley, around 1924 in Cincinnati, Ohio. Last known address for Claire and Shirley was Cincinnati, Ohio. Claire Disser is my husband's natural grandmother, and Shirley Disser would be his natural aunt. Any info appreciated."

On the third of July, my youngest son and his wife came to the house bearing food in preparation for the Fourth of July holiday. She was beaming and couldn't seem to control herself. Seconds later, she exploded with the news that she had found my sister, Shirley.

I had to sit down. *Now what do I do?* I thought. I heard my son say, "Do you want to meet her, Mom?"

"Well, I was the one who asked you to try and find her, now, wasn't I? Does she want to meet me?"

"Well, we don't know yet. She is visiting her eldest daughter in Lexington. Her youngest daughter will tell them both about you tomorrow."

The night of the Fourth of July, 2000, I heard my sister's voice for the first time. When the phone rang, I knew I had to answer it. I could barely say hello. We introduced ourselves and then laughed and cried. We talked and laughed and cried some more. I still get goose bumps when I think of anticipating that first conversation. I don't remember anything we said. What I do remember was a kaleidoscope of my life's fragments moving into place, securing a final image of peace.

> **A sister can be seen as someone who is both ourselves and very much not ourselves—a special kind of double.**
>
> —Toni Morrison

Shirley

My distant cousin Valerie Price-Knost, granddaughter of cousin John's sister Emma Doppler, had been in recent contact with me. She was researching the Doppler genealogy and was curious if I could help to fill in the blanks of a family tree. I received her request on June 27, 2000, and turned it over to my youngest daughter. She was driving me to the home of my eldest daughter in Lexington, Kentucky, where I was going to spend the weekend before the Fourth of July holiday.

On Sunday, July 2, in the evening, my youngest felt challenged by my cousin's query and settled down in front of her home computer with a glass of chardonnay. She had never searched for the Disser lineage before and was struck by the hundreds of sites offering information. The third site she chose, and what she had decided would be the last one, was ancestry.com. When prompted, she entered the last name Disser and was intrigued to see a request for information.

She clicked on the request. It had been posted on June 27, the same day I had received my cousin's genealogy request. The request asked for information on Shirley and Claire Disser. In disbelief, she closed the request, took a sip of chardonnay, and then clicked on it again.

She typed her excited response: "SHIRLEY DISSER IS MY MOTHER!" Then she rapidly keyed a second reply: "CLAIRE DISSER WAS MY GRANDMOTHER!" The very next day, July 3, Janet's daughter-in-law saw the message and responded.

"Wow, I do not know how to respond. Do we have the right Shirley and Claire? Was your mother born in the Cincinnati area? Does she have any knowledge of a sibling?"

My daughter responded, "It's true! Mother is Shirley Disser and Grandmother was Claire Disser. Please e-mail or call me!"

Back and forth, the messages continued that day. "Is your mother still living?"

"Mother is alive and well in Cincinnati and lives about ten minutes from me. Please e-mail or call so I can hear more about Jennette and her father."

My youngest daughter called her older sister the evening of July 3 to ask if we could alter plans. She wanted to pick me up midday on the fourth of July, half-way between Cincinnati and Lexington so that all of us could have lunch together. My eldest daughter and I easily changed our plans for the day of my return. On Tuesday, we met at the Cracker Barrel in Dry Ridge, Kentucky. When our drinks had come to the table, my youngest reached over to grab both of my hands and said, "I have wonderful news. Your sister Janet wants to meet you!"

All three of us started to cry. "Really, you found her? She wants to meet me?" I was incredulous.

"Do you want to meet her?"

"Why, I think so—at least, I don't know why not." I didn't know what I was going to say. After all these years, I could know my sister.

I kept waking up in the night. In my dreams, Janet is calling to me and I am smiling. What a thrill to have the other half to my family. We had spoken that evening on the phone, laughing, crying and sharing bits of information about Mother, and Father!

The real voyage of discovery consists not in seeking new landscapes, but in having new eyes.

—Marcel Proust

Janet

We met privately one week after our first telephone conversation. It was a fragmented sharing of recollections and questions, photographs and facts. Our disjointed conversations have continued.

In our own way, we are piecing together a family that has endured, separate and parallel.

THE END

That private meeting took place when Janet was seventy-three and Shirley was seventy. They are now ninety-two and eighty-nine years of age.

This book was Shirley's story. The one thing of which she is most proud, is defending Claire's endurance and love of life.

THE BEGINNING

And now we come to Janct's story... Before us stretches a new perspective on this family history, the chronicles of Sam.

Printed in Great Britain
by Amazon